## PRAISE FOR JOHN PHILLIPS

"When I first met John Phillips, his real talent was obscured by meeting the immediate demands of a wire service. But fish gotta swim and real writers gotta write. Phillips' debut collection of short stories, *Dress Whites*, was worth the wait. Not since Hemingway's 'Twenty Grand' and Algren's 'A Bottle of Milk for Mother' have I realized how much power is in the mastery of a short story. With Phillips it is the people—a woman becomes a war widow at age 23, a returning Vietnam vet turns to the brutal world of boxing to fund the search for his missing daughter left behind in Vietnam, the occupants of a run-down Vegas hotel battle their private demons. It's not fancy. It's not pretty. It's a journey through the dark end of real life, where people battle for a second chance. It makes you want more."

JERRY IZENBERG, AWARD-WINNING COLUMNIST
AND AUTHOR OF *ONCE THERE WERE GIANTS*

"Evocatively and poignantly written, *Dress Whites* recreates slices of life in America as it was a half century ago."

THOMAS HAUSER, AUTHOR OF *MISSING* AND
*MUHAMMAD ALI: HIS LIFE AND TIMES*

"Beneath the nostalgic memories of lava lamps and tie dye of the 1960s was a grittier era unfolding in the blue-collar bars of Staten Island, the swamplands of the south and the jungles of Vietnam. John Phillips' new book *Dress Whites* is a cinematic collection of fascinating interlocking stories told in the styles of Quentin Tarantino and Raymond Chandler. It's a new, must-read look at how the Vietnam era shaped the lives of those who served and those left behind."

JODY HEAPS, TV PRODUCER, WRITER; FIVE-TIME<br>EMMY WINNER

# DRESS WHITES

JOHN PHILLIPS

*These stories are dedicated to the tens of thousands of parents, wives, brothers, sisters, children, and friends forced to carry incredible losses for the rest of their lives because of the Vietnam War. Personally, I think of Doug Ford, a school friend, and Nick Lia, a fellow Staten Islander, both Marines wanting to make a difference in the world and paying the ultimate price for it.*

*It's mind boggling to think of the 58,220 lost Americans and impossible to comprehend the estimated two to three million Vietnamese innocent women, children, and men, slaughtered in their own country for just being there.*

*Finally, a debt is owed by all of us to those journalists, writers, courageous veterans, and even those too few politicians who finally told the truth about old men sending young men to die for very wrong reasons.*

# DRESS WHITES

## AND OTHER STORIES

# JOHN PHILLIPS

www.admissionpress.com

# CONTENTS

# G&T

"WHY? TELL ME WHY," Nicky's mother asked him and spun her head to catch a waiter's eye. Acknowledged, she pointed to her empty gin and tonic glass, then swiveled to lock back onto Nicky's eyes, a look between quizzical and accusing.

"Really, Nicky, I'm serious. Tell me why? You have options. Try to get into the National Guard for one. We'll figure a way for you to stay out of it. The Marines? Vietnam? Why?"

The Trocadero family—Nicky, his younger brother, Bobby, mother, and father—sat in a red Naugahyde booth at Jackie "Jackie Pink" Marino's restaurant on one of their fancy nights out every couple of months. It was pink all over at Jackie's— pink tablecloths, napkins, ties, blouses, pink roses at the host's stand. He picked up the nickname from his laughing friends after the camera lenses he thought were going to fall off the truck turned out to be three gross of pink napkins and table- cloths. He figured the deed had already been done, so he'd make the best of it.

In a flash of red fingernails, their mother pulled the breadbasket over and unwrapped the pink napkin covering Jackie's famous garlic bread.

"Canada. Italy even," she said, tearing a piece of bread from the loaf. "Remember my second cousin, Gina? She married a man from Palermo. She's always writing that you should come over for a long visit so you can see where you originally came from."

He leaned over his plate toward her. "Stop, Mom. Stop! I'm from here and I'm no draft dodger. I live here, I gotta stand up for my country! I don't wanna be just another guy on a street corner. I wanna do something special, something that matters!"

She covered the far rim of her gin and tonic glass as she squeezed the lime.

"There're lots of ways to do that, baby," she said. "You don't have to shoot someone or get shot to be special. And—don't roll your eyes—you're already special and you'll always be special."

He shrugged.

"Mom, I know you mean it, but mothers are supposed to say that. We need to show 'em what's what, that we help people, you know, live the way they want. Self-determination and all. Like us."

"You know, Nicky," she said, lifting a gold cross from her neck to lay over her shimmering green blouse, "not everybody wants to be like us. Not everyone wants to live the way we do. There are millions of people who like their lives just the way they are. And not all people respect us or even like us."

The Old Man slapped the table.

"That's just commie speak, Marie. Everyone dreams of coming to America. For good reason. Don't twist what your son's saying! That's not what he's talking about. He's talking about the right to vote—freedom to say what we want to whoever we want. They all want what we have. You should know that."

"I should know that?" she said, narrowing her eyes. Then louder: "I should know that? I know what they want me to know so I won't know what's really going on. I know what I know, Mike, not what they want me to know."

She wrenched off a piece of bread with her side teeth.

Bobby paused in sucking up the last of his soda through a straw.

He turned to the Old Man. "So when're we gonna go to Yankee Stadium? And we can go into the dugout, like you took Nicky. You said we would. You promised."

The Old Man reached over to the antipasto plate in the middle of the table and speared a slice of prosciutto. "I dunno. I don't have the connection I used to, now that Jimbo Riley gave up the hot dogs."

"Why'd he do that? He gets to see all the games and all," Bobby said, sticking two fingers into his glass, pulling up an ice cube and slipping it into his mouth.

"His knees and back were starting to go, all those games up and down the stairs, carrying dogs. Rough on your body. Take care of your body, Bobby. You only get one."

He reached for the antipasto dish again and with a fork raked an artichoke heart and three small mozzarella balls onto his plate. Their mother shook her head, sending long black curls fluttering, and dismissed their conversation with a backhand slap in the air.

"Seriously, Nicky, think about it," his mother said. "Really think about it. They're shooting real bullets."

"And they're killing our guys with real bullets, Mom," Nicky said, pushing farther back against the booth and sitting straighter. "I'm not an idiot kid anymore, you know."

"C'mon, you two. Give it a rest," the Old Man said.

"Give it a rest?" she said, raising her drink to her lips. She lowered her glass and put it down hard and off center, sloshing some of it onto the pink tablecloth. "We're talking about your son risking his life! And for what?

"Seriously, Nicky, think about it, really think about it," she said, blotting the spilled drink with her napkin. "This isn't a game with toy guns in the woods. Boys—young men—are being killed. Legs and arms blown off!"

"And we gotta stop that," Nicky said, brushing the palm of his hand against the front of his dark crew cut that stood straight up—a tic of his when he was anxious. "Ma, we're the biggest country in the world. We can't let them get away with it. We gotta show 'em what's what."

Jackie himself, tall and lithe with a river-boat gambler's narrow mustache and sideburns down to mid cheek, delivered a fresh basket of bread, a new sour on the rocks for the Old Man, sodas for Bobby and Nicky, another G&T for their mother. He took away the depleted glasses. The Old Man motioned for Jackie to give him back his glass and plucked out two cherries. When the boys were young, the Old Man would give them a cherry each from his sour. Now, for the first time in a long time he dangled cherries for each boy to take one. Grinning, they did.

Hanging on the wall over the booth was a large, framed poster from *Roman Holiday*—Gregory Peck sitting behind a laughing Audrey Hepburn, steering a red Vespa as they careened through Rome, the Colosseum in the background.

"You know, Jackie," the Old Man said, tipping his glass at the poster, "I always wanted to see the Colosseum. See where gladiators had to fight for their lives and Caesar giving thumbs up or down, deciding if the loser should live or die, depending on if he put up a good fight. Those fights. Real *mano-a-mano*! A real test of what they had."

"What's 'ma no ma no'?" Bobby asked.

"It's one-on-one, you against the other guy," the Old Man

said, churning his fists. "It's who's the toughest. You get to show everyone. You get to strut your stuff, big time. Like our guys in Vietnam—Marines, anyway."

Their mother glared at him, controlling herself.

"You know, Jackie," the Old Man said, sipping his drink, then smacking his lips and tilting his head in satisfaction, "not many people know it but we—the movies, really—got it all wrong about the thumb thing. Thumbs up actually meant kill the loser and send him to heaven and thumbs down was to keep him alive on earth."

Jackie pushed out his bottom lip, nodding, educated. Their mother rolled her eyes.

"Baby, you sound like a politician when you talk about wanting to go to Vietnam, you have to—"

"But that doesn't mean I'm wrong, Mom!" Nicky said, staring at his mother and brushing his crew cut. "I mean, we get a say in it all—like we're doing now—'cause we vote for who we want. They don't," he said, gently putting his hands on the table and lacing his fingers. "And if we don't stand up now, those people will get to be told how to live with no say about how they want to, you know? Who knows what'll happen to all of us if the commies win."

"Oh, the domino effect?" she said with a snort. "If the communists take Vietnam, it won't be long before they'll be surfing Malibu? C'mon, Nicky. Listen to what they're really saying and why. And what you're saying."

She flicked her hair back from her cheek and sat up straighter.

"Nicky," she said, giving up proper posture to plant her elbows on the table, jutting her head toward him and holding up the jagged piece of bread. "It's a made-up war, made up by politicians and generals," she said, hammering the air with the bread (*Bam!*), "to make money (*Bam!*) and names for themselves." (*Bam! Bam!*)

Nicky drew his head back and turned over his hands in exasperation. "Ma, that's over the top, don'tcha think?"

"Over the top?" she said, pausing as she held up her drink. "Think about it, Nicky. What do generals train for? What do they think about their whole lives? War! (*Bam!*) That's what they do. They do war." (*Bam!*)

She paused to take a sip, put down her glass, and stared at him.

"And to do what they like to do they have to curry favor with politicians and their money people and rile everyone up to go to war."

She picked up another piece of bread.

"War is good for business. (*Bam!*) It's all propaganda. (*Bam!*) You know, tell a lie often enough and people believe it. Viet Cong in Santa Barbara? Christ!" (*Bam!*)

"That's not—"

"I'm not finished," she said, staring hard at Nicky. "And to do what they're bred to do, they have to be in cahoots with politicians like D'Alesandro and their money people in Washington." (*Bam!*)

"Where do you come off saying that?" the Old Man said, slathering butter on a piece of soft bread he always asked for instead of the famous garlic bread Jackie's mother makes. He raised his head slightly from pushing a pile of manicotti onto his fork with a piece of bread to glower at their mother.

"All of a sudden you're an expert about it all?" he said. "You know more than the President or Vic, down in Washington looking out for us? You think he couldn't spot a hustle?"

"Little snot-nosed Vic? He couldn't find his rear end if it didn't have a dollar bill stuck on it. C'mon, Mike."

She grabbed the pepper mill, tightening her lips as she twisted its neck over her salad.

"How'd he get that big house on Todt Hill? Kickbacks on contracts!" she said, twisting the grater. "That's how! Government contracts. Contracts handed out by those generals and politicians who love war."

"He's a good guy, Marie. He sponsors three teams in the American Legion league. And he ran that dinner for little Joey Gregorio after his accident and built a ramp for his wheelchair and all."

"Yeah, the dinner was at his cousin's restaurant. How much did he kick back to Vic? Vic never did anything for anybody without a buck in it for himself."

She slowly shook her head at her husband, sadness to it.

"C'mon, Mike. He's just another smiling fraud. Why do you get taken in by these types? Everything about him and his family is an act. The same old act."

She raised her hand with her forefinger extended upward—a teacher signaling students to take notes. "Case in point: that monument to Korea veterans on Manor Road with his father's name on it, like he was a hero. Real hero. My mother knew him. He was a fat Navy clerk in Washington who died during the war of a heart attack in bed with some chippy." She tossed her salad, mixing in the layer of pepper flakes from the pile she'd made. "A fraudster begets a fraudster."

The Old Man looked around and waved his hand to shush her. "Marie, you don't know that about the contracts and Vic," he said quietly. "So tell me, how do you think you know so much about Vic's business?"

"You told me about the contracts after you drank up everything at the Knights, the night you got inducted," she said, spearing a stalk of asparagus with her fork. "Of course you don't remember. Besides, it doesn't take a genius to figure out his angles or Vietnam and how stupid it all is. History, anyone? You should know that, Mike."

"Marie, he's a grown man, for Chrissake," the Old Man said through a mouthful of manicotti, sitting up straight and quickly chewing while holding up his forefinger for her to pause until he swallowed.

Their mother drew an imaginary zipper across her lips, folded her arms, and smirked.

After swallowing hard, the Old Man said, "Nicky's not stupid! Marie. He's getting a college degree in May! He's gotta make his own decisions, his own mistakes. Besides, it's the right thing to do. For generations, men have been standing tall for their country."

Bobby chewed another ice cube and reached for the breadbasket.

"Is Clay, uh, I mean Ali, better than Marciano was or Joe Louis?" he asked through the ice. "He's always saying he's the greatest."

"Don't talk with your mouth full," the Old Man said. "He's just a loudmouth, doesn't know his place. Definitely not a credit to his race, yelling all that stuff, changing his name to something foreign and all."

Their mother waved away their conversation.

"Oh," she said, raising her eyebrows to the Old Man, "your son has to make his own mistakes? Yes, like what job he wants. What car to buy or girl to marry. No! We're talking about life and death mistakes. Boys come back in coffins, for Chrissake!"

She paused as she raised her glass.

"You know, it's easy, real easy, Mike, to dream of your son being a war hero when you're sitting in a La-Z-Boy. You missed your hero-boy chance with your deaf ear. Give it up! You don't get to be a war hero if your son is."

The Old Man slammed the table with his fist, shaking

dishes, knives, and forks. Jackie and a waiter rushed from the other side of the room to see what was wrong.

"That's it! I'm outta here," the Old Man said, throwing his pink napkin onto the pink tablecloth. "You can't resist running that smart-ass mouth of yours. Never could. Never will."

The Old Man stomped out of the room. Just past the bar, he quickly about-faced, marched back. went to Jackie, wiggling a cork on a champagne bottle at a table on the other side of the room, and put a ten dollar bill on the table.

"Please get them a cab. I'll settle the tab tomorrow."

He strode out of the room again. As he passed her, a woman sitting with a man looked up at him and shook her head. The man smiled, head down, twirling spaghetti around his fork.

Bobby took the last piece of garlic bread, and Nicky reached over for a piece of soft bread in front of the Old Man's plate.

Bobby dipped his bread into the extra sauce on the side that the Old Man had ordered. He brought it over his plate, dribbling sauce on the way. He was left with only a faint stain of sauce on the bread's hard crust.

"This is how you do it, dummy," Nicky said. He bobbed the last piece of the Old Man's soft bread up and down in the sauce, brought it over to his plate, stuck his head over the plate, and sucked in the gravy-logged bread.

Their mother slowly shook her head, pushed her plate to the center of the table, took a long swig of her G&T, and looked for a waiter.

# WINGED VICTORY

IT WAS the first time Nicky had actually suggested to his little brother that they go anywhere in Nicky's red Oldsmobile convertible with the loud pipes. Usually, Nicky's mother would have to insist he pick up his brother after school to take him to the dentist or somewhere else Nicky, a college senior now, didn't want to go.

But there Bobby was in the Olds at Nicky's invitation, riding shotgun, his arm meticulously casual, dangling over the edge of the door. They were going to the green-and-white bandstand on Manor Road for Fourth of July ceremonies to remember Staten Island's war dead.

Bobby had turned up the radio—The Mamas & the Papas' "California Dreamin'"—to signal their arrival as they cruised past the park. Nicky made a U-turn to grab a spot across the street where he could keep an eye on the Olds, its white top tucked and snapped into the well behind the back seats. The bandstand was set in the center of the park, bordered by waist-high hedges and forsythia, dull green again until next spring when they'd glow daisy-yellow, drawing people to the park for a few weeks anyway.

It was a typical July day for Staten Island, hot-breath ripples of air slicking necks and backs of the forty or so people gathered in front of the bandstand. To the right, four Marines stood at attention in front of the obelisk, maybe ten feet tall, topped by a copy of the headless Winged Victory, commissioned by the local chapter of The Daughters of the American Revolution. Four more Marines stood at parade rest in front of the hedges, their rifles upright on the ground in front of them, held by stiff arms ending in white gloves.

It was the first time Nicky and Bobby had seen soldiers with real rifles up close. A stylized bronze scroll with raised letters—oxidized now to algae-green—showed the names of Staten Islanders killed in WWI. On another side were the dead in WWII; a third plaque named dead Korean War soldiers. The fourth scroll was blank.

U.S. Representative Victor D'Alessandro, secreted behind the dark windows of a black Lincoln Continental, arrived after the Marine Honor Guard had been waiting for fifteen minutes in 93 degrees. He emerged, wearing a light blue summer suit, crisp white shirt, and a red-white-and-blue tie. He made a show of plucking a white handkerchief from an inside pocket, shaking it open, surveying the crowd, and dabbing at his dry face.

The Marines wore high-peaked white caps with black brims, navy blue tunics embossed with red-and-gold chevrons, navy pants with scarlet stripes, and white belts, brass buttons and belt buckles glinting in the noon sun.

"Man, they look cool, huh?" Nicky said to Bobby. "Look at that guy with all those stripes on his sleeves and the rows of medals. A Marine lifer! Got a neck like Godzilla. Imagine the stories he could tell. Cool! Very, very cool!"

One Marine held a U.S flag, its staff supported by white straps over his shoulder and around his waist, ending in a heart-shaped white cup just above his groin. Next to him a Marine held aloft the Marine Corps banner the same way, perspiration running down the sides of his face, a bead of sweat hanging from the end of his nose.

The bugler blew "Taps." Mrs. Henry had made Bobby's class look up the words.

*Day is done, gone the sun,*
*From the hills, from the lake,*
*From the skies.*
*All is well, safely rest,*
*God is nigh.*

At a barked command, the Marines standing by the hedges brought their rifles in front of their chests. At "ready" they clicked—kind of scary, Bobby would say later—rounds into their rifles' chambers. Another command had them aiming into the air and then the order to fire. At the sound of the first shots, birds that had been roosting in the bandstand's rafters exploded from under the roof, furiously making their getaway.

# DRESS WHITES

BOBBY HEARD the muffler before he saw Nicky, wearing the Dress Whites of a brand-new Marine Corps Second Lieutenant, ease his red Oldsmobile convertible into the curb between the two chestnut trees that were foul-ball markers when they'd played stickball against the steps.

Tara, tiny in a pale blue summer sweater over a pink blouse, sat thigh-close to Nicky. The Olds's white top was carefully snapped into place behind the rear seats. The late-afternoon sun popped the edge of a taillight ruby red.

Nicky loved the Olds with a passion. He'd bought it with money he'd made working the graveyard shift at the gypsum plant his college sophomore and junior summers, supplementing his pay by loading Tommy's truck twice a week at 3 a.m. with gypsum boards Nicky had stashed behind the loud machine nobody wanted to go near.

"Free money. Who's to know?" Nicky told Bobby. "I mean they're polluting the river big time, dumping hunks of broken gypsum boards into it every night. So why not?"

Nicky revved the engine, teasing out one more growl. He

got out and stood in the street next to the driver's door in the shade of the trees. He tugged down his white tunic and carefully reset his billowed white cap, tilting its glossy black brim low on his forehead. He walked around the car to the passenger's side, looked up at Bobby standing at the top of the steps, and grinned. He opened the car door for Tara. She swiveled from the seat, legs firmly together beneath her short, white, pleated skirt, and stepped onto the curb.

Holding hands, they walked up the path—Nicky, shoulders erect, narrow waist, solid pecs, an officer's gold bar on each shoulder, the Corps globe and anchor emblems and brass belt buckle sparkling just so.

Years later when Bobby could joke about any of it, he'd admit that when he first saw Nicky in that uniform, white down even to his shoes, he thought of the pictures of old-time milkmen he'd seen in the ancient *Life* magazines the Old Man collected. Bobby never got around to teasing Nicky about looking like a dweeby milkman.

Tara's skirt stopped just above her knees and was whiter even than Nicky's Dress Whites. She wore pale-blue flats, matching her sweater. Walking up the path to the house, she tugged Nicky's hand to slow him as she looked down to avoid tripping on uneven flagstones the Old Man had said for years he should fix before someone fell and sued him.

At the bottom of the steps, Nicky freed his hand from Tara's and climbed them two at a time ahead of her. At the top, he widened his grin, saluted Bobby and hugged him for the first time ever. Their father and mother stood in the doorway waiting for their hugs, their mother blinking quickly several times.

Nicky snapped off a salute for the Old Man, who hugged him even harder than he had after Nicky'd juked his way off tackle to score the winning touchdown against New Dorp on Thanksgiving Day four years earlier.

"Nicholas Trocadero, Second Lieutenant, United States Marine Corps! You've done us proud! Really proud!" his father said, breaking off the hug to hold his son at arm's length to scan him. He released Nicky with a slap on his shoulder. Nicky turned and hugged his mother, who clung to him before Nicky pulled away to turn to Tara.

She walked up the steps and stood beside Nicky. Bobby's eyes roamed to her small breasts nudging her blouse and to her skirt, its pleats hugging muscled thighs—he knew from watching her jump at basketball and football games in a short red-and-white cheerleader's skirt. A pink headband cinched her dark hair, gathering it into a crest before cascading down her neck. Her nose was close to but not classically aquiline—nostrils slightly flared, as if in the first stage of stimulation that could be good or bad. Her chin hinted at a cleft. The parents stood aside to let her through the doorway but she lingered on the landing.

"Hi, Mr. and Mrs. Trocadero. Hi, Bobby. Doesn't your big brother look cool? You know, he polishes his brass every day. Look at that belt buckle—it's so shiny, almost as shiny as this!" she said, her voice approaching a squeal as she brought her left hand up to her face, twisting it so the small diamond ring and gold wedding band next to it caught the fading sun.

The Old Man, who'd put on his new tan polo shirt, with white stitching around the collar and sleeves that displayed impressive biceps, stepped down from the doorway toward Tara.

"C'mere, you," he said, enveloping her in a bear hug. "Welcome to the family."

"When? How? Why now? Oh, Nicky. I didn't see that coming. Why didn't you tell us?" their mother said, staring at

Nicky. "You never said anything in your letters that this might happen."

"We didn't want to wait and we didn't want to spoil the surprise, Mom. I thought Tara should decide when word got out."

Their mother pursed her lips, spun away, and walked into the house. The Old Man ushered Nicky and Tara through the foyer into the living room. Bobby trailed in his bell-bottomed dungarees and tie-dyed T-shirt the Old Man never failed to shake his head at. The Old Man motioned for Nicky and Tara to sit on the rose-dappled love seat facing the fireplace and plopped onto his La-Z-Boy.

"So. Here we are, celebrating a new adventure and a great addition to the family," the Old Man said with a broad smile. Bobby sat facing them in his grandmother's maroon Victorian wingchair that hardly anyone ever sat in. The Old Man always said he bet the chair would be worth something someday and winced whenever anyone sat in it.

"Wait! Wait! Wait a minute! Just a minute. I gotta get this down for posterity," the Old Man said.

He lowered the fold-up desktop of the secretary he'd won in a bowling tournament in Buffalo and picked up his new Polaroid camera. He told Nicky and Tara to stand close to each other. Nicky put his arm around Tara's waist and she snuggled into him.

"A momentous occasion! For the ages! Get ready! At the count of ninety-three," the Old Man said, grinning, delivering the same line whenever he took a picture.

The flash fired and a piece of white paper disgorged from the camera's lip. The Old Man put it on the secretary's dropped lid and stood watch over it. After about a minute, he smiled. "Got it!" He slid a tiny brush out of a tube and ran a coating of a transparent film across the photo they said would keep the picture from fading over the years. He didn't show it to anyone and put it in a drawer on top of a stack of other pictures.

A tea kettle whistled from the kitchen, and a dinner bell rang.

"Let's go into the dining room. Your mother said something about tea earlier—high tea now with our new princess in the family."

Tara blushed and smiled. Nicky smiled. Bobby got up from his chair, and they went into the dining room. Nicky and Tara sat on one side of the table, opposite Bobby, and the Old Man sat at an end opposite their mother's chair.

Their mother, in navy slacks and cream blouse tied at her waist, bumped open the kitchen's swinging door with her hips and backed into the room. She carried a tray with a teapot, cups and saucers, bottles of Coke, and glasses with ice cubes. She set a cup and saucer in front of Tara and distributed the Cokes and glasses to the Old Man and the boys. She went back into the kitchen and came out with a plate of chocolate chip cookies and put them in the middle of the table.

"The Olds runs great," Nicky told his father. "Tommy started it once a week when I was gone. A real friend. Kept it in his garage and parked his own car on the street the whole time."

The Old Man leaned on his elbows toward Nicky. "I always liked that kid. His father, not so much. Big-shot cop always has his hand out."

"Thanks, Bobby, for polishing her up. Turtle wax, right?" Nicky said, pulling up his collar, raising the Marine Corps emblems.

"Yeah. You said you'd only use that on her. Really shines her up."

"Sure does. And those white walls look cherry—nice job."

Tara put down her cup and fluffed her hair. "Nicky

proposed on the phone from Quantico and said he didn't want to wait." Tara sat up straighter and put her left hand flat onto the table, the diamond catching a flicker of light from the chandelier. "So I went down, and we got married in a Marine chapel a day after his graduation parade." She gazed at Nicky, then turned to their mother. "Your son is sooooo romantic. We're going to the Poconos for a mini honeymoon. We'll have a proper one when he gets home. He'll be a captain by then."

Their mother stared at Nicky.

"Maybe more than that," the Old Man said, pouring Coke into his glass. "Johnson just sent in something like a hundred thousand more men—lotsa them Marines—to teach those little commie bastards who's boss. Great chance for Nicky to show his stuff."

"I thought you had to work today," Bobby said to Tara, as he snatched two cookies from the plate. "Another teachers' day off?"

"I took a sick day. I thought we all should be together as a family now," she said, glancing at her ring. "What about you, Bobby? Hooky?"

"I got the afternoon off when I told coach Nicky was coming home. He said to say hi, Nicky, and that you should come by to say hello."

Tara told Bobby she'd met Flora Whalen, a teacher at her school. "Her brother, Johnny, was in your class, wasn't he? Sad, he was killed by a truck. Did you know him, Bobby?"

"A little."

"Flora said she's saved his yellow pencils to remember him by. So sad to not get a full life."

"Are you still going to keep up your writing, Nicky?" their mother said. She topped off her cup and passed the pot to Tara.

"You know," their mother said after sipping her tea and gently putting the delicate, yellow-flowered cup that had been her mother's onto the saucer, "I loved your descriptions of the boys in your barracks. That ignorant boy from Arkansas who made the anti-Semitic remark to your friend stands out in my memory, and the way you stood up for him. And the detail about the other boy from Iowa never having been on an escalator before—how you described his legs 'wet noodling' and his accent brought him to life. I could see him so clearly. Please keep writing, Nicky."

"Nicky wrote wonderful love letters to me, Mrs. Trocadero," Tara said, putting her hand on top of Nicky's. "I'll treasure them forever."

"I think I will," Nicky said, withdrawing his hand from under Tara's and brushing phantom crumbs from his tunic. "If I have time. A kind of diary, I guess."

"A diary? Sounds kinda girly, Ace," the Old Man said.

"Writing and expressing yourself is not girly," their mother said, pausing her cup in front of her mouth, staring at the Old Man over the rim. She put down the cup without taking a sip. "Anyone who knows anything knows that."

The Old Man held a stare on their mother, slowly shook his head and lifted his shoulders in a mini shrug.

"Well, even if it is girly, you'll have earned the right to write about it."

Tara tilted her cup with sunflowers circling it and sipped the last of her tea.

"We should go, Nicky, to meet Richie and Susie. This has been lovely, Mrs. T. I look forward to doing it again," she said with a perfectly decorous smile. She dabbed her lips with a paper napkin, folded it, and slipped it under her plate.

The family stood on the landing, watching Nicky and Tara amble down the walkway, swinging clasped hands, her white skirt sashaying its pleats.

Bobby held the Old Man's camera. Nicky opened the car

door for Tara. She dipped into the seat sideways and pivoted to bring her legs into the car without revealing too much—but enough—thigh. She wiggled back into her seat and turned to wave goodbye to Bobby, the Old Man, and their mother, bunched together on the landing.

She draped a gauzy, pale-pink kerchief speckled with navy polka dots over her hair and tied it beneath her chin just like Audrey Hepburn might have in *Breakfast at Tiffany's*, so much her all-time favorite movie that she'd even read the book.

The sun flared over the top of the hill behind them, rimming the back of the car and their heads in a lopsided halo. Nicky started the engine, setting off the muffler. Tara tugged her sweater tightly around her shoulders. The Olds eased away from the curb, the muffler growing louder as Nicky shifted.

Bobby pressed the shutter button and paper oozed from the camera. He left it dangling as it developed. After Nicky and Tara disappeared around the corner, the picture had finished exposing itself and Bobby gently tore it from the camera.

The Olds had turned a dull orange along with the taillights, and the halo was gone.

The Old Man told Bobby later that the camera was only good for closeups, not for distance.

# FLYING THE STOOP

SEVEN-YEAR-OLD COUSIN EDUARDO wanted to impress his mother's new boyfriend—the one who would toss him a candy bar or a quarter on his way up the stoop to visit her and tell him to stay outside until he came out.

Afterward, there might be another quarter or maybe even a walk together to Benito's over on 116th Street for a Good Humor ice cream sandwich, Cousin Eduardo looking around to see if his friends saw him with his new *compañero*. He'd tell them the boyfriend said they'd go to the park to play catch when the field dried up.

Cousin Eduardo sat on the top step, waiting for the boyfriend to come up the block. He'd tied to his neck one of his mother's red satin sheets he knew would be in the hamper Saturday mornings after her Friday nights for herself, she'd say, when he had to stay at his aunt's place. He saw the boyfriend swaggering up the street, wearing a white *guayabera* shirt over bright blue slacks, a thin black mustache and a tan, straw fedora, its brim turned up.

"*Mira! Mira!*" Cousin Eduardo shouted as the boyfriend

turned to come up the stoop. Cousin Eduardo jumped, reaching for the sky.

He broke his arm, cracked a rib, chipped two teeth, and bloodied his nose.

Cousin Eduardo wouldn't let anyone but the boyfriend sign his cast. It was a big, bragging signature—all loops and swirls that Cousin Eduardo had outlined in "red violet" from a 24-pack Crayola box the boyfriend had given him for his birthday when he first started coming around.

The day before Cousin Eduardo was to have his cast cut off, the boyfriend moved back to Ponce with his wife.

# THREE-CARD MONTE

"THIS HUSTLE IS OLD TIME. Older than fuckin' Jesus," Manny told his son and Cousin Eduardo when they reached the top of the steps coming up from the 4 train at Union Square. Each of the boys carried two large cardboard boxes.

They were on the east side of the park and headed west. It was one of the first warm days of spring and packs of students from nearby schools—NYU, The New School, Parsons, FIT— were hanging out on the fringes of the small park along with "bridge and tunnel" guys from New Jersey and Queens, pretending they were students and looking to score drugs and girls. Along the path through the park, they were perched on the backs of benches and railings and sunbathing on small plots of grass. A guitar player leaned against the base of a statue of a triumphant George Washington, towering over the park atop a fierce-looking king-of-the-herd horse in mid prance.

Young women were out in bikini tops. Others stood, hips cocked, watching a tall, skinny guy, wearing a red, green, and yellow fool's cap, dangling tiny, tinkling bells and juggling long-necked bowling pins. A guitar player stood in the shadow of big, bad George and his horse trying to rough-sing "Blowin' in the Wind" like Dylan. A guy sitting on a bench was slapping bongo drums set between his legs, a lone dollar bill in his tip jar. Another was acapella-riffing Vietnam protest songs—one about old men "sending young men not their sons to die in the sun."

Card tables were set up on the sidewalk on the south end of the park, displaying incense, T-shirts in a full-range of psychedelic colors (several with Che Guevara's likeness screened on the front), beaded wristbands, and necklaces. About ten feet in front of a table devoted to bongs, a young blond woman, eyes closed, head back to the sun, twirled like a ballerina, her long hair swishing around her face.

"Lookit," Manny said loudly, as if Carlos and Cousin Eduardo hadn't noticed, "alla them white girls, no bras, *tetas* hanging loose, bouncing like little lemons."

Two girls sitting on a bench looked at each other as if they'd spotted a cockroach. The one in frayed denim shorts and a Kelly-green bikini top shot him a middle finger, its nail flashing matching green.

Manny grinned at her. She countered with the middle finger of her other hand, jabbing both into the air like pistons.

"You know, I been thinkin'," Manny said, louder for the girls' benefit. "How come do skinny white girls have tiny *tetas* and Spanish *mamacitas*, even if they're skinny, they got real big melons? I mean, *grande*! *Grande*! Gotta find out why. Maybe ask Santiago. He did almost a year at community college.

"And lookit all them college *gringos*," Manny said, pointing with his head. "No rent to make and nothin'—nothin' to worry about. Not even worried the *Federales* are coming for them and gonna send 'em to that Chink place. As long as their *papis* pay to keep 'em in college, the draft board's gotta leave 'em alone. Law says so. A'course, that don't do nothin' for us."

"*Tio*, I saw on the TV *gringos* fighting down Wall Street," Cousin Eduardo said. "They were yelling to stop the war. It was kinda funny—guys in hard hats punching other guys carrying signs. No one knew how to punch. Not like Carlos."

"You got that right, C.E. That's because I taught him how to punch. Me!"

"One a the signs," Cousin Eduardo said with a grin, "was, 'Bombing for peace is like fucking for virginity.'"

"Now that's funny, you think about it," Manny said. "And don't forget the ones that say, 'Make Love, not War.' I can feel that one."

They crossed the cobblestone side street bordering the west side of the park.

"*Si*, I'm doing this hustle to get us by," Manny said. "But don't forget what I am. I train boxers, not fighters—boxers. I taught you, Carlito. Me. I know how to teach. They say I got no schoolin' for a real job, but I know things they don't see. I give you things you ain't gonna forget 'cause I put them in your bones—takin' a punch and givin' a punch. You know, knowing how to do that is what life's about in and outta the ring."

He grinned.

"And *tetas* and *culos*, a'course."

"Papi, lookit that one waiting for the bus," Carlos said. "She's got big ones!"

Manny acknowledged with a nod. "I took those stupid toy animals outta your crib and put boxing gloves in it. Your *mami* cried, but she stopped when I made her know my son would be a man, not a *maricon*, like her brother. Remember when you got suspended for hitting that *pendejo* teacher in the *cojones*? Remember? I took you two to Little San Juan to celebrate. You sittin' at the bar all grown up for your first drinks, at, what? Twelve? Remember? I took you."

"*Si, Tio*. We got free peanuts and got to take home coasters," Cousin Eduardo said. "I still use them for my *leche con chocolate* and now for *cafe con leche* all the time—each day a different one 'cause I don't want them to get worn out. Maybe, *Tio*, you can come over and we'll play dominoes."

"Carlos is gonna be a champ some day," Manny said. "So we gotta figure out a way to keep him—you, too—outta the gringos' hustle of making big coin by making us go shoot them people over there."

Manny and the boys crossed 14th Street on the way to a shady corner of Broadway, to a spot Manny had claimed after rousting a guy, who thought the corner was his.

"Just hadda flash a blade," Manny said. "Pussy got all bug-eyed and turned whiter than Albi Sanchez."

Manny glowered at a driver blowing his horn, taking exception to Manny holding up his hand like a traffic cop while he and the boys crossed the street to a Sabrett cart. As they waited for the Sabrett guy to load mustard and stewed onions onto their dogs—"don't be comin' up small, hot dog man"—Manny told the boys that the plan for Monte was beautiful in its simplicity: no start-up costs, just a couple of cardboard boxes, some playing cards, a roll of singles, a few fives, and a ringer looking like he's winning legit.

Manny chomped off half of his dog and licked mustard from his fingers. Cousin Eduardo took his dog out of the bun and vacuumed off the toppings. Carlos bit into a big, doughy pretzel, pimpled with salt.

"Everything's Three-Card Monte, you think about it," Manny said, spreading his arm over the 14th Street scene. "Like, you know, teachers and all saying you can be a winner at life if you just follow the rules. Their rules we don't know nothin' about and they keep changin' 'em. So where're we at then?

"But take it to the bank we got the rules for Monte. Let 'em win a couple of times and think they're smarter than anyone and can follow the card. Then *bing!* They lose and then they pony up even more, their *putas* looking at them. And *bing! bing! bing!* they lose even more!

"They wonder how that happened. 'How could this dirtbag Spic win?' Dumbass! You don't know that you had no clue from the jump what was happening. It's life, sucka—you gotta look out for the hustle of those making you think you're in the game when you're not. Same types down Wall Street—think they're special. Think they got the code for everything. Up here, I got the code!"

Manny stuffed the rest of the dog into his mouth, swiped the back of his hand across his lips, and turned around to watch a girl bending over to pick up after her poodle.

"Check it out!" Manny said. "Now that is *primo culo, hijos. Primo!* Born to be on her stomach."

She turned around, saw Manny staring at her *culo* and shot him the finger. He smiled through a mouthful of dog, mustard, kraut, and onions and spread his arms, palms up, and shrugged. Whaaa?

"Kinda funny, you think about it," Manny said, taking a swig of cream soda and extending his arm toward a group of whooping college kids.

"College boys think it's a sure thing they gonna win, 'cause they're smarter than us 'cause we gotta work the streets to survive. But that puts us ahead from the jump—not that we need it 'cause we can't lose, long run.

"So when they start losing, they keep bettin' bigger 'cause they got boners seeing their *chicas'* little *tetas* bouncin' and thinkin' they gonna get some extra 'cause their *chicas* so turned on, so they keep on bettin'.

"Anyways, you know, think about it. We're part of history. Our line a business goes way, way back to them olden guys wearin' sheets in Rome on the way to steam baths and Guinea pussy and stoppin' off to try to win some coin offa street guys like us.

"Lotsa suckers then too, a'course, like these Richie Riches, ten-dollar haircuts and those dumb-ass shoes they freakin' call wingtips.

"Think about it. We're hustling the future hustlers," he said, flipping over his heavy silver cross hanging on his chest so a crucified Jesus was right-side up. "We should get a cut a teachers' coin. These gringo college boys learning about jukin' and jivin' for bread down Wall Street are getting' a better education from us teachin' 'em the ropes a hustlin' so they get ready for hustles they gonna do."

Manny told the boys to set up the cardboard boxes on top of each other next to a newspaper stand. He told them that after the Monte suckers lose, they're candidates to look for a cop.

"They tell *policia*," Manny said, raising his voice an octave and enunciating with clean Rs and ringing "ings" out of Greenwich, Connecticut, "to 'Arrest those people, officer—uh, officer Jones, is it? Surely they do not possess a license to establish a gambling operation on the streets.'"

The boys laughed at the accent they'd heard in old-time movies, showing rich *gringos* driving convertibles through leafy streets.

"*Policia* mostly ignore us," Manny said. "But when someone bitches enough and talks like he maybe knows someone big, they gotta roust us.

"So the cops stake us out and sometimes bring us in or give us DAPs—freakin' lame-ass Desk Appearance tickets, which we can beat easy but cost us time off the score. So, we gotta have lookouts.

"That's where you two come in hanging down the street,

lookin' out," he said, demonstrating by swiveling his head to look up and down and across 14th Street.

"Hear me now. You see anyone wearing loafers or a nice suit that actually fits, forget about him. Not a cop. Can't run in loafers and cops' threads don't never fit.

"And if the shirt's tucked, move your eyes to the next guy 'cause street cops in civvies always wear shirts over pants to hide guns and cuffs. *Comprende?* This is important what I teach you. It's your college. It'll always be with you. Always help you.

"C.E., gimme the whistle again how you gonna warn us."

Cousin Eduardo spread his mouth with his forefinger and pinky and let loose a two-tone ear splitter.

"C.E., you got the greatest sound! You could break glass like that fat *mami* in that TV ad. The Memorex tape one. You know, the famous jazzy singer—*cafe con leche* skin—with the Irish name, uh, uh, Fitz something. She's a bitchin'-good singer when she's singin' legit."

For months, Manny brought the boys to the Square to work the crowd with him and to dispense his wisdom.

He'd drill them about which roofs were best to hide from cops downtown and in the *barrio* where they live off First and 112th. As a special gift, he told them how to find the rooftop hideout he uses around the corner from their building where he and his girlfriend of the moment would blow up an air mattress.

"But stay away on Fridays after school or Sunday nights, her *mami* thinking she's studying with her *amiga*."

After he taught the boys the Monte hustle, Manny sent his girlfriend to the hospital after he found out she was doing Arturo on Manny's roof. He left her with a scar running down the side of her mouth and two false teeth that looked it.

"Thought she could have anything she wanted," Manny

told Carlos when he visited him at Rikers, on assault and battery charges the girlfriend's teacher pressed her to file. "Well, she ain't looking so good now. And you know that *pendejo* she was with? His time's gonna come. Thinks he's a big man, owns 115th from the river to Park, hustling primo shit—you know, Gringo Mike's Panama Red and Blue Magic H. Payback's comin' when the time's right."

Manny was still in jail when Carlos's time was coming for the draft. But Father Oscar, who ran a clinic to advise guys how to duck Uncle Sam, told Carlito to tell the Draft Board that he was the sole support for his family. No lie there. He worked two jobs: one at the Fulton Street fish market and one at a chop-shop in the Bronx.

Reluctantly, because there was a quota to meet, the draft board gave Carlito a hardship exemption. As for Cousin Eduardo, after he was caught with a stash of heroin, the judge offered two options: a likely jail sentence or signing up for the Marines to go to Vietnam.

"Way it goes," Manny told his friends in Benito's backroom, where they'd play dominoes and drink Colt .45. Cousin Eduardo just couldn't go to jail, couldn't live in a cage, so he took that *pendejo* judge's deal.

"Alla it's a crapshoot—for him, for alla us. C.E. knows that now. Sometimes you make your point, sometimes ya crap out! Way a the world. I taught those kids that. Me! And not for nuthin', but this whole thing over there. Like, why? What'd they ever do to us? What's in it for any of us to take it to 'em?

"You know, that guy Stokely—who names his son Stokely? —last name'a Carmickle or something. Anyway, he's always shoutin' Black Power and all. He had it right when he said no way he was gonna fight the Honkies' made-up war. He told 'em, 'No Viet Cong never called me nigger.'

"Spic, neither."

# MEADOW GREEN

"LUSH, I gotta get outta here before I do something I go to jail for or worse," Calvin said, standing at the edge of the pond, shimmying against a towel across his back.

"What you talkin' 'bout?" Luscious said, sitting waist deep just a few feet from shore in his safe spot, aligned with his markers—a tree at one end of the pond and a boulder at the other end, indicating where the water gets three-feet deep. He can't swim and won't let anyone teach him no matter how much he's teased.

The first time Luscious waded into the pond four years earlier he slipped down the sloping bottom into deep muck. He tried to yank his feet free but the more he struggled, the more mud oozed through his toes, sucking his feet even deeper. Panicked, he swiveled toward shore, furiously windmilling his arms until he finally pulled his feet free. He groped his way with his feet to shallow water, fell onto his hands and knees, and crawled to sit in about a foot of water.

"Now that was funny, Lush," Calvin said, a towel hanging from his neck. "You splashing around like a drunk octopus. No way you gonna drown with me on the job, but you were funny, spinning your arms and all."

From then on, whenever Luscious went into the pond, he'd moor himself in the shallows, sluicing water over his back. He said it reminded him of when he was a little boy, sitting in a tub, Momma lathering his back.

Luscious and Calvin had discovered the pond when they were ten, playing their game—"Slaves and Crackers"—in the thick woods separating the town's Black and White neighborhoods. On the far side of the pond were charred remains of a cabin and a dock that had tumbled into the water. Stories that skeletons were under the collapsed timbers kept most people away from the pond.

"I don't leave, I'm gonna slit Daddy's throat like a fat pig," Calvin said.

He dried his legs, grabbed his pants from a tree limb next to the pond and stepped into them. He cinched his belt, its end drooping from his narrow waist, closed his eyes, and raised his face toward the sun. After a minute or so, he turned away.

"Cal, you gotta stop even thinkin' about something like that," Luscious said, unfolding his lanky body from the pond, sloshing his way toward shore, gingerly stepping around rocks.

"You know it's a sin even to be thinkin' that," Luscious said, coming through an opening between a stand of cattails. "Besides, he's Joe Jackson. Nobody—son neither—should be messin' with that big-ass mean streak."

"But it's different now," Calvin said, stretching to reach a sleeveless, white T-shirt from the top of the rock. He pulled it over his head, tugging it down over raised scars on his back, and adjusted its straps to sit evenly on his wide shoulders. "He used to be mean mostly outside the house, but now he's mean inside all the time. If I'da had a blade last night, I'da cut him sure as you get wet in water.

"We're sittin' at the table—and he asks Momma where the meat is. She says there ain't none 'cause Mr. Thomas said we ain't paid the bill for a month. Then it was like watching a runaway train. He slams the table and yells at Momma to stop talkin' back at him, makin' him look bad."

Calvin slowly shook his head, bent to pick up his left work boot and took a deep breath. He slipped his foot into the boot and began lacing it.

"Then Daddy got quiet like he's listening to himself. Then he stares at the bowl all pretty next to the biscuits. Momma loved that bowl with periwinkles on it she got from her Momma so much she wouldn't allow for anyone to handle it 'cause they might drop it. She'd serve us outta it herself."

Calvin grabbed his other boot and held it still, suspended above his foot.

"Then, without sayin' nothin', Daddy, he right-crosses Momma outta her chair and swipes the bowl onta the floor—mess a potatoes and chips of periwinkles all over.

"And there's Momma laid out on the floor," Calvin said, putting the boot down, his eyes on the ground between Luscious and him, "covering her nose—blood leakin' through her fingers."

"Holy shit, Cal," Luscious said, pulling on his pants.

"Daddy steps over her like she's a log and heads to the back door on the way to Boo Boo's. Didn't even look at her. Then he stops on the way out and turns back to Momma. I'm thinking he's coming back to hit her again. But he goes to the ice box and rips off the magazine picture of a 'zeebo Momma always dreamin' about and put on the door. He crushes it and hook-shoots it into the garbage can. Takes the sample of the way the paint would look on the 'zeebo she ever got one—Meadow Green it was called. Got it from Paint-O-Rama. Daddy rips it up and throws the pieces into the air like snow fallin' in one of those round glass things."

Calvin blinked rapidly, put his boot on and laced it up.

"Man, o' man! He's takin' mean to a whole 'nother level. Whadya do?" Luscious said, sitting on a rock letting the sun soak in.

Calvin slowly shook his head. "I take a run at him, thinkin' I'll knock him down from behind when he's bookin' to the back door and clip him upside his head when he's going down," Calvin said, standing up, staring at the woods. "I jump on his back, but he shakes me off like a bad smell and throws me up against the wall. Says if I wasn't blood he'd kill me. Then he rolls his fat ass out the door."

"That some sorry shit," Luscious said. "But you gotta know he ain't never gonna change. You gotta stop hopin' for that." Luscious reached down and rubbed his legs with a towel. "Might as well be waiting on Jesus to walk across the pond. Mean's a thing once you get it you can count on it always be there so deep even Jesus ain't gonna get at it. Lottsa people say what goes around comes around. Sounds nice to hear, 'specially in church and all, but people like your Daddy don't change 'cause they thinkin' they always can duck the come around."

"He ain't seen no come around for nothin' he ever did," Calvin said.

"Yeah. Lottsa times the come around hits the wrong person, you know, like when somebody gets shot or sliced without doing nothin' . . . innocent stand-byer."

"That's what I'm talkin', Lush. I can't stick around waitin' for the come around to hit him or Momma again. I'll dice him up like an onion."

"Cal, you talkin' serious shit—adult shit—cuttin' your daddy. Be careful what you thinkin', Cal, real careful," Luscious said, folding his towel. "'Cause sometimes you promisin' yourself to do something, it got a way a workin' inside your head like a tapeworm that gets fat and takes over and you got no say and you gotta do what it says, even though you know you shouldn't."

Calvin walked toward the pond's shady end and grabbed a rope anchored by a rock and running into the water at the other end. He fished out four cans of Mountain Dew bound together by plastic rings, then walked toward Luscious, dangling the cans from a finger. He ripped off two cans and set the remaining two on the ground in a sliver of shade next to the rock.

Luscious wiped the top with his shirt and popped the tab.

"I'm already thinkin' I got no choice," Calvin said, tilting his head back and chugging half of the soda. He looked at the ground, slowly shaking his head. "I don't see another way—either cuttin' him or bookin'."

Luscious drank from his Mountain Dew.

"You ready?" Calvin asked, grabbing his towel from the rock. "Let's go."

Luscious ran his towel through his hair and flipped the towel over his shoulder. They walked past a fat weeping willow and down the path through the woods.

"You know, Cal, if you book, I'm bookin' with," Luscious said, kicking a branch off the path. "Remember. We don't never split up. Calvin Jackson and Luscious Banks. Calvin and Luscious. Luscious and Calvin. I got the blood paper under my bed in my box."

Calvin sipped his soda.

"My daddy been saying ain't nothin' gonna change for us 'round here," Luscious said. "He says, 'Sure Rev King's saying true stuff and we gotta hope. But nothin' gonna change our life-times around here for us.' Daddy says we'll overcome but gotta be careful how we overcome. Says White people don't like bein' overcome a little bit, 'bout nothin'. Like Daddy say, 'Gets tiring always stopping ourselves from overcomin' 'em on lotsa things.'"

Luscious turns around, looks at the weeping willow and turns toward Calvin. "You ever wonder what that tree's weepin' 'bout?"

Calvin didn't answer.

"Anyway, Daddy says I could work my way up to assistant school janitor, I watch my Qs and Ps. Yeah, shuckin' along not looking anybody in the eye. Sheet, I think it's honkies not wanting to look us in the eye, you know, like it's not healthy to look at someone in the eye you got trapped and you not sure you can beat."

Calvin picked up a stone and fired it at a tire leaning against a tree. It curved on him and sailed into the weeds.

"Yeah, that gets real tirin', you know?" Luscious said. "I mean sometimes I wanna be someone who doesn't have to make sure no one thinks I'm disrespecting them 'cause I look straight at 'em. You know, sometimes I just wanna be able to not have to say 'yes, sir' and 'thank you, sir' for getting my own damn change from some cracker. My change I'm due! Sometimes I just want to be able to cop an attitude like White people get to do and just snatch the bill from 'em like I gotta be careful not to touch his hand, like they do."

"You do that to the wrong one, Lush, a heap of grief coming down on you. Look at what it got Emmett for just lookin'. Crackers with tiny dicks thinkin' they'll get bigger ones they put down Emmett. Way it is, Lush, they still doin' it. Ain't gonna change—not in time for us, anyways."

The path curved around weeds growing alongside a clump of bald tires, some leaning against trees, others laying flat with yellow and purple weeds sprouting from their centers. To the side of the tires were two mattresses, one lying crosswise on top of the other, oozing dirty gray stuffing. Empty beer cans and green-glass wine jugs lay scattered next to the mattresses. Farther into the brush a rusting burn barrel on its side was splattered with bullet holes.

Calvin was suckered again by the sun glinting off something between the tires and the mattresses. For a mini-second he thought it was something worth something or something he might want. Then his brain caught up to his eyes, telling him again that it was only the bottom of the same beer can he always saw, still somehow shiny-peeking from weeds. Fooling him. He shook his head and jump-shot his empty can at the middle of a tire and missed, sending the can tumbling farther into the weeds.

"You know Rufus, right?" Luscious said, swatting at a horsefly as they followed the path around the rubble. "Elji's cousin?"

"Yeah, kinda," Calvin said, slapping his shoulder. "I know he lookin' to get cut himself, Sally Mae's daddy finds out he gets with her."

"Well, he finally did find out, and Rufus takes off like the Roadrunner on moonshine after her daddy found out they'd been in Tyrone's backseat. Elji was so scared, Tyrone said, he nearly turned White and took off for Kinston. "Anyways, Elji says Rufus says work's there for asking. Tobacco work. Elji says Rufus says they need guys to work so bad they give a big discount to stay in houses they got for 'em."

"You sayin' we should go?" Calvin asks.

"Well, what we got here? Especially you thinkin' what you shouldn't be thinkin'.""

"That's a big idea. Bookin' to there," Calvin said.

Calvin stopped before they reached the grove of trees that would block the sky for a while before they came out onto the hardtop. He scanned the sky to see if his turkey vulture was on the wind yet. Often he'd go to the pond by himself to sit dead still on his boulder like he belonged. Then he'd slowly raise his head to not disturb what was going on and try to spot frogs, sitting mostly underwater on the edge of the pond. He liked to see their yellow-green eyes staring just above the surface, waiting for the tiniest movement that didn't belong and with a plop disappear under water. Sometimes Calvin thought they'd locked eyeballs on each other, recognizing something.

Then he'd look for double-winged dragonflies, flitting from cattail to cattail, landing on top of them just long enough to catch their breaths. Sometimes, Calvin would sit so still for so long that his turkey vulture would start circling him. He'd watch the ugly, graceful bird, wings dark against the sky, spread wide like Dracula's cloak, its wings filling and spilling wind to tighten its downward spiral.

He'd watch the bird gradually shrink his circle, checking whether there was something about to give up life on the ground so it would be safe to land and rip off still-warm flesh.

Calvin and Luscious reached the hardtop.

"Later," Luscious said and turned right. Calvin went left. Their houses were on opposite ends of the south section of town, separated from White "Upper Tompkins" by the new two-lane blacktop.

Calvin checked for any sign of Muncy before cutting across the old man's field instead of walking clear around his thirty acres. Calvin's daddy was still seething about Muncy shooting two of his cows five years ago for wandering onto Muncy's land. The sheriff said technically Muncy had a point when he said for the record, "That boy's cows came onto my land not for the first time. So ipso facto I had a right to shoot 'em and eat 'em."

Calvin's daddy would bellow through the years about how

he hated Muncy with a passion and was making plans for revenge.

Calvin cut across the field, deer-twitchy alert for any sign of Muncy. He came out on the other side onto Old Mill Road, down a bit from his white house with its short white picket fence in front. Every year Daddy would paint it and the taller fence bordering the back of the house, enclosing the side yard.

In the front yard, beyond the low show-off fence was a fake well with a green shingled roof. It was like the one Momma had seen in a magazine in a White lady's house she cleaned back when she was first married. Husband Joe had built an exact replica for Momma, complete with a spinning brass weathervane on top that she kept shiny.

Calvin stepped over the small fence and across the yard to the gate on the larger fence. He unlatched it and walked across the backyard where—out of sight from passersby—sat two dented, chipped clothes-washing tubs, their wringer rollers hanging off-kilter on top. A newly painted, sunflower-yellow 1954 Chevy was on blocks, a black tarp blown back, exposing the guts of the chassis and webs of dangling wires. On a picnic table nearby, splotched with black mold, were two mufflers, a half dozen sections of tailpipes, a car radiator, and assorted tools.

Calvin was twelve when Daddy turned him into a mule after he'd killed their mule, overworking and underfeeding it.

"You offa ya momma's titty for a long time now," Daddy said the first day he hooked his son to the plow. "You gots to earn your keep, now, boy."

Daddy would walk behind Calvin, slinging his whip at him with one hand, the other guiding the plow's dirt-polished steel blade through the hard-packed red dirt. The whip hit Calvin so often, especially when he slowed, trying to churn a particularly hard part of the red soil, that he couldn't sleep on his back for a week until the slashes scabbed over.

When Calvin became a mule, he decided that he didn't want to sleep on the living room couch any longer. The chickens were long gone, so he cleaned out the coop against the big fence on the far corner of the backyard, put up plywood walls and added an alcove for his clothes and treasured transistor radio, behind which Momma would put a sandwich and an apple, hiding them from Joe, in case he went into the coop. In front of his chicken coop, Calvin had put a sign he'd found in the woods by the pond. "Beware of the Dog." A line was drawn through "Dog," next to which Calvin had painted "Mule."

———

The night after he'd jumped Daddy, Calvin had fallen asleep in his coop and was dreaming of his vulture swooping down on him. He was struggling in the dream to move his body so the vulture would know he wasn't dead. He woke when Daddy burst through the door, yelling and shaking the flimsy walls, trembling the movie poster on the wall, showing Jim Brown hugging Raquel Welch, her now quivering breasts close to bursting over the top of her blouse.

"You ain't a man, yet, boy! You best remember that. You even think a beatin' on your daddy again, you be floating belly up in that pond you and Luscious sneak off to."

Joe spun around, fists still clenched at his sides, walked out the door, and punched the side of the coop, shaking the walls and Raquel's breasts again.

Calvin lay awake on his bed for two hours with an ax handle next to him, ready if Daddy came back. Calvin figured the knees first and then home-run swings at Daddy's head. He thought of the funeral and the closed casket.

He lay there. How did he get from there to here?

One Saturday when Calvin was eight, Daddy had relented to Momma's pleas to let Calvin tag along downtown to the boxing ring Daddy had built in the narrow lot between Tilde's second-hand store and Tutti Fruitti's Men's Shoppe.

Daddy was perched on an oak-topped stool at the edge of the ring, collecting bets on fight cards he organized on the first and last Saturdays of the month. The grand prize for winning five fights in a row was a suit, shirt, tie, and, if the winner wanted, shoes to go with it—for a 10% discount at Tilde's. Losers would get slips of papers giving them 10% off at J.D's liquor store, where, on fight Saturdays, J.D. would raise prices 15%.

The day Calvin tagged along, Daddy ordered him to stand next to the stool while he went on a beer run. Calvin, wearing his first long pants Momma got for Easter at Tilde's, reached up to put his assortment of twigs in various shapes that, with a powerful imagination, could look kinda like toy soldiers, on top of the stool.

He spun the seat to lower it to get a better look at how he should position his troops. When Daddy came back, he discovered that Calvin had changed the stool's perfect height and gave his son his first bloody nose.

Then there was the summer night when he was eleven and went with Momma for the first and last time to see Daddy play center field for the Tompkins's Bollweevils Single A team. Calvin watched mosquitos, gnats and an occasional bat zigzagging through the haze of light beams, streaming from poles at the top of the stands.

On their way into the ballpark, Momma had pointed out

the plaque that said the stadium with its latticework of steel had been built in 1921.

Calvin was proud, seeing Daddy trot in from centerfield in his white uniform trimmed in red and blue, the big red "T" at a slight angle on his blue cap. Joe's batting average that summer was .167, without a home run and only one extra-base hit—a bloop double just past first base.

That night, Joe struck out in the second inning and in the fifth hit a weak come-backer. A group of long-time season ticket holders decided they'd suffered too long in silence. When Joe came out of the dugout toward the on-deck circle for his third at bat, five fans rose, raised their beers to him, and off-key sere-naded him with "Joltin' Joe-Oh, DiMaggi-oh-oh"—a take-off of that old song that praised the real Joltin' Joe—for hitting in 56 straight games way back when. One guy yelled, "Hey, Joe! Where's Marilyn?"

Joe struck out on a curve in the dirt, prompting another chorus. This time the song was picked up by the rest of the 75 or so fans. Momma forced a half smile at Calvin—scrunched down in his seat—and nudged him to take a handful of popcorn.

After the final out of the game, in which Joe went 0-4, accompanied by the usual jeers and song, he walked into the locker room, grabbed his civilian clothes and, still wearing spikes and his uniform, click-clacked across the cement floor and out the other door leading to the street.

At two in the morning that night, Joe eased his old Chevy, a taillight dangling from tape, up to the locker room door and threw his uniform on the ground in front of it.

A few years later, Joe was sitting on his stool, tipped back against Tilde's brick wall, waiting for the second fight to begin.

He righted the stool, looked down the street, and saw Calvin coming out of Creamer's Candy Store carrying a little brown paper bag. Wayne Burson, much bigger than Calvin and three years older, blocked his way, shoved Calvin against the window, told him he was a worthless piece of shit and had to pay with his licorice to get past him. To emphasize the point, Wayne punched Calvin in the stomach.

Calvin twisted away from Wayne, who pursued him while Calvin pleaded to be left alone, his voice quavering. Wayne turned to his friends and laughed, then closed in on Calvin.

Calvin planted his right leg, spun back toward Wayne, and threw an overhand right with all of his weight behind it, slamming into his temple. Wayne staggered. Calvin rushed him, throwing a flurry of punches that dropped Wayne to his knees. Calvin kept hitting him, flattening Wayne onto his back. Calvin kneeled on Wayne's chest and raised his fist over him. "You give? You give?"

When he didn't answer immediately, Calvin broke his nose.

"You give now?" Calvin shouted, cocking his fist over Wayne's face.

"Yes! Yes! Stop!"

"Louder! Say it loud!" Calvin shouted, raising his knee and thumping it down on Wayne's chest. "Say it! Say it! Say it loud!"

"I give! I give!" he said, his eyes bugging.

"Again!"

"I give! I give!"

Calvin stood up, picked up the bag he'd dropped, pulled out a rope of licorice, ripped off a chaw, and swaggered down the sidewalk, the black licorice dangling from his mouth.

*Bingo!* Joe had his very own fighter. Maybe he'd call his son "Kid Dynamite" or maybe "The Punchin' Prince of Boxing." Maybe "Kid Chocolate" after the old-time Cuban world champion. Joe knew he was onto something. A son who replaced his mule and now, with his quick hands and ferocity, a good draw for his Saturday afternoon fights.

Joe never gave his son boxing lessons, because he didn't know anything about the finer points of boxing, but he knew how to draw a crowd. Calvin quickly learned on his own to not get backed against the ropes, because two sides of the ring were only a couple of inches from the stores' brick walls and his head easily could be smashed against them. He fought mid-ring, which fans appreciated: slugfests, no feinting and covering up against the ropes.

Joe declared that his son would take on all comers. Of course, he knew his son—tall and big all around for his age with long arms that allowed his jabs to open the way for him to get inside to work the body—would lose some fights, especially against older, bigger, more experienced brawlers.

But this boy with wide shoulders whaling away at big guys was a good draw, win or lose. *Gotta admire the kid's guts*, they'd say, as blood oozed from his mouth and nose.

After one bout that drew blood, gushing from Calvin's nose and from a cut over an eye, Tyrone asked Joe, "How can you let your kid take a beatin' like that?"

"Teaching him 'bout life, the old man said. "Teachin' him nothin' free in life, 'specially his life. So he gotta punch for lunch. No punch, no lunch."

———

At dawn, two days before Calvin's 16th birthday, he and Luscious left home. Luscious didn't say anything to his family before leaving. He couldn't bring himself to tell his daddy and momma that working his way up to be head janitor was not his idea of the good life.

Calvin took Momma and and his little sister Sissy aside the

night before to tell them he was leaving. Momma told him through tears that she didn't want him to go but that she understood why. Sissy stared at him, eyes wide open, hands at her sides. Calvin bent to hug her. She threw her arms around his neck and hung on tightly as he picked her up. He burrowed his head into her neck, he set her down, and pulled her arms from his neck, tears rolling down her cheeks.

Calvin and Luscious took the bus about seventy miles to Kinston. The bus drove along Main Street lined with cars, angle-parked into the curb. They passed the Ritz Theatre, Uncle Bob's five and dime with its red-white-and-blue awning, and Momma Delora's cafe next to a Marine Corps recruiting station with an American flag and a Marine Corps flag flanking the door. Pop's feed store with a Holstein and a pig painted on his window was next door. Mid-street they passed Growers' Bank, the biggest building in the county, with two tall, white, wooden columns on the sides of the entrance. Hanging from one of the columns was a huge round clock with Roman numerals that was always eight minutes slow.

On the outskirts of town, three long, narrow shacks left over from slave days lined a field overgrown with weeds and prickly bushes. The president of the local chapter of the Daughters of the American Revolution pushed to have the shacks preserved just as they were, as memorials to the good-old days. But the tobacco farmers who dominated the town said there had to be some kind of cheap housing for their workers. The growers said economics had to rule the day. With money from the Kinston Heritage Fund they replaced some of the shacks' rotted clapboards, cut in a few more windows, and dug three more outhouses. As a sop to the Daughters, the farmers put up a large bronze plaque with a relief, depicting two slaves in frayed straw hats hunched over tobacco plants.

The barracks' location near town allowed the doctor easy

access when he'd finally respond to imploring phone calls to come and treat a worker's tobacco sickness, which came with spasms of vomiting, diarrhea, and crushing headaches—symptoms of nicotine poisoning from days spent handling damp tobacco leaves.

Luscious was gangly and didn't look all that strong, but Calvin's muscled arms and wide shoulders got them work, and he assured the bosses that Luscious was strong, too. And, of course, lots of "no, sirs" and "yes, sirs" and minimal eye contact.

Early in the season, Calvin and Luscious would patrol the rows of budding tobacco leaves, scanning undersides for green hornworm larvae, crushing them between their fingers. They'd sucker the leaves to let others grow big and when the leaves were big enough for harvesting, Calvin and Luscious would cut them down and stack them flat on wagons. They'd haul them to curing sheds behind Main Street, draping them over long poles, and hoist them to dangle from the rafters to dry. After auction, they'd take down the poles and pack the leaves for delivery.

Calvin and Luscious had cubicles next to each other in the middle barracks of the former slave shacks. Three days into their jobs, Leroy, one of the workers, told Calvin he was kind of a sheriff of the barracks and that Calvin and Luscious had to pay five dollars a week as dues to those who were there before them. Luscious and Calvin laughed at Leroy. That night on the way back from the outhouse, Luscious was jumped and beaten by three guys wearing stockings over their heads. The next morning Calvin saw Leroy walking to the outhouse. Calvin ran ahead of him, stopped in front of the door, his arms at his side and clenched fists.

"That'll be five dollars a crap, starting now, my man," Calvin said.

Leroy raised his arms to push Calvin to the side. Calvin

popped him with two jabs Leroy never saw followed by a right that broke his nose, sending a flood of blood over his shirt.

"Sure hope for your sake you got a five-spot on you, boy."

Leroy reached into his pocket and pulled out a ten-dollar bill.

"I'll take an extra five on account," Calvin said.

Three days later the foreman told Calvin and Luscious to move their things to the shack farthest from the outhouses and cut their pay, saying the pay they were getting was a miscalculation—the new wages were in keeping with what newcomers should be paid until they proved themselves.

So, Calvin and Luscious needed money. From time to time, posters would be tacked up around town, advertising carnivals and strongman contests featuring boxing matches with few rules. Calvin had resisted entering them for a while, but now they had no other options. It turned out that Calvin had, indeed, learned a thing or two in Daddy's boxing ring.

His victories—usually by knockouts or surrender towels thrown over the ropes—soon dwindled the pool of opponents. So Calvin was urged by promoters to carry White opponents for a few rounds or risk losing White audiences that paid the freight.

Sometimes he'd let a White fighter last the full six rounds and, of course, White referees would give their boys the victory.

Most fans, though, knew that Calvin was the best fighter on any given night. They appreciated his unrelenting style—always stalking, unfazed by punches he took to get inside, where he worked on kidneys and livers before throwing his shotgun-blast left hook for the kill. His style was to never head-hunt before its time. He believed the old boxing adage: "Kill the body and the head will fall."

Intent counts, he'd been told by a man who'd watched one

of his fights in Daddy's ring. "You gotta believe you're gonna stick your fist into his guts and come out the other side."

One night, Calvin entered a ring in a tent that had been used to auction hogs that day. Sitting ringside was a contingent of "toy soldiers," as Luscious called them, from Robert E. Lee Military Academy. They came—some in Black face and red lipstick—to cheer on their guy, who would "show the Coon a thing or two."

Calvin always hunched his shoulders under his robe when he got into the ring, dipped his knees a little, and kept his robe on during introductions, trying to look smaller as Luscious roamed the audience taking bets.

"C'mon, folks, who thinks this White boy can knock the shine offa the shine? Money talks, bullshit walks!" Luscious would shout, careful to finish with an impish grin.

Some bettors laid down money just to shut up this uppity Black boy with the big mouth and "those long eyelashes that make you look like a girl, boy."

One night, Calvin was in no mood to carry the White boy and midway through the first round caught the toy soldier against the ropes and sunk a left hook into his liver. He went down and stayed down, curled into a whimpering ball. The crowd of cadets, college frat boys, and assorted locals quieted, murmuring about Calvin's "raw power," meaning it was strength straight from the jungle—not quite human.

"So whatta you gonna do with your cut?" Calvin asked Luscious when they were walking back to their cubicles in the old shacks after the fight.

"Some new threads and a proper date with Gertie," Luscious said. "Now I can do it up, proper like. Bones said I could borrow his uncle's car 'cause he's laid up with the shakes so who's gonna know?"

"What's that mean to 'do it up proper'? You never gonna be

able to do it up proper for her and her momma. Just wasting money."

"What're you talkin'? What? I got nothin' she likes?"

"I'm just saying you're field and she's house, and her momma thinks that's a big difference. No Saturday bath and perfume you pour on your neck is gonna change that."

"You just jealous Gertie never liked you boyfriend-like and she did me. You a hoodoo man, now? Sayin' you seein' the future?"

"I see enough to know there ain't no future for you and Gertie—Gertrude her momma always sure to call her. Proper like."

"And you," Luscious said, "a boy who fights in a pig pen—knows all about proper?"

"Leastwise I know where I fit and where I don't. Been shown that all my life—you too. And Gertie's momma thinks she knows where Gertie fits and it ain't with you. Gertie might not think that now but she will, even if she doesn't want to think that."

"You talkin' shit!"

"C'mon, look at us and look at them. Two shades darker, for starters. And that means something to someone lives in the house."

"Shows what you know, Boxing Boy. They live in a house behind the house."

"C'mon, Lush. It's a real house. You got one with running water, for starters? You gotta know who you are and where you're at. We gotta make it with what we got, not what we want to have."

Luscious glowered. After a long silence, Calvin said softly, "Now I don't have nothing against Gertie, herself. She's nice and all, but you gotta . . . Aw, c'mon, whatta I know 'bout anything? Just don't fall too deep into those eyes of hers or you never be climbin' out."

Calvin playfully punched Luscious on his arm. "Besides," he smiled, "you get with her, where'm I at?"

Luscious moved his shoulder away from Calvin's attempted hug.

"You know, Cal, I can do things by myself, and a girl can like me, too. Why not?"

"What're you takin'? Who says different, Luscious? I'm just sayin' for your own good to think about what she really thinks of you deep down."

"Maybe she likes me. Maybe she likes me better than you or anybody likes you. I'm gonna make somethin' of me."

"I'm just saying, Lush, you gotta pick careful like. She's not the only one looking your way. Her momma looking hard, too."

Calvin and Luscious were making money on the fights. But one night when Luscious was counting their winnings and Calvin was changing clothes behind a tent, three sheriff's deputies—one carrying a double-barreled shotgun—showed up. He waved a paper at Luscious and said it authorized the seizure of all funds involved with gambling and that they had to appear in court for their offenses. "So hand it over, boy. You'd only throw it away anyways on purple hats and moonshine."

Two days later, Calvin and Luscious were sitting at one of the five white, Formica-topped tables squeezed into the back room of Momma Delora's Kitchen café, next to the Marine recruiting office. Above the table was a framed *Life* magazine cover of Muhammad Ali, standing over Sonny Liston—flat on the canvas—taunting him, curling his arm to urge him to get up, his right bicep bulging.

They slurped the last of their Royal Crown Colas to wash down Momma's Friday special of fried catfish, mac'n cheese, mustard greens, and sweet potato pie. Calvin had suggested the meal and offered to pay for it—a kind of secret penance because he had accurately predicted that Gertie would come around to believe her momma that she could do better than Luscious.

Walter Cronkite on the TV screen hanging from the wall was reading the news. He said President Johnson had increased the monthly quota of draftees from 17,000 to 35,000.

As if on cue, a White soldier—block-shouldered in his cocky uniform with all those doodads on it—strode, parade-straight, past the counter up front and pushed aside the plastic curtain of amber beads into the back room. He dragged a chair, screeching it along the floor from another table to theirs. He stood over them all smiley. On the sleeves of his tan shirt were sergeant's insignias, and scarlet stripes ran down the sides of his blue pants. His black shoes glistened.

Calvin and Luscious tucked their work boots under their chairs.

"Hope you boys're doin' okay," the Marine said. "Mind if I sit a spell with you?"

They had learned about "rhetorical questions" in night school. Luscious and Calvin knew enough not to answer the sergeant's question because that would seem uppity, even if they said, "No, sir, we don't mind at all" because that would imply that they thought they had an option.

The big Marine took off his cap and placed it on the table, the shiny Marine Corps logo—a rope wrapped around a globe and an anchor on the front—aimed at Calvin and Luscious.

"I wanna talk to you about gettin' ahead of the game," the sergeant said, "by not waitin' to get drafted and havin' no say what happens to you."

Calvin and Luscious were only sixteen but had said they were eighteen to get their jobs. So they were added to the list the recruiter had of eighteen-year-olds in town.

The Marine rearranged the sugar bowl so it was dead

center on the table and put the salt and pepper shakers on opposite sides of it. Satisfied, he looked up at Calvin and Luscious.

"You heard the news that our Commander in Chief sent one hundred thousand troops to show those commie fucks what's what? He doubled the number of guys he's gonna draft. Doubled! So, for sure, Uncle Sam'll be callin' you boys to do your duty too and go kill those little commie Gooks. Sure as shit," he said, switching several times from Calvin's face to Luscious's.

"Now listen up! The draft board's meetin' tonight and," he said, looking side to side as if looking for eavesdroppers. "I have it on good information that your names are on the list, and it's in the Army you'll go. You'll have no say how, or when, or what you're gonna do in the Army, where everyone's dumped—the dumb, the lazy, the cowards. And, I gotta say, the ugly. It's something to be proud of—being a Marine—the best of 'em all. You can be that, too. You boys ever been told you're the best? At anything?"

Calvin and Luscious sipped their sodas.

"The Marines offer schooling and a trade that you can use after you finish your tours. And, boys, an added bennie is girls spread 'em for this old uni. Believe you me. Even White skanks for you boys. You just gotta show up. Plus you boys can go on the buddy system, which means you can be together, if you want."

Calvin and Luscious said they'd for sure think about it, sir.

After a few seconds of silence, the Marine shrugged his shoulders and stood up over them while he adjusted his white cap on his head.

"You know where I'm at, you choose to do the smart thing."

He executed a perfect about-face, slapped the doorway beads aside, and left the room.

"Ya know, Calvin," Luscious said after a final slurp of his soda and while crunching ice in his mouth, "I don't even like White girls. Skin looks like Milk a Mag-neesh-ah, like being sick. Why they all think we like White girls?"

"'Cause they got 'em and so they think we hafta want what they got 'cause they think we wanna be like them."

Luscious slowly shook his head, slipped a toothpick out of its cellophane, and probed his teeth.

"You know, Cal, maybe we should think about signing up. Maybe not the Marines, though. Maybe the Navy. Those commies ain't got no big boats to fight with so not likely they'll be coming after us we're on a boat."

"The Navy? Luscious, you're crazy! You can't even swim. You're afraid of the water—afraid of even our little ol' pond. 'Sides, I sign up for anything, it'll be the Marines. They're tough in and outta uniform. Even we'd get respect."

"We gotta decide 'cause that cracker just told us we're due," Luscious said, breaking the toothpick and dropping it onto his plate. "Signing up to have a choice of what we do is something to think about and three squares a day, free room, and they pay you something, too. Maybe Whitey has something we should listen to."

"Yeah, to go get killed instead a him. Not that there's much for us around here keeping us," Calvin said, pushing his chair from the table. "And don't know where there is, neither. And we're both not the dumbest guys, so maybe we can show we could do somethin' other than shoot people in the jungle. Ya know?"

Calvin and Luscious didn't think for a second it was coincidence that three days after they told the Marine recruiter they'd think about it, they got their greetings-from-Uncle-Sam letter, telling them they'd been drafted.

"There's still time, I guess," the sergeant told them, after rushing from his office without his cap when he spotted them going into Momma's, "before they get hold of you and you not gettin' any say about it. But you gotta sign right here, right now."

Calvin and Luscious had shown fake birth certificates to get work and so were on the town's list of guys eligible for the draft. They weren't great fakes, but they were good enough for the sergeant's captain to look the other way.

They signed and took the bus together on the buddy plan to boot camp on Parris Island, South Carolina, an 8,000-acre Marine Corps training camp riddled with tidal swamps. Luscious and Calvin got off the bus and were sent to different barracks. They never saw each other again.

Calvin was shipped out to DaNang on his way to Khe Sanh just in time to be one of the 6,000 defenders encircled by some 20,000 North Vietnamese troops for 77 days before Army troops broke the siege that killed more than 1,000 U.S. troops, mostly Marines. Calvin always wondered how and why he survived. Just plain old luck.

Two weeks after Luscious arrived on Parris Island, his drill instructor called him "an uppity, arrogant Black son of a bitch," for not saluting quickly and crisply enough when a White officer had passed him. That led the D.I. two nights later to take Luscious on a nighttime punishment exercise. The D.I. had drunk two six-packs of Dixie beer, misread the map, and ordered Luscious into the wrong canal in the swamp.

Luscious tentatively waded into the water, trying to feel with his boots where the shore fell off the way he had in the pond back home. A memory twitch of that day told him he would be okay; he'd reach the shallows if he set to windmilling the water as hard as he could just like he had at the pond when Calvin had laughed so hard.

The D.I. stood on shore, screaming: "You 'fraid of a little

water, boy? You fuckin' candy-ass! Get out there, deeper, boy, you fuckin' fuckup!"

The water was the coldest Luscious had ever felt. After all, it had come from the Atlantic Ocean down river only about five miles. Luscious stood as tall as he could, straining to pull his feet from the muck. Water rose up his back under his rucksack, soaking it, making it weigh even more than its original eighty pounds.

"Alright, you fucking fuckup, get the fuck outta the water," the D.I's disembodied voice shouted in the darkness. "Find your way back, boy. Have a nice walk. I'm fuckin' outta here," he said, throwing an empty beer can at Luscious.

Luscious tried to turn to shore but with his heavy boots, he hadn't felt the muck working its way up his ankles. His feet couldn't turn the boots. He could only claw at the water. He lifted his chin as far as he could toward the bright full moon that was pushing the tide up his back.

He drowned standing up, rooted in his boots stuck in the muck.

# TIMEX

COUSIN EDUARDO TOOK his eyes from the elephant grass about a hundred yards away where the Viet Cong were likely hiding. He looked up at a tree with wide leaves like those in the Bronx Botanical Garden where Algie took him junior year and then to Arthur Avenue for calzones and Cokes.

That's what you think of when you're 8,000 miles from home, knowing you might die any second. You think of home. You make everything back there as sweet as you can. A lot sweeter than it was.

Algie had turned those black sparkly eyes on him, just short of tears, tilting her head in a silent plea to get him to go with her. The Garden had been on her list since she'd missed a fifth-grade class trip because her mother had thrown out the permission slip, telling her that school was for sitting in a classroom and learning, not for a bus trip to look at flowers.

Algie was delighted by all of the species of trees, flowers, and grasses of so many colors of green and yellow, so pretty and graceful—even spiky zebra grasses, they call them. Cousin Eduardo particularly liked the orchids, so many shapes, some "kinda having tongues loafing out of kinda mouths."

In one of the little glass hot houses, she pointed out with a broad smile that sank her dimples, a Venus flytrap. She told him it was a carnivore, and that she'd feed him to it if he turned out to be just another barrio player, using girls as playthings, like her cousin Julio and the guys he ran with.

She had him look at the symmetry of leaves on both sides of every leaf's spine. She said nature left alone is perfectly balanced. From then on, Cousin Eduardo had tried to find an exception—uneven sides, something showing nature out of sync. He couldn't and that meant he had a guarantee that he'd be able to find beauty whenever he needed it. Who knew? Maybe she'd be there if he made it home.

But then again, maybe Carlos was right.

"You gotta get over her, 'cause sure as shit she over you," he told Cousin Eduardo the night before he left for Vietnam when they were in the back dining room at Little Ponce on 119th Street, Spanish Harlem.

"You gotta take the fall for it, too," Carlos said, pulling on a Schlitz beer bottle before reinserting his hand between Rosita's thighs as she sat on his lap. "Don't go all country music and say you were done wrong by some kinda devil woman. Not all girls are the same, C.E. Some got us figured out. She figured you out and didn't like her figurin'," he said with a grin as Rosita put her tongue in his ear. "You gotta face it. You were too busy trying to prove you could have it all even after she warned you.

"You were bookin' on Algie's smile always there for you while you're playing with all those show-me-why-I-should-let-you-fuck-me girls who love swishing and bouncing it all around to see what you gonna spring for to get some," he said as Rosita massaged his ear lobe. "Algie's made different. C'mon, you shoulda known that. Am I right, Rosita?"

Rosita smiled, nodded her head, and ran her tongue over her lips.

But that was then, and now in the real world of trying to duck bullets, Lieutenant Belson gathered the platoon, told them to take a knee, and said they were going out in the bush to bring back more enemy ears than his rival platoon lieutenant's guys had brought in last week. The idea was the Colonel would drape the ears on strings and spotlight them like Christmas ornaments, dangling over the front of his tent for everyone to admire and to be jealous.

Paulie Lupe and Fish in the third row were smoking weed as Belson paced in front of his troops going over the details of the ear hunt. Belson came to ignore his men lighting up in downtime, since he'd busted Schnerson for it and Belson's sergeant advised him that it was, "like asking to be fragged, sir."

"Guys," Belson said, holding up a map of their route, "I asked the Colonel to let us go out tonight and said we'd make him proud—show him what we can do. He said he liked my enthusiasm. Said he'll come up with medals for us if we come back with a dozen ears. So, of course, I said we'd do just that."

"We saddle up at seventeen hundred," Belson said, checking his Timex watch before heading back into the mess tent for another coffee and a slice of blueberry pie.

"Un-fuckin'-believable," Cousin Eduardo told Smiley. "Fuckin' medals? C'mon, he's putting our asses on the line for fuckin' two-bit medals?"

"Yeah," Smiley said, "what good are they? Can't fuck 'em. Can't eat 'em."

After humping for about two hours, they found a spot where they could set up for the night with decent visibility around them. All eyes were on the tree line behind elephant grass that was about seven feet tall. Was it moving? Cousin Eduardo blinked rapidly to clear his eyes. Maybe it was one of the wild boars coming out to forage. Or a man-eating tiger on the hunt. Maybe even one of those humongous snakes they grow here wiggling through the grass. Maybe the V.C. waiting to hit when it got darker.

Of course, it could have been the effects of the Dexedrine included in the "lunch boxes" they handed out to keep them pumped.

"Keeps you guys alert. Could keep you outta body bags," Belson said.

A couple of years later, in his first bid at Rikers for possession with intent to sell, Cousin Eduardo would see on the TV news that from '66 to '69 the Army alone doled out more than two hundred million tabs of Dexedrine to keep grunts wired—chomping on the bit to be John Wayne heroes.

A journalist who'd gone on a patrol with them told him that officers have a centuries-long history of juicing troops—some as young as ten, back when they stormed castles. Officers would send kids in the first charge—target practice for archers—who'd whiz arrows into their guts and/or pour boiling water on them. Then adult soldiers would follow, stepping over and onto the kids' bodies.

"And by the way," the reporter said, "think about the word —it's *infant-ry*—from the French for babies. For centuries now, young grunts have been canon fodder. The younger the better because they think they're immortal—you know—death is for somebody else."

The tall grass was getting darker, fuzzier, turning into whatever your imagination grabbed onto. Enchilada and Tomlison were convinced a human was moving the grass. No optical illusion, no doped-up weirdness. Stoned, they ripped off two clips apiece into the gently swaying blur of grass. Then they took off, running over the open field toward the grass. Enchilada wasn't wearing a helmet.

"C'mon, c'mon!" Tomlison screamed. "You little fucks. I'll waste all ya motherfuckers!"

Enchilada was running about ten yards to Tomlison's right. "You dickless fucks! C'mon out, cocksuckers!"

Enchilada's head snapped back like he had been hit with a sledgehammer and fell flat onto his back. One shot. Tomlison went another twenty yards before being spun by a round through his shoulder. He landed turned around facing his guys —their heads sticking up above the rims of their foxholes, watching. Then another round ripped through his leg. He tumbled onto his face.

"I'm hit! I'm hit! Muthaa-fuckaa! I'm hit!"

Maloney grabbed his medic's bag and got about twenty-five yards before a round took out the back of his head.

"Stay back! Stay back! Sniper! Sniper! Locked in!" Belson shouted.

As night took hold, Tomlison kept screaming, pleading for someone to come get him. Then for someone to shoot him.

Ten minutes later: "No! No! No! My balls! My balls! No! No! No! She's gonna cut 'em off! Kill me. Please! Please! Someone shoot me!"

Then, "Oh my God! Oh my God! Mommy! Mommy!"

He screamed for another long minute or so. Then about thirty seconds of silence. Then a sing-song, girlish voice wafted through the mist to the Marines in their holes.

"*Dem thit nop mieng hum. Dem thit nop mieng hum. Dem thit nop mieng hum.*" Then: "The tiger been brought his meat."

She repeated that every five minutes for an hour. Some of the guys covered their ears. Others shouted every obscenity they could think of in every possible combination.

———

After Enchilada, Tomlison, and Maloney, Cousin Eduardo and his guys stopped taking the "pep pills."

"Instead of those pills," Paulie Lupe said, "why the fuck don't they give us rifles that you can fuckin' count on when you need 'em? Like those tough AK-47s the Gooks got. None a these pieces-of-shit we got—jam, you look at 'em. Get us dead!"

"Rat bastard officers," Cousin Eduardo said, back at base camp, sticking a rod with a cotton pad on it down the barrel of his weapon. "Never pressed command hard enough to make sure these pieces-of-shit rifles we got didn't kill more Marines, jamming when gooks are coming for us.

"Yeah," he said, shaking his head, "too expensive to give us good guns 'cause it would eat into profits'a the gun guys. Besides, nobody likes a squeaky wheel in the Marines or anywhere. End of complaints. *Semper Fi*, sucka!"

Cousin Eduardo would learn later in the *Daily News* that the jam-prone rifles found in the hands of dead Marines had different gunpowder than previous versions and so the rifles needed custom-cleaning kits or chances were they'd jam. They didn't get the kits before plenty of guys died with dead rifles in their hands.

———

After that night of the tiger getting his meat, Belson's platoon spat on the ground or grabbed their crotches when Belson walked past them. If looks could kill, Belson's corpse would be rotting away, joyously unlamented in the jungle's smothering heat.

"Belson orders us out there again to collect fuckin' ears, we should just frag his ass," Harris told Cousin Eduardo. "Asshole should be lookin' out for us and let us coop—just fuckin' coop. What's the fuckin' difference in the end?"

"The difference," Simanski said, "is we bring in enough ears, he moves up the asshole ladder."

"Yeah," said Tony D, digging dirt out from under his fingernails with his bayonet, "that's the deal. But, you know, their guys're not looking for us. We should just stay the fuck away from 'em, just coop."

Paulie Lupe was whizzing against a tree.

"Yeah," he said over his shoulder. "Lucky fucks. Least they get to fuck their own women, get laid in appreciation. Leave 'em alone and they'll leave us alone! Cuts one more day off before we get the fuck outta this shit-hole for good."

"Ain't the way it works," Ahearn said, untying his boot, taking the laces out and straightening them. Whenever they took a significant break he'd do that to both boots and then re-lace them, pulling them into a bow, draping them just so. "We hump jungles and paddies, dig, wait, maybe get off a few rounds, and hump back," he said, tugging his laces. "We get lucky and have a joint and a couple of beers. Not so lucky, we get zipped into a bag. Way it is."

"Trade you for them peaches?" Tool asked Paulie Lupe.

"You ain't got nothin' I want," Paulie said. He slowly cut open the can of peaches, looked at Tool, grinned, and sluiced the juice down his throat.

"But whatta the Slopes gettin' promised?" Paulie said, wiping his mouth with the back of his hand. "Must be some powerful shit they live like they do. Think about it."

"They live here," Cousin Eduardo said, sitting splayed against a tree. "Nowhere to go so they fight their balls off."

Before they left camp for their next ear hunt, Belson gathered his platoon around him, ordered them to take a knee, and handed out the lunch boxes.

"Look, Marines, this is our time. Our time!" he said, running a hard look across the faces of the first two rows of his troops. "I asked the Colonel if we could go back out and told him we'd do him proud. After all, we didn't get any ears that night 'cause of our guys buying it. So we're gonna make up for that. There's gotta be beaucoup Gooks out there. Let's go get us some ears! Balls, too—for Tomlison! *Semper Fi!*"

Cousin Eduardo was more than a little unnerved by the idea of standing for at least an hour waist deep in a river again. The last time he did that a leech latched onto his nipple like it was digging for mother's milk. He couldn't burn it off with his cigarette lighter because the V.C. would see the flame. So the leech kept sucking away.

"He asked the Colonel if we could go out again?" Paulie Lupe said as they were digging in for the night. "He fuckin' asked for this? I personally am gonna cut off his balls when we're out there!"

"And eat 'em," Ju Ju said. "Fuckin' barbecue 'em!"

This time as they moved out on the ear hunt, Belson dropped back, telling them to keep going, he'd catch up. "My pack's fucked up."

Cousin Eduardo looked back to see Belson on one knee, fussing with his pack's straps as his troops went ahead.

*Again? Again? He's gonna be way behind us. Again?*

Cousin Eduardo, twitching his head side to side, dropped back to last in line, took off his pack and pretended he was adjusting his own straps. Ahead of him, the last of the squad turned a corner of the trail out of camp and out of sight.

Cousin Eduardo lobbed the grenade at Belson, gently like a pitcher beginning his warm-ups. The ground shook. Smoke billowed. Bloody chunks of flesh rolled around. Dirt sucked down pools of blood.

Cousin Eduardo ran toward his squad down the path a bit, and timed it just right to turn around and run back toward Belson so the guys double-timing it back toward the explosion would see him going back too. Cousin Eduardo knelt in front of pieces of Belson, his pack obscuring his hand reaching out into the mess. As luck would have it, Belson's wrist was intact.

Cousin Eduardo smiled, ripped off Belson's watch, and put it in his chest pocket.

With a bigger smile, he intoned the old ad: "Timex: takes a licking and keeps on ticking."

# WAYS OF THE WORLD

COUSIN EDUARDO JUST SHOWED UP. All of a sudden he was just there.

117th Street off First Avenue—*El Barrio* to its people, Spanish Harlem to Anglos, who wouldn't go north of 96th Street without Uzis.

He reappeared after a year in Vietnam. A year of only a handful of letters home, some enclosed with Polaroids of him in Saigon with bar girls draped over him in his favorite spot off Tu Do Street, Saigon's G.I. playground. Cousin Eduardo usually had a cigarette dangling from his mouth, a bottle of beer raised in toast, and devil-red-eyes from the flash.

His mother had one of the pictures enlarged—not the one with one of the girl's breasts hanging out. She squeezed a family-rated one on top of the television in front of the rabbit ears antenna next to the silver, scalloped-edged frame that held her wedding picture—her dead ex-husband cut out of it. It faced Carmelita's and Rosalita's confirmation photos.

Cousin Eduardo sat on the sidewalk, his back against a wall beneath a maroon awning—B-B, for Benito's Bodega, stenciled in white, old-English script on the front flap. His Marine Corps garrison cap lay flat on the gum-studded sidewalk next to him. A Baby Ruth wrapper skittered past his feet. He was clean-shaven except for shadows of newly conceived civilian side-burns. Dribbled beer had wet his tan Marine blouse. Next to him a paper bag was crimped over a can of Ballantine Ale. A Timex watch peeked out from a cuff.

"*Si, Mami*, he just sat there. Din't know who I was," said Carlos, who had to step around Cousin Eduardo to get into Benito's to buy a six-pack of Colt .45 and a couple of Slim Jims for his mother. "He was just staring across the street like he was froze. Then he kinda waked up and said weird stuff over and over. Kept saying *el tigre* got his meat. Then he says, 'She cut off their *cojones.*' *Loco!* Then he says he gotta get ears for beers. Then he cried."

"I have *simpatico* for him," said his mother, peeling off a Slim Jim wrapper. "But you know he was always sometimes loco—not bad loco—but loco from the time he was *el niño pequeno.*"

Since coming home from Vietnam, Cousin Eduardo had become an embarrassment—a mini-scourge in his own neigh-borhood.

In his first two weeks back, Cousin Eduardo snatched Mrs. Gomez's purse as she struggled with grocery bags in A&P's doorway, stole car batteries out of parked cars, including Father Gomez's Lincoln Continental, copped his sister Rosalita's high school ring, his mother's gold crucifix, and sister Carmelita's tiny 14-carat gold earrings she got for her first communion. He also made off with the gold-rimmed, cherry-wood box that held his father's ashes, which he'd hidden in his closet when he was twelve because his mother said her bad luck was because of his father's ashes in the house and she wanted to pour them down the garbage chute.

On the way down the block to pawn the box, Cousin Eduardo blew his father's ashes into the gutter.

"So? So what? A hit makes the day go quick. So fuck you! Fuck him too!" he shouted over his father's floating ashes.

Cousin Eduardo came home to find he wasn't set up to live large by all the dope he'd shipped home in false bottoms of bamboo tables, chair arms and legs, and thick bamboo crucifixes. He had shipped them to Ernesto, his pal and partner, who sold the junk, pocketed the money, and moved back to San Juan.

Bottom line was that Cousin Eduardo didn't have the soft landing he thought all that merch would give him. His life wasn't any different. Actually, it was worse. Getting out of Nam alive wasn't close to being as sweet as it was supposed to be by surviving when "no one gave a rat's ass if I came home in a box."

Some people said he should catch a break. After all, he had been forced to fight those people in that place over there, where he got hooked on junk. Those on the other side of the Cousin Eduardo equation said he was just a generic scumbag back at it.

Every time Cousin Eduardo saw the lion roaring in the Metro-Goldwyn Mayer circle before a movie began, he thought of that disembodied voice in the jungle night—a sing-song voiceover to the screams of a wounded Marine being castrated by a female Viet Cong.

"*Dem thit nop mieng hum. Dem thit nop mieng hum. Dem thit nop mieng hum.* The tiger been brought his meat."

He didn't have to see the big cat with the long teeth to wake up shaking in the middle of the night. Sometimes he woke after dreaming of corpses with bloody cavities where their ears used to be. Sometimes he was stringing dark, blood-encrusted ears for the Christmas tree—hanging them next to an angel blowing a golden trumpet toward heaven.

"Don't take Einstein to figure that one out," Santiago said when he and Cousin Eduardo were setting up to play dominoes in the back of Little Ponce and trading fantasies about what they were going to do next.

"You knew you shouldn'ta cut off them ears," said Santiago, who'd had almost a year in community college and really liked Psychology 101. "So somewhere inside you, you feel guilty for it," Santiago said, turning tiles face down to set up the game.

"You know, we come outta our *mami* with ears, we should have 'em when we go inta the ground. Everyone should," Santiago said, mixing the tiles up and laying down the first one. "Now Jesus is pissed at you, and he's thinking you gotta pay for it."

"Yeah, maybe. But I think I should catch a break for it—you know, war and all."

Cousin Eduardo played a tile.

"But Jesus knows you traded ears for extra beers officers promised you. You din't turn down any cold ones, right?"

"Of course not."

"There you go," Santiago said, shrugging his shoulders and taking a toke of Maui Wowie that his cousin had brought back from Hawaii.

"You know," Cousin Eduardo said, looking up from the card table and staring into Santiago's eyes, "if I'm telling the truth, cuttin' them off felt good. I put my knife flat against the sides of their heads so I'd get all of the ear when I sliced down. Sometimes they were still warm, so it was like they can feel it even though they're dead," he said, squinting, as if savoring the memory. "I wanted them to feel it. You gotta remember one a their *putas* cut off the cojones of guys still alive. Guys I knew. Still alive, *amigo*! Still fuckin' alive! Somebody gotta pay. So I kept cuttin'."

"I hear you, C.E., but Jesus don't care why. It's what you

did that counts for him." Santiago shook his head. His shoulders quivered. "Anyways, tell me how you ducked jail after you got caught with all that dope before you got shipped to Nam."

"Got caught with two bricks of Arturo's Bombita. I got no lawyer proof he set me up, but he din't show at the drop, and I'm there and *policia* came outta, like, nowhere and pull me over. They know exactly where to look in the trunk. Asides from getting a good bust, they get to skim a piece for themselves."

"That's a lot of product," Santiago said, shaking his head. "You facin' a long bid for that. How'd you slip it?"

"I got a smart lawyer for free who pled it down to a couple of misdemeanors, saying *policia* din't have cause to stop and search me and he said they busted me up just for kicks. But the real reason I ducked the big charge was my lawyer was gonna go public with more stuff that they wouldn't want on the vine, being an election year for the mayor."

"What lawyer works for free? You got somethin' on him?"

"Nah, my sister, Carmelita, like, knows him from being in court with me those times, and he was nice to her when he saw her waiting with me for my case to come up. She's a good kid and loyal to family and me, no matter what I do. So this gringo lawyer told her that the free lawyer the city gave me is *stupido* and said he'd be my lawyer if she wanted."

Santiago played a tile. "I get it about lawyers, thinkin' they gotta make up for all the shit they do. So sometimes they do free work even for us Spics 'cause it lets them lie to themselves that they're good people. On top of that, lotsa gringos like brown skin—I mean they spend all that time in the sun trying to brown up—so I guess Carmelita smiling at him with those dimples made him dream big."

———

Indeed, Sean W. Murphy, Esq., who called himself "The King of Plea Bargains" and took Cousin Eduardo's case pro bono, had a thing for Carmelita.

More specifically for her *culo*, widely admired as she walked through the courthouse. Always quick to seize an opportunity, Murphy pounced—a lion sinking claws into a zebra—taking Carmelita to a far corner where he said that Eduardo's public defender was not doing the best for her brother. She begged Murphy to help.

So intent was Murphy on Carmelita's *culo*, that he used some of the best leverage he'd ever had to persuade the Assistant D.A. to bargain down Cousin Eduardo's latest charge to an expired inspection sticker and no driver's license.

Murphy's magic took place in the judge's chambers, where he told the judge and the dweeby ADA—hired by the mayor as a favor for the mayor's second cousin by marriage—that he'd argue Cousin Eduardo was a victim of the mayor running for re-election. The mayor, Murphy would say, was targeting Puerto Ricans—actually, all Brown and Black people—to look tough on crime. Murphy backed up his charge with statistics of minority arrests he'd invented.

Murphy added, "And I want to go on record that I will not be responsible if, as a civic duty, someone were to secure maximum exposure—pun intended—to have the public view expertly focused photos of the mayor's nephew receiving oral satisfaction at the precinct from a lady of the evening his uncle's police officers had brought in. Pants down to his ankles is not a flattering pose."

"Cops," Murphy explained after the judge raised a skeptical eye at his story, "always look for leverage on their bosses and there are lots of cameras where they shouldn't be. That's how they got rid of their last C.O. who was cutting back on overtime and actually investigating civilian complaints about cops shaking them down and handing out beatings just because they could."

"And, if I remember correctly, counselor," the judge said, "you won a corruption case and got a bad-shoot charge dismissed for a grateful police officer and of course his union. All after you received copies of said pictures? Curious."

"All I can say, your honor, is that serendipity is unfathomable. I will say, though, that headlines stemming from such photographs and stories regardless of their provenance, have a way"—Murphy glanced at the judge and the picture on a shelf of him shaking the hand of the mayor, with whom he was running again on the same ticket—"of redounding on the long chain of city officials and really anyone, however much they are merely on the periphery of the issue at hand. Simply put, schadenfreude—that enduring and perhaps most persistent of human traits—sells papers and garners airtime."

Murphy stared at the ADA, whose mouth was open, and slowly pushed his glasses up on his nose with his middle finger and smiled. The 24-year-old prosecutor, bobbing his head up and down like a yo-yo, agreed to the plea deal. The judge frowned but nodded his approval.

At The Gavel, a lawyers' watering hole two blocks from the courthouse, Murphy was asked about the Spanish girl they'd seen him huddling with in a corner of the courthouse—the one that looked like a young Rita Moreno but with "more meat on her in all the right places," said one of Murphy's fellow lawyers, soon to be a judge.

"Ahh, me boys," Murphy said, plucking the last of three cocktail onions from his Gibson, popping it into his mouth, and licking his fingers, "we have indeed made a connection. I am her Perry Mason in the flesh, miraculously bargaining her beloved brother Eduardo's charges down to the proverbial slap on the wrist," he said, tossing down the rest of his martini and sliding the glass toward the edge of the bar for a refill.

He turned, scanning his three-deep audience and leaned back against the bar. "Let's just say I am mentoring her in the ways of the law and, I might add, the ways of the world. I also must say, counselors," he said, grinning and flicking his bushy blond-gray eyebrows, "she has that rare and most coveted combination you could ever hope for in the fair sex: a body that won't quit and a mind that won't start."

After the laughter eased, he said, "Look, it's inevitable—sad but inevitable—that these people more often than not will graduate from minor to more serious crime and punishment. Meanwhile, luscious Carmelita gets more and more desperate to help her brother. And there I am! She is ever so grateful."

Murphy had started with dinner at Del Monico's and then took Carmelita on a shopping spree at Bloomingdales. They would go on to earn Murphy a discount on the hourly room rate for so often taking grateful Carmelita to the Flying High motel near LaGuardia Airport with vibrating beds.

After spending the better part of a year at Murphy's disposal, Carmelita began pressing Murphy that they at least could go out to dinner and even a movie once in a while. Murphy stopped taking her calls and used his discounts to take Juanita, whom he met at her *quinceañera* as Carmilita's guest a few months earlier, to the Flying High.

———

Back then, Cousin Eduardo had only been vaguely aware of Vietnam and his vulnerability to getting sucked into the war. He was too busy trying to graduate from selling a couple of baggies of dope here and there to having a larger number of customers on his way to actually having a territory. But then he was busted for having close to a kilo of baggies of smack in his car, worth a felony charge for intent to sell that, combined with previous offenses, would mean serious jail time.

The same judge that Murphy had played presided over Cousin Eduardo this time too, but without Murphy as his lawyer. After the public defender stumbled through a preview of his weak defense, the judge said that Cousin Eduardo could choose a jury trial, over which the judge also would preside, or join the Marines and ask to go to Vietnam.

Without Murphy's services and having to duck various people he'd stiffed, Cousin Eduardo opted for the Marines.

After that, if he survived, he promised himself that he would move to Vegas, where it was warm, there would be lots of action, and where he'd heard his ex-girlfriend Algie had moved.

———

To her mother's delight, Carmelita told her mother that she'd ditched the Gringo lawyer, whom their mother had called slimy-fat and sneaky looking and had begged her daughter to stop seeing before something happened. She warned her daughter that she would not help bring up a half-gringo kid.

Carmelita dropped out of school six weeks after Murphy dropped her. She sought out Carlos, who was always sweet on her. They would go up on a roof Carlos knew about and lie on a blow-up mattress, listen to his transistor radio and try to see stars through the glow of city lights.

# WHAT'S MY NAME?

CALVIN JOGS in place in front of the Desert Song motel on the edge of downtown Las Vegas, the pink neon "S" and "O" on the marquee flickering faintly behind him. A black gym bag is strapped across his back. He's wearing black shorts and a gray sleeveless T-shirt, showing thick, ropey triceps and cut biceps. He's waiting for a break in traffic before sprinting across the Strip and heading to Johnny Tocco's, 1.2 miles deeper into Old Vegas funk.

"C'mon," Calvin had said to Buttsie last week before they'd clocked the distance in Buttsie's gold Cougar the day before it was repossessed, "I run it six days a week. I know how long it is —I know every freakin' foot! One point two miles on the nose. Not the smartest bet you ever made."

Traffic slows after a billboard truck passes, advertising "Girls, Girls, Girls" with photos of grinning, glossy-lipped, big-breasted women in bikinis and lingerie and the phone number that'll order up one or more to a hotel room.

Calvin darts across the road just ahead of a stretch white limo. He reaches the other side of the street as two sets of heads, shoulders, and arms pop out of the roof hatch like whack-a-moles, waving bottles of Bud and whooping him.

Three weeks earlier Calvin had been jogging his route when two cops in a patrol car, flashing lights and shrieking siren, jumped the curb and cut him off.

"Where you running to, boy? Who's chasing you?"

There'd been a spate of snatch-and-run thefts of tourists' necklaces and shopping bags downtown on scuzzy Fremont Street, and Calvin was carrying a bag and running while Black. He'd also left his wallet at the Song. He was released after he used his phone call to ask Johnny to vouch for him. Johnny told the cops that Calvin was a Vietnam vet and reminded them that the police commissioner is a friend and his sons work out in his gym for free and "I got your boss's direct line."

A week later, after Calvin had calmed down some, he invited the chief of detectives to watch Marvelous Marvin Hagler train in Johnny's. From then on when cops passed him, they'd burp their sirens in friendly acknowledgment.

Calvin usually would do roadwork after training at Johnny's, but he jogs there anyway, his arms tucked against his sides, occasionally flicking punches into the air. He pushes himself to stay on pace, prodded by the old trainers' adage that "somewhere someone's runnin' harder and more than you, so you don't match him it'll come back on you late, make you a coward, looking for a soft place to fall. Then you just be a broke-down gym bum."

———

Calvin and Cousin Eduardo had bonded over being Marine Vietnam vets.

They were part of a crew of six—give or take—pay-by-the-week Song residents who hang out for the most part to pool their drugs. Being a boxer always in training, Calvin is the only one who doesn't use.

One Saturday afternoon back a few months when they first met, Calvin and Cousin Eduardo were leaning against the Song's railing on the outside walkway, watching a couple in the backseat of a '59 pink Caddy convertible getting married by an Elvis impersonator wearing lifts in his shoes. Cousin Eduardo was telling Calvin about the first meal he'd had back in the States to celebrate surviving Vietnam. Calvin said he knew what he'd order someday when a promoter took him to dinner to celebrate signing him.

"First, we're gonna eat at Union Hotel in that restaurant where you sit in, like, a glass dome and you're looking over downtown with all that screaming neon and that cowgirl flashing her legs up on the side of that building.

"'Get what you want, champ,' he'll tell me. I'm gonna order up oysters Rockefeller, medium-rare ribeye, stuffed baked potato, glazed carrots, and New York-style cheesecake. Too bad I don't drink or smoke 'cause I'd top it off with a Grand Marnier and a Havana. Maybe I will anyway. I could pay for it now, I guess, but it'll be sweeter he picks up the tab."

---

Richie Munson's Blood of Jesus storefront church next to Helpful Herman's bail-bond office is Calvin's marker to kick into high gear for the last hundred yards to Johnny's. As he gets closer, crude sketches of fighters on the side of Johnny's come into focus.

They're boxers who have worked in Johnny's, others he's trained, and some he just admires: Liston—the first boxer Johnny had trained in Vegas—Ali, Frazier, Sugar Ray Robinson —the original Sugar Ray—Hagler, Johnny Tapia, 1931 featherweight champion Kid Chocolate out of Cuba, and an assortment of Latino fighters, obscure to many but never to Johnny, who respects all boxers until proven wrong.

"You got the *cojones* to walk up those three little steps to see who'll be the hurt one, you're my kinda bum," Johnny tells fighters on their first day in his gym.

"But I got rules and you follow 'em—all of 'em—or you're out on your ass. They're simple: no drugs, no broads unless they train here, and no disrespecting anyone inside this joint. You got a beef with someone in here, you lace 'em up or take it down the block. No credit! You pay on the first of the month. I give you three days' grace."

Calvin stops in front of Johnny's and walks around the building to the rear door. A concrete block sits on the ground to the right of the steps.

A long chain encased in plastic runs from a bicycle lock through one of the block's holes, through front and rear spokes, and around the frame of a sparkly purple mountain bike, purple plastic ribbons drooping from its handlebars. Calvin yanks open the steel door into the locker room and hits a wall of Mr. Clean, rubbing alcohol, and musky bodies. He changes into black boxing trunks with white stripes along their sides, the letters "NGOC" written on the stripes. He pulls on a gray sleeveless T-shirt, laces up black boxing shoes, and fishes out speed-bag gloves and a jump rope from his bag. He slams shut the bent orange locker door that's decorated with a black Magic Marker drawing of a vagina, a dick, and a partially inked-over peace sign. He spins the combination lock and heads toward the two-ring gym.

About two dozen foldable wooden chairs are in front of the ring near the front door that Johnny assigns the gym's top fighters for sparring. The walls behind the rings are plastered with old-time posters in color and older ones in black and white, for fights in Tijuana, Laredo, Panama City, Philly's Blue Horizon, L.A., Stockton, and the Bronx.

After ten minutes of jumping rope, Calvin walks to a corner where a speed bag dangles from a round wooden platform overhead. He cranks it up to six feet, level with his forehead. He gently slaps the bag for a few seconds. When his eyes and hands sync, he speeds up the churn of his fists until the fat leather teardrop is a blur bouncing against the platform and back to his fists, its rat-tat-tatting echoing throughout the gym.

Next to Calvin, a pretty girl is whaling away at a heavy bag. She's maybe sixteen—about the age he thinks his daughter would be. The girl is about five foot eight and solidly built with heavily muscled thighs and long arms. Her face is broad, set off by flickering studs in her ears.

Her almond-shaped eyes are wide open as she attacks the torso-sized red leather bag, its midsection permanently dented and cracked from years of punches. Perspiration slicks her face and arms and is beginning to spread on the front of a purple T-shirt, where white script says, "Jesus Saves." On the back, "Follow His Word." She's all church purple: purple shoes, white socks edged in purple, pigtails tipped with bows of purple yarn, and purple lipstick. She's rooted in a wide stance in front of the bag. Every power punch she throws comes with a grunt, ending in a squeal.

"Hey, there, little sister," Calvin says, dropping his hands, letting the speed bag wobble into gravity. He turns to face her. "I don't wanna get up in your business, but I think you can get more power out of your punches. Want me to show you what I mean?"

"Uh, yes! I mean, yes, sir!" she says, dropping her hands, twisting, hunching and releasing her shoulders to keep them loose. "I surely would appreciate that."

Shaking out his arms, Calvin walks over to her heavy bag.

"You could have some real power. But you gotta use your legs better—set them quick and wide enough so you can stick your jabs but not too wide so you can't shift in a hurry to move fast to get outta range of a counter and get another angle to throw your shots. Of course, getting angles is not just moving to another spot. Takes work to learn how to do that right. Another time, maybe. And not for nothing, think about losing those grunts—too much energy."

Calvin twists his torso and shakes out his arms. "Now, I'm not gonna hit too hard 'cause I got on speed gloves, but this is what I mean."

He dances in place for a few beats, sets his legs, and fires three jabs. He gets back onto the balls of his feet, slides to his right, sets his legs again, and slams a four-punch combination— a left hook to the top, a right to its side where the liver would be, and a combination left-right at head level.

Landing the first punch, he grunts, "No." He moves to his right, landing the second with "punch." The last two are punctuated with "no" and "lunch." He drops his hands, steps back, and looks at her.

"Uh, no disrespect, but you were saying words, kinda grunting when you were punching."

"Ha!" he says, grinning and throwing back his head with a laugh. "You're right on that one. Got me! Sometimes I just can't catch myself. It just comes outta me. Guess it's, like, printed on my mind like lotsa stuff you're filled with when you're a kid.

"It's kind of, uh, what they call a mantra—something you say to yourself. Something familiar—something to help push you when you need it, when you gotta extra-believe in yourself, you know, tell yourself you're good enough. Like, good enough to grab something worth something."

"What does 'no punch, no lunch' mean?"

"Got it from my daddy. Something to motivate me even

more. You know, remind me that this is a serious business, just like Daddy was serious about me not getting lunch if I don't put on a good show. Anyway, you see what I did—sticking and moving, setting my feet quick, and getting back on the balls of my feet after unloading so I can get another angle? We'll work on that. You want to do that safe and efficient. So? You think you got what I showed you? Wanna try like I showed you?"

She steps to the bag, rocks sideways a couple of times, plants her feet, crouches, and fires three hard jabs, a left hook, and then a right cross. All without a grunt or a squeal.

"Like that?"

She stops and faces Calvin, raising her eyebrows.

"Get lower before throwing your follow-up to the jab so you're coming up with leverage and more power offa your legs. And remember to breathe through your nose, not your mouth. An open mouth can easy lead to a broken jaw. But yep, you got it for right now. But you'll lose it quick, you don't keep doing it until you're dreaming it, it's so deep in you."

Calvin takes a couple of steps back toward the speed bag, stops, and turns around.

"What's your name?

"Jaylene."

"Just one name?"

"Jaylene Taylor Carson."

"There you go! Respect who you are, who you come from," Calvin said, his eyes hard on hers.

"You got a full name and a full history that comes with it—grammies and grandpappies and their grammies and grandpappies. Be proud a that. If you're not, nobody is.

"And you gotta always understand, always remind yourself, Jaylene Taylor Carson," he said, cutting off his smile, "that boxing is a business, a rough business. You gotta protect yourself at all times."

"Like they say before a fight?"

"That, too, a'course, but I mean protect yourself in the business side of this game," he says, bringing his fists up in front of his face, peekaboo-style. "It's a lot rougher than the boxing part. You got so many people runnin' riffs to pick your pockets and more. And they know you're hustlin' to get some kinda recognition, someone to see you.

"We all been there, right? Us, I mean," he says, searching her eyes, "hoping someone sees us. So they'll be dangling that out there, you know, the respect thing, the movin'-up-maybe promise. But you gotta ask yourself what their real game is. You feeling that?"

"My mama be saying that to me all the time."

"Well, listen to your mama, baby girl. Uh, I don't mean any disrespect calling you that."

"None taken," she says with a broad, beautiful smile.

"And while I'm at it, be careful of that beautiful face." He winks.

"Uh, I appreciate that. Surely do, sir," she says, again with her wide smile, flashing a mouthful of sparkling, perfectly level teeth. "Appreciate it all. So, are you, like, a professional fighter?"

"Well, yeah. I'm trying, Miss Jaylene. Trying to move on up," he says, shrugging and tilting his head while looking at her. "Tryin' to see and be seen. You know that one, right?"

"Yep. My whole life. What's your name, you know, so I can follow you?"

"Calvin. Calvin Jackson."

"I surely do wish you good luck, Mr. Calvin."

"Yeah. Me too. Take care of yourself, Miss Jaylene."

She spins away to set up in front of the bag, her purple-tipped pigtails dancing to keep up.

It's media day at Johnny's and there are about a dozen

reporters sitting or just hanging out near the ring apron. The AP's Fast Freddie Steinberg is making plans with Pat Putnam of *Sports Illustrated* to meet at the Flame, an un-touristy bar and steakhouse downtown with a back room and an occasional casino cocktail waitress stopping by after her shift.

The reporters are in Johnny's to watch Ivan "The Terrible" Rodriguez's last sparring session before fighting Carlos "The Cannibal" Seguro in a highly touted elimination bout for a shot at the WBA heavyweight title. In the year Calvin's been in Vegas, he's drawn attention mostly from gym rats for his ring smarts, left hook, and long, hard jabs.

But he needs to step it up, get noticed by a fight guy who's a player in Vegas boxing who could put him on a legit undercard, even a walk-out fight—so called because most fans are walking out of the arena after the main event. So, he's in Johnny's after four hours of sleep following his shift, bouncing at the Lost Indian saloon downtown.

Calvin's in boxing's no-man's-land: too experienced and too good at 9-to-1—the loss in Reno to a hometown favorite—to be matched by anyone just starting out and too dangerous for a serious contender looking to pad his record.

In the one loss, Calvin had been ducking the guy's punches and effectively countering with an assortment of shots from all angles. Judging from the guy's bloody face and fans' reactions after Calvin lost in a split decision, he'd really won going away.

Calvin had changed his routine to be in the gym early for media day—be where the action is. And, after Vietnam and all and carrying some age, although he didn't look it, he couldn't waste any time.

———

Rodriguez's posse sits in a clump of ringside chairs behind their guy's corner, except for two guys leaning against the dinged steel front door, their faces carefully set to glower. They're wearing matching sky-blue nylon sweat suits with white stripes and cloud-white sneakers with blood-red laces.

Sitting in the middle of Rodriguez's crew is his promoter, Clarence "The Chief" Clearwater.

He's a Don King knockoff, except he wears braids down to his waist. In the gym, he's not wearing the long headdress he sports in ring introductions and at formal press conferences. Fast Freddie says he thinks Clearwater uses makeup to darken his face to match the Paiute genes he claims to have.

Calvin is back on the speed bag, slowly circling it, keeping its beat going. From the Chief's crew on the other side of the room, Bed-Bugs Benny marches over and forms a T with his hands for time-out.

"Hey, tough guy, wanna buy yourself more bling?"

"Who you talking to, Dough Boy?" Calvin says, sliding a quarter-turn away from Benny. "You don't see a *man* working here?"

Benny had hazed Calvin when he'd started at Johnny's. They'd sparred twice, Calvin outsmarting and outpunching Benny each time. Calvin ended their last session with a particularly vicious assault, in retribution for Benny throwing two low blows that drew cheers from his guys and a smirk from Benny. Calvin's onslaught forced Benny to take a knee. Benny went on to defeat a career tomato can, but after three consecutive beatings, trying to step up against slightly better competition, he opted for a job as the Chief's all-around "gofer."

"Always the wiseass mouth with you," he says now. "Someday someone gonna shut it for you."

"We both know it ain't gonna be you, Chubs," Calvin says, his fists churning against the bag. Benny follows him.

"You wanna chance to earn despite your mouth or not?" Benny says. "Just gotta work Rigo for five rounds. You got the balls to do that?"

Calvin keeps rapping the bag. "First, what're you paying? Careful not to come up small, 'cause you need me, especially today 'cause your usual sparring guy's either sleeping it off or's back in lockup. So you're stuck for someone to work your clown in front of these pencil-neck reporters." Calvin ratchets up the speed. "And second, Chubs, you gotta have balls to ask a question about balls."

"Fuck you! Hundred fifty for five rounds, wiseass."

"Lose yourself, Humpty."

Calvin slides another quarter turn around the bag.

Benny follows. "Alright, two."

"Three, and I get it upfront."

"Three? I grant you, you got balls—a fuckin' wannabe walk-out guy, lives in a fleabag motel, passing up two that should be one."

"Get outta my face, fat boy, before you get hurt by this boxin' bum. Again."

Calvin keeps at the bag, finishing with a hard right. The bag hits the bottom of the platform twice more before stopping. He steps back, puts his right hand under his left armpit, squeezes, and pulls off the elastic-sleeved glove and yanks off the other glove with his freed hand. He winks at Jaylene, who's taking a breather she doesn't need so that she can listen in.

"I'm done for the day. Have a good one, Chubs. 'Bout time you be stuffin' your face with more pie."

Benny looks over to Rodriguez's crew on the other side of the room. One of them holds his hands out palms up.

"Looks like your massa wants to know what's keeping you, Doughy. You best be jiggling back to him and report in how you couldn't close the deal."

Calvin towels off his face and head. Benny goes back to his guys, listens in a huddle with his head down, and comes back with three hundred-dollar bills. Calvin flips the towel onto his shoulder and holds the bills up to the light.

"You drive a hard bargain, Chubs."

"Fuck you, no-hope sparring bum!"

"What's my name, Chubs? What's my name?"

"What the fuck that got to do with it? You got your money!"

"What's my name, Chubs? What's my name?"

"Jackson. What the fuck?"

"What's my name? What's my name, Chubs? Say it!"

"I just did."

"No, you didn't. You said half of it."

"Jackson. Calvin Jackson."

Calvin spins away from Bugs and walks over to Johnny sitting at his desk on a platform next to the locker room and asks him to lace up his gloves.

"Look out for his 'Sweet Pea' clown show and play along," Johnny says quietly, as he tugs on Calvin's gloves and begins to lace them up. "You gotta play along, you want more paydays from Clearwater. Who knows, maybe he'll see you as more than a gym guy. He could be your ticket."

It's old-school in Johnny's so there's no bell to signal rounds. Someone in Rodriguez's corner yells, "Time!" to begin sparring. Rodriguez skips to the middle of the ring. Calvin shuffles forward, hands up. For the first minute or so they feel each other out—flicking range-finder jabs and dancing some to see how the other guy moves. They trade two jabs.

Rodriguez throws a roundhouse lead right. Calvin merely pulls his head back a few inches to avoid it, steps back in, and hits Rodriguez with a right below his heart that catches him flat-footed and a left hook to his ribs that draws a wince. Calvin holds off for a half beat on throwing another hook, so he only grazes Rodriguez's head. Calvin tilts his head and winks at Rodriguez to let him know that in a real fight that follow-up punch would have done serious damage.

Predictably, Rodriguez goes into his version of four-time champion Pernell "Sweet Pea" Whitaker's act, consisting of squatting nearly as low as his opponent's knees and bobbing his head away from punches. The idea is to make the other guy look befuddled in front of reporters. Rodriguez has been showing off his Whitaker bit since the media started watching his sparring sessions.

A lot of fighters have tried to come up with hot-dog moves since Ali introduced his fast shuffle in real fights.

Calvin knows his role. He drops his hands and stands still, looking confused. Reporters snicker. Then he waits for Rodriguez to square up to him again.

Finally, Rodriguez sets himself and rushes Calvin, landing a left that Calvin catches on his arm. Rodriguez clinches. After they separate with a showy macho push by Rodriguez, Calvin breaks off a four-piece combo, running from Rodriguez's stomach to his head, ending with a left hook, stutter-stepping him, bringing him down off the balls of his feet. It was the punch Rodriguez had been working on avoiding.

"C'mon, Rigo, counter that move!" One of his cornermen shouted. "Move your damn head! Come back with your hook."

Clearwater takes his always-present toothpick out of his mouth and asks Benny, "Who's this guy? And what does 'N-G —O-C' mean down the side of his trunks?"

"He's just a sparring guy. Dunno, really, about the name. Heard it's something to do with a girl in Nam, where he did time."

Calvin nods at Rodriguez and half smiles around his black

mouthpiece as he allows Rodriguez to bob and weave under and away from punches.

After a couple more exchanges in which Calvin brushes away punches without countering, Rodriguez again goes into his act. Calvin looks around, playing the confused fool, and sees Jaylene, who's left the heavy bag and is standing closer to the ring, watching it all.

Maybe it's his disgust with Rodriguez or with himself for having to play the patsy. Maybe it's that Jaylene is watching. Maybe he's watching himself, and he's embarrassed. Maybe it's the boxer's primordial need to strike when he sees vulnerability. Maybe it's a "no punch, no lunch" warning from his daddy telling him when he was a kid that he better put up a good fight against these older, bigger guys his daddy's making him fight or he won't eat.

Whatever. It begins as an electric jolt in Calvin's brain, fires to the top of his shoulders, races down his biceps and forearms to his fists.

At the same time, another connection between synapses is getting ready to anchor his feet to gather power to throw punches when the target's in place. Calvin feints a right, sets his feet, drops his left shoulder, and steps in with a left hook to the head—"No"—then a straight right—"Punch." As Rodriguez is teetering, Calvin lands another hook—"No"—and as Rodriguez is going down, Calvin chops him on top of his head with a right—"Lunch."

Rodriguez sinks to his knees and slowly falls forward, landing on his forehead as if he's bowing to Mecca. He lingers there for a second before keeling onto his right side.

"Motherfucker! You motherfucking piece of shit!" Benny screams as he hops into the ring. "You're dead! You hear me? Dead!"

Benny and another guy lift Rodriguez by his armpits, drag

him to his corner, and plop him onto his stool. Without support, he lists to his right and oozes to the floor.

The cornermen scramble as if they'd dropped their meal ticket—which they had—and prop him back onto his stool. One guy kneels in front of Rodriguez, holding him by his shoulders to keep him upright, while another passes smelling salts under his nose.

Calvin spits out his mouthpiece and gnaws at the laces of his right glove. He drops one glove to the canvas, then the other, steps on the bottom rope, yanks up the rope above that one, ducks through the gap, and jumps to the floor. He walks past Jaylene, who's staring at him google-eyed, gloves dangling at her sides, the words "Jesus Saves" dark with sweat.

Clearwater rushes to the side of the ring, peers up at Rodriguez, sitting on his stool glassy-eyed. Shaking his head in disgust, he turns away from his fighter, flips his braids over his shoulders and down his back, and huddles with his crew. The pack moves toward the door—held open by one of the sweatsuit guys.

"Wait! Chief! Wait!" Fast Freddie shouts as reporters jump to their feet. "C'mon, Chief, don't just walk out. You gotta give us something."

Clearwater pauses, turns around, and heads back toward them. A photographer is approaching. Clearwater pulls the braids from behind his back so they hang down his chest.

"Of course, this is not what I expected," Clearwater tells the reporters. "In due time I'll announce my plans. You know me. I always have a plan. I always come out on top. No cheap-shot, no-hope, sparring-partner clown's gonna upset my plans. I'm The Chief!"

Calvin had stopped on the way to the locker room, ostensibly to listen but really to make himself available for reporters to approach, to ask his name, at least. Something.

When they all rush out of the gym, following Clearwater, Calvin leans against the ring apron waiting for them to come back. After twenty minutes, he walks around the ring, the room empty now except for Jaylene skipping rope and a guy in the far corner shadow-boxing in front of a mirror.

Calvin heads for the locker room. He passes Jaylene stretching against the wall. She lowers her head as he passes. He unwinds layers of tape from his hands and drops them onto the floor in long strips like entrails.

# FOR THE AGES

"If any question why we died,
Tell them, because our fathers lied."

RUDYARD KIPLING

TAKING deep breaths standing on the porch of McNeil & Sons funeral home where his brother lay in a shiny brown wooden casket, Bobby remembered fifth grade when Johnny Whalen and his Schwinn were crushed by a Smiler's oil truck on his way home from catechism class.

No one said anything the next day when Johnny hadn't come to school. Johnny just never showed up again. No one ever told any of the kids why Johnny wasn't there anymore. How could someone just disappear and he was the only one to notice? Bobby found out what happened to Johnny when he listened at the door to the teachers' break room and told only Anthony, swearing him to secrecy. Bobby didn't know why he told only Anthony.

As far as any of the other kids knew, Johnny had simply disappeared. There was no mention of a funeral or of anyone missing him. He just evaporated. His desk was empty for two weeks before the teacher had everyone in his row move up a seat. Then Johnny wasn't even an empty desk. It was as if he had never been there, had never stolen the two new school-bus-yellow pencils Bobby had carefully sharpened the night before Johnny snatched them. Bobby would remember Johnny as a pencil thief who wouldn't let him cheat off him in math class.

Beneath Bobby on the porch was the garage, where they brought bodies to be unloaded out of sight. Nicky's family originally received a dented aluminum casket, military shipping hieroglyphics stenciled on it. It followed a letter from Nicky's commanding officer, saying Bobby's older brother had died valiantly defending his country while securing a perimeter in the Vietnam highlands west of Da Nang, Vietnam. Bobby knew that "valiant" often is overused.

From the porch, Bobby could see Clove Lakes Park's Diamond Number 1, where Nicky once went five-for-five, including a homer, against New Dorp, earning a feature story in the Staten Island *Advance* that called him a five-tool talent who surely would draw big league scouts. Beyond right field was a pond and boats tethered to a dock splayed out like a string of fish barely kept alive in the cold water. Farther to the right was a grove of trees where Nicky told Bobby he'd first felt up Mary Beth Stankowski. Two years later, Mary Beth was a sophomore in that college upstate when her drunk boyfriend went over a dip in the road at ninety. Mary Beth hit the roof and snapped her neck.

The night before the funeral home's first visiting hours, Bobby and Tara, a widow at twenty-three, had huddled on the couch in her basement, looking at pictures of Nicky they'd found stashed in books and a drawer of his parents' secretary.

They wanted to display them on a cork board in Nicky's room at the funeral home.

Some of the pictures were from Tara's photo album, a gift for her ninth birthday with Cinderella on the pink cover in a ball gown, holding a sparkling wand. In the center they'd agreed would be two pictures—one of Nicky in his smudged football uniform after a game next to one of Nicky and Tara that same night all dressed up for the senior prom, posing for the Old Man's new Polaroid camera. Tara was in a white dress with iridescent blue threads shot through it, a pink orchid pinned over her left breast. Nicky, his crew cut waxed and standing stiff, wore a white tux jacket over black pants, red plaid cummerbund and matching bow tie, his arm around Tara's waist.

Another photo was of Tara and Nicky—specks against the sky, sitting atop the Coney Island Ferris wheel. There was one of Nicky grinning while rubbing baby oil onto Mary Beth's back, Tara kneeling to the side, smiling a conqueror's smile and holding up two rabbit-ear fingers behind Mary Beth's head. There was another of Nicky and Bobby in a rowboat on one of the Clove Lakes, waving to their mother and father. There was one of Nicky and Tara eating hot dogs on the Staten Island Ferry. Of course, there was a photo of Nicky, a brand-new Marine second lieutenant in Dress Whites, his arm around Tara, smiling like she'd just been coronated.

As they reviewed the photos in the basement, Tara tilted her head at them like a puppy trying to understand a new sound and laid her head on Bobby's shoulder, her eyes watering. Bobby put his arm around her and kissed her cheek. She turned her head upward and kissed his lips. Sweet Chanel No. 5—the perfume Nicky had given her for her birthday—wafted around their heads. They weakened the kiss at the same time, pulled apart, and quickly went back to sorting photos.

In the first session at the funeral home, Tara—Nicky's wife of three months and five days—had stood next to Bobby, his parents on the other side of him. But after that, she sat in the far corner of the room with her friends, gathered on folding chairs in a semicircle in front of the easel holding the cork board with a collage of snapshots from their lives with Nicky stuck onto it.

Bobby took a deep breath before going inside the room where Nicky's casket was against a wall for the first of three days—two sessions a day—of people coming to pay respects. Bobby, wearing a charcoal-gray suit, white shirt, and black tie, stood next to his mother and father to the side of Nicky's flag-draped coffin. At the foot of Nicky's casket, a Marine Corps banner drooped on a stand.

Heavy maroon drapes over the windows of the dimmed room kept out most daylight except for a sliver of sun where they hadn't been drawn tightly. A buzz of subdued voices came from the other side of the door, where people were gathering before the doors opened for visiting hours. Bobby counted the gray foldable chairs set in rows—eight back and ten across. He knew that two days later jokey guys in green work clothes would fold up the chairs as soon as Nicky's casket had been wheeled out to a long black car to go to the cemetery. Then a day or so after that, the chairs would be unfolded for another funeral for someone, probably alive now.

The slice of sunlight had crept across the wood floor and onto the edge of the rug. When Bobby was twelve, Nicky had taken him camping. Nicky stuck a twig into the ground, drew a circle around it, scratched a clockface into the dirt, and calibrated its shadow to the time on the Timex watch he got for his birthday. Every half hour Bobby asked Nicky what time it was according to his watch and compared it with Nicky's sundial that was always behind real time by fifteen minutes.

———

Bobby left the receiving line now and then to bring his mother water in small paper cups from the cooler next to the door. After gulping the water, she'd crush each cup, turning her knuckles white before putting it back in his hand.

"Nicky's a hero for the ages, Mike. Nicky's a giant of a man," Jackie Pink said to Bobby's father.

"Thank you, Jackie. That means a lot."

"Was, Jackie! Was!" Nicky's mother said, her head down. "He's a dead boy for the ages now. That's what he is. Dead! Dead for the ages. Dead forever."

"I'm . . . I'm sorry, Marie. I didn't mean to upset you. I meant he gave his life for his country. He's a hero with the medal and all."

"I know what you meant, Jackie," the Old Man said. "Appreciate it."

"Medal?" she said, raising her head to stare at Jackie with dark eyes piercing through gathering tears. "What does that mean? Purple Heart? They get that for nicking themselves shaving."

Jackie grimaced and slipped away to the far end of the room where Tara sat next to the cork board. She wore a navy-blue wraparound skirt, almost matching top, navy pumps, tortoiseshell headband, and Marine Corps globe-and-anchor earrings Nicky had sent her from Officer Candidate School. Jackie, hands clasped behind his back, bent to quickly survey the pictures on the cork board, nodded to Tara, and left the room.

The Old Man stooped and whispered to their mother out of the side of his mouth, "What was that? At your own son's funeral?"

Bobby's mother stared straight ahead. Her face was dusted

with last-minute makeup too white for her olive skin. Her heart-shaped lips, for which people often complimented her, were a deep red. She'd overshot her lips on both sides, turning her mouth into a tiny Joker's grin. All three turned to the door when they heard shoes clomping on the worn wooden steps.

Six Marines strode into the room in a line, wearing dress blue uniforms—scarlet stripes running down the sides of trousers, and high, stiff collars studded with the Marine Corps' shiny emblem.

After crossing the threshold, they snatched off their white caps with glistening black brims and tucked them under their arms. Two of the Marines wore rectangular maroon-white-and-blue combat ribbons pinned above their hearts and took places in the reception line, standing erect among slouched-shouldered civilians.

Bobby didn't know many of the mourners, but he was sure most of them hadn't seen Nicky cut around would-be tacklers, laughing his way to a touchdown. Of course none of them saw Nicky grind it out later that night with Tara at a cheerleaders' party. They hadn't seen Bobby whiff Nicky with a new Spaldeen that dipped like a spitball because Bobby had left the powder it came with on the ball and added Vaseline to it from a blob on his belt. They hadn't seen Nicky throw his broomstick bat at him after Bobby struck him out with imaginary bases loaded. They hadn't seen him take in that dog and nurse her back to health or seen him writhing in pain from the sunburn he got from sitting on a towel all afternoon with Tara at South Beach.

The last Marine offered a slight bow to their mother.

"Nicky did you and the Marine Corps proud, ma'am," the second lieutenant said. "He's a Marine hero forever."

Their mother tilted her head back to stare up at the tall Marine, as if she were a tourist trying to take in the entirety of the Empire State Building, her forehead crinkling as she held her stare.

"Son, do you know what that means? What you just said? What does that even mean? You don't think everyone for forever has said that to mothers like me? So many mothers like me. Nothing changes. Nothing. Not you. Not my son. Nothing. Nothing changes."

"Ma'am?"

"My son got blown to pieces thousands of miles from home. Blown to pieces! For what?" She shrugged. "That is not an honor. That is nothing to be proud of. That is just plain dead. Buried with military honors is still buried." She tugged his sleeve. "Don't let that happen to you, son."

"Excuse me, ma'am. I'm sorry for your loss." The Marine bowed slightly, right-faced, put on his cap, took four steps, pivoted left to face Nicky's coffin, saluted crisply, about-faced, and marched to the door.

The Old Man leaned down to his wife and cupped his hand behind her ear, the backs of his ears red. "That's it, Marie! Get the fuck outta my sight! That young man could have been our son!"

Their mother pulled her head back a few inches like a turtle retracting its head, crimped her brow, scrunched her eyes, and looked at her husband as if seeing him for the first time. Her lips tightened. She said loudly enough to be heard at the end of the line: "So, does getting blown up as a Marine somehow make it better? You, our dead son, and me—all of us," she said, sweeping her arm across the line of people, "we are just plain stupid. Domino effect? Protect America? Dumb! Dumb! Dumb!

"Some of these boys are going to die too," she said, extending her hand toward the Marines in line, her voice quavering. "And for what? What are they dying for?"

Her voice grew stronger, louder.

"Shame! Shame! Shame!"

She turned back to her husband.

"You encouraged them. You encouraged Nicky to live your hero fantasy where only other kids get killed. Everyone's fantasy. Shame on me for letting you infect him with your stunted ego."

She slowly walked away, shaking her head.

"Shame. Shame. Forever, shame."

Those on line stared at the floor as she passed them, her head up, eyes focused on the draped window, leaking fading daylight.

She took a seat alone in the middle of the last row of the gray metal chairs facing Nicky's coffin. She stared at it, hands clasped in her lap, shoulders erect in perfect posture the way the nuns had taught her.

# GONE THE SUN

"RINKY-DINK!"

That's what Bobby said his big brother, Nicky, would have called the tiny playground that Staten Island pols finally got around to dedicating to Nicky all those years after he was killed in Vietnam.

"I'm telling you, Danny," Bobby said, taking a hit from his second whiskey sour on the rocks at Ray Ray's. "Guarantee that's what Nicky would say. Absolutely low-rent. One seesaw, one hoop, a tiny jungle gym, a bench, and a water fountain that'll break in two months. Not even a sprinkler for little kids to run through in the summer? Nicky loved little kids. I can hear him: 'Yo! Take my name the fuck offa it!'"

"They wait all these years to do it and they do that?" said Bobby, shaking his head. "They preach about respect for Nicky and his guys who never came back? I mean, fuck 'em where they breathe." He funneled peanuts into his mouth.

"Way it always goes, Bobby," Danny said, pulling a *Daily News* over from in front of the empty stool next to him. "They show sad when everyone's looking but then it's 'Whew! I kept my kid outta it all.' Everyone's in amnesia about the whole war like it's ancient history. Which I gotta say it is. You know, 'cause everyone wants it to be. No one wants to think about how fucked up it was and that we lost. Ran away, you wanna tell it right."

Danny opened the paper to the horse racing results and ran his finger down to Aqueduct racetrack's total money bet—the handle, the last three digits that decide the winning number for betting with a bookie.

Danny tossed the paper to the end of the bar.

"Of course. Of course. Why would I think today would be any different?" he said and spun around on his stool for a long look at a strutting Lynn Steinberg, unanimously elected by his board of directors for the inaugural "Staten Island Derriere Hall of Fame."

"Man oh man. Check it out, Bobby! Look at her swinging it all around. And lookit Ray Ray," Danny said, head pointing to Ray Ray, practically running—hopping was more like it with his limp—to the table where her girlfriends were sitting. "He's white-on-rice all over them, smiling, practically drooling. He's even putting on a new tablecloth."

"Anyway," Bobby said, taking another hit of his sour. "It was not fun waiting for D'Alessandro to show, all puffed up to take credit for the park. Fuckin' guy comes in like way late, we're waiting for him in that heat that's so hot my toenails are sweating. And you up in Lucy's pool chillin'.'"

"Hey! You're the one said I should skip it, 'cause the park was so lame. Besides, she's got an ass I'm sayin' is sweeter than Lynn's. And in a bikini, I mean, for the ages, that ass."

Bobby told his Old Man a couple of weeks before the dedication that he'd remember and honor his brother his own way, "without a cheap politician and a rummy priest smarming up the place, looking so pleased with themselves."

"He's your brother! Wear the freakin' jersey at the dedication or get outta my house!"

Bobby had never seen the Old Man that angry. Not even the day when Nicky was fifteen, put on the Old Man's fedora to look older, stole the car keys, and put the Buick in a ditch. That caper cost the Old Man fifty bucks so the cops wouldn't report it and Nicky wouldn't get a Juvenile Delinquent card.

That melting day at the dedication, Bobby was standing front-row-center, wearing Nicky's No. 25 red-and-white high school football jersey. Next to Bobby waiting for Congressman Victor D'Alessandro was Tara, Nicky's wife of three months when a Marine sergeant—brass buttons and belt buckle glistening, spit-shined shoes slick as black ice—rang her doorbell, called her "Ma'am" at twenty-three, and told her she'd been made a widow.

Tara wasn't all that keen about being in the park that day either. She'd been struggling to put together a life after Nicky without help—actually open disdain—from some of Nicky's friends. That went back to a year or so after Nicky hadn't come home and Jimmy Graffano, the center on Nicky's high school team, spotted Tara walking down the Avenue arm-in-arm with a guy.

Jimmy knew that guys didn't walk down the street on a sweltering day with a girl with a great body without some kind of promise. Jimmy swerved his car into the curb and got out. He shouted, "Hoe-ahh! Skank! *Puttana!*" before coughing up a huge loogie and spitting, just missing her shoes. Tara tugged the guy's arm, pleading that he not go after Jimmy. It turned out the guy was her cousin on the way to change a tire on her car. But that wouldn't have mattered to Jimmy because she was still swinging her ass down the Avenue with a guy.

After Nicky's pals had taunted her for all those months, Tara dyed her hair bright red, bought a couple of push-up bras, and swished herself up and down the Avenue in mini skirts, laughing and pushing a baby carriage with lots of guys not her cousins.

Around the same time that Tara was driving Nicky's friends crazy with her audacity, Bobby's draft deferments ran out. Bobby's first deferment was for being in college. The second was because his Old Man had cancer and he'd signed— without saying a word—a letter Bobby had written, saying he needed to run the bar for the family to survive.

Then the Old Man got better for a while and returned to the bar part-time. The draft board said the bar and the family could survive without Bobby. Bobby had concluded, with help from Pete Hamill, a columnist for the *New York Post*, that no way was he going to volunteer. Hamill kept up a drumbeat about officers lying about their progress in the war and about almost everything else in Vietnam—the everything else running from rewarding troops with extra cases of beer for bringing back enemy ears to running black markets for stolen P.X. merch to handing out unearned medals to pals who fathered children they'd abandon to generals and politicians lying about the war. So no way was Bobby following Nicky into volunteering.

"Greeting: You are hereby ordered for induction into the Armed Forces of the United States."

Lyndon Baines Johnson was ordering him to go to the Whitehall Street Induction Center in Manhattan's Financial District. There Bobby and hundreds of guys would be prodded, poked, and observed for any obvious—they had to be very obvious—issues that would disqualify them from humping a gun through Vietnam's rice paddies and jungles.

If you had money to pay a doctor to say you had something like bone spurs or fallen arches or some other get-out-of-Vietnam card money could buy, you'd just mail the information to your draft board and be done with even thinking about Vietnam.

Bobby had none of that.

Instead, the morning of his Whitehall Street exam Bobby scraped poppy seeds from six bagels and ate them in one handful. Then he put a copper penny under his tongue. He'd heard they were supposed to screw up your urine tests or something like that and get you the gold ring—classified 4-F, not fit for the service. Some guys went to Canada. Others skipped the war by getting married and/or knocking up someone before that exemption was ended because too many guys were ducking it all. Some guys with family money went to graduate school and beyond to keep the government's hands off them. Others with connections, as a last resort—other than skipping the country— would get into the National Guard, virtually assuring you'd never hear a gun fired in anger. Homosexuality was another hustle.

Tommy Doyle, a legendary swordsman around Staten Island, opted for the "homo" bit. His nickname was "Tool," which, if you were in a locker room with him, you'd know why. Tool had a plan "to get me the fuck outta that stupid fuckin' war. I ain't a fighter, I'm a lover. And the best, I gotta say."

The first instruction at Whitehall was to strip down to skivvies. Absolutely no hats, the sign said. But no way were the Black guys about to give up their lids, so the guards—not wanting any more turmoil than the war protesters outside Whitehall shouting, "Hey, hey, hey, LBJ! How many babies did you kill today?"—looked the other way.

So, you had dozens of guys, Black, White, Brown and everything in between in their underwear—many wearing their favorite I-don't-give-a-shit hats, brims turned up porkpie-style— parading up and down stairwells and along corridors, stopping along the way at dingy stations where alleged doctors kind of examined them.

That morning, Tool had put on his sister's red panties, mascara, a touch of rouge, and pink nail polish, and laid on swishing hips that would have had Marilyn Monroe taking notes.

There were sneers, shaking heads, and flat-out laughter as he swayed through the building. Tool was convinced he'd earned an Academy Award. For sure he'd get thrown out of Whitehall by lunchtime, stroll a few blocks down to Battery Park by the Staten Island Ferry, buy himself a dog with all the trimmings and a Nedicks soda, and sit on a bench, watching miniskirted secretaries parade their stuff.

He just knew the Oscar was his when a guy behind him called him sweetie and winked. Tool smiled back, fluttering his eyelashes. Then the guy puckered his lips, ran his hand over Tommy's sister's red panties, and grabbed Tommy's crotch. The guy may have been doing his own homo con to get a 4-F, but touching Tool was a big mistake—for both of them. By the time they pulled him off the guy, Tool had broken the guy's nose, leaving him writhing on the floor cupping his groin.

With that display of testosterone, Tool proved himself just the kind of guy needed to fly 8,000 miles to protect America. With much less drama, Bobby earned the same 1-A—poppy seeds and copper penny notwithstanding.

At a time when the military and its politicians were pouring more and more guys into Vietnam's rice paddies and jungles, it would only be a matter of days—a couple of weeks on the outside—before Bobby could expect a draft notice. He took a final "Hail Mary" pass to duck the draft.

*Dear Honorable Congressman D'Alessandro,*

> *I am perplexed about a situation that seems obviously unfair. I've applied to join the Air National Guard at McGuire Air Force Base in New Jersey. But to my dismay I have received no word on my application, while other young men my age who applied much later than I did have been accepted by the Guard.*
>
> *I realize that I am neither as wealthy nor as connected a constituent as many of my contemporaries, but in all fairness surely you agree that I should be considered for the New Jersey National Guard in the same priority as my peers.*
>
> *I hesitate to write that, frankly, I am concerned there might be some chicanery involved.*

(Bobby had fallen in love with "chicanery" in an English class discussing Shakespeare or somebody, writing about plots and double-agent rat bastards.)

> *I would appreciate it more than I can express if you would inquire into my status and the reasons why I seemingly have been ignored.*
>
> *Thank you for any help you may be able to offer.*
>
> *P.S. Thank you so much for dedicating the park in honor of my late brother, Nicky, who, as you know, gave his life in Vietnam as a U.S. Marine.*

Nicky would understand using his name to try to slip the draft. He'd just call Bobby a candy-ass and let it go. But Bobby could never tell the Old Man. Years later, in an attempt to get him to think better of him, Bobby told the Old Man that more than half of the twenty-seven million guys eligible to be drafted got exemptions or were disqualified. His father, sitting in his La-Z-Boy, nodded and went back to the sports pages.

The line about chicanery very well could backfire, pushing D'Alessandro to just deep-six his letter out of pique for the not-too-subtle reference to his possible favoritism and turn to help other guys and their parents with real connections—read that "money."

Waiting for a response from D'Alessandro was tougher than a year earlier waiting to see if Donna would get her period. Back then, he'd had a nightmare where he was wearing a tuxedo with a red plaid bowtie and matching cummerbund, kneeling at the altar for Communion next to Donna, wearing Snoopy pajamas. Along with the body-of-Christ wafer, the priest handed Bobby a very ugly baby with a Marine Corps tattoo on its arm, a halo dripping blood and hitting a blunt.

Six days after writing to D'Alessandro, Bobby got a letter telling him to report in two weeks if he still wanted to join the Guard. Three days later he received a draft notice.

Not a believer in the story of a dead guy on a cross flying out of a cave on his way to be the enforcer for his Old Man, Bobby thought he should be thankful to someone, something, for getting him out of the draft—maybe designate a shrine for what surely was his patron saint. Could be that old oak tree in Clove Lakes Park where Nicky said he'd felt up Mary Beth Stankowski big time. Maybe he'd call it GM—Goddess of Menstruation—for making Donna's body finally do the right thing.

Bobby was neither proud of nor ashamed of ducking the draft. But he was always proud that he'd figured out by himself —no help from the Old Man—how to avoid the war that anyone with a functioning brain cell could figure out was a hustle.

Bobby's father, of course, never said he was disappointed in Bobby for avoiding the draft and never mentioned it to Nicky's mother, the only one who tried to talk Nicky out of wanting to be a hero. She never forgave the Old Man for encouraging Nicky.

"Yeah, I guess I gotta say that Bobby ducked the war," he'd say after a few pops years after Nicky died and his marriage had collapsed. "But, you know, he's his own man and made his own decisions. I'm sure it wasn't an easy one, but he made it the way he saw it. And, you know, he's just different than Nicky . . . was . . . and I get it, you know? Different strokes."

But Bobby knew what was in the Old Man's heart of hearts. Bobby knew at some level he thought Bobby simply was less than Nicky. Bobby also knew he could never change that because you can never win a popularity contest with a dead hero—especially a dead hero son. But Bobby was alive and "Fuck all of you! I'm not gonna feel guilty about that."

At the dedication of Nicky's park, D'Alessandro's dye job just wouldn't run. Bobby wanted—really, really wanted—it to pour down his face.

Bottom line: D'Alessandro was a first-class scumbag. A West Point graduate who rode a couple of easy-to-get WWII medals and a bright smile to Washington, D'Alessandro always had his hand out to push through zoning changes for real estate deals in which he had a stake. He also took a monthly kickback for having cops look the other way from his cousin Marty's bookmaking and the girls Terry pimped out of the Dew Drop Inn.

A few years later, Bobby, to his delight, came to think that maybe he should include another object of his affections to worship. He'd call it "Saint What Goes Around, Comes Around." That was after big-ass chickens came home to roost in the congressman's backyard: D'Alessandro went to prison on charges of corruption and bribery for helping rich Arabs get immigration papers and licenses to build and run casinos in

Atlantic City. The feds had called their undercover sting to nail D'Alessandro and six other dirty congressmen Operation Abscam. After Arab organizations complained that the moniker's contraction of "Arab" and "scam" demeaned Arabs, the feds changed it to Abdul Scam.

The last time Bobby had been in the park before Nicky's dedication, he was thirteen and had felt up Angela Cremonesie while boosting her onto the jungle gym. She decided it was kinda offensive, so with a subtlety way beyond her years she asked Bobby if his father was a bum like her father said. That night Bobby asked Nicky if that was true. Nicky punched him in the gut for asking.

Now, Nicky's mother stands at the back of the crowd in Nicky's park just inside the wrought-iron gate. She pushes her oversized sunglasses onto the top of her head à la Audrey Hepburn in *Breakfast at Tiffany's* and surveys the gathering.

D'Alessandro taps the mic, nods, and begins: "We are here to celebrate and thank from the bottom of our hearts our American hero—Nicholas Anthony Trocadero. Nicky answered the call of his country . . ."

Nicky's mother shakes her head, purses her lips, pulls sunglasses down over her eyes, spins around, and marches out of the park through the spiked gates. She thinks of traitors' heads she read about in history class impaled on London Bridge's spikes.

Father Dolan steps to the mic and asks the crowd to lower heads for the Lord's Prayer. A photographer's motor drive rips off shots of D'Alessandro and Dolan, heads bowed. At "amen," the photographer turns his camera toward Nicky's father.

With a nod from Dolan, the Old Man smashes the bottle— wrapped in a towel Nicky had snatched with "YMCA" written in red on the bottom—against the jungle gym that Nicky's friends had repainted three days earlier in shiny green Rust-Oleum.

"For Nicky! For Nicky!" a voice from the middle of the crowd shouts. Several more people pick it up and for a few seconds it seems it might become a chant. When it doesn't, a young man wearing a baseball cap shouts, "For Nicky! Always! Always! *Semper Fi!*"

A man dressed in Parks Department green pushes himself from the fence he'd been leaning against, spits out a toothpick, and presses a button on a boom box, set on one of the jungle gym's crossbars. It plays "Taps." Bobby knows the words from music class.

*Day is done, gone the sun,*
*from the hills, from the lake, from the skies;*
*All is well, safely rest, God is nigh.*

Walking down the block, Nicky's mother sees the Old Man's new red Mustang. She takes out her keys, chooses the biggest one, and, holding it tightly, scrapes it along the length of the car. She pauses at the front fender, shakes her head, sticks the key out again, and walks the rest of the way around the car gouging it, flakes of red paint floating in the air like dried blood.

She sighs, squares her shoulders, and jaywalks across the Avenue to Ray Ray's for G&Ts.

# KILLING MCNAMARA

AT 0700 BOBBY put on Nicky's Marine camouflage fatigues he'd pressed the night before at the Colonial Brick motel just off the interstate in Pennsylvania in the middle of what they liked to call "the Endless Mountains" that were really just hills. He knew Marine rules banned fatigues in public, but decided Nicky would be okay about a little rule-bending.

He lined up the belt buckle perfectly with his fly, even though his blouse would cover it. He tugged on spit-shined boots and topped off the look with a fatigue cap, its crown sharply creased and Marine jaunty—tilted down just so above his eyes the way Nicky had worn it. He looked in the mirror and patted the name tag over his chest—"Trocadero."

He looked out the window and across the parking lot at the Elk diner, turned into "E k iner" by two dead, formerly red, neon letters, now milky blind. Just past the diner was the dirt road that led to the boat ramp where he and Nicky used to slip the ancient aluminum Grumman canoe into the Susquehanna River. On their last trip ever upriver to get to their island beyond the humming highway traffic, Nicky taught Bobby the

J-stroke that would keep the canoe moving straight if only one of them was paddling. They tooled around some and landed on the tiny island, ate bologna and American cheese sandwiches, and drank Pepsis before throwing out lines.

Bobby drove across the parking lot to the Elk. At the counter, he ordered Nicky's favorite—two fried eggs over medium, American cheese, crisp bacon on a roll, and coffee. He leaned against the wall next to the bulletin board to wait. Thumbtacked on it were notes about lawn sales, a used John Deere, a turkey dinner to benefit the Great Bend volunteer fire department, a new, never-used steel-framed deer stand, mixed shepherd-collie pups, a nearly mint two-year-old side-by-side, and a fabulous opportunity to become a Mary Kay representative.

"Here you go, sweetheart," said the waitress, done up in a frosted-blond, '6os-style beehive hairdo, and handed Bobby a paper bag and the check.

The kitchen door burst open and a skinny guy with a long apron tied way above his waist zigzagged around the counter toward Bobby. Bobby thought the cook had made him for one of those out-of-staters who'd bolt on the bill and hit the highway. He snatched the check from Bobby's hand and said, "Your money's no good here." He wiped his hand on his apron before offering it. "Thank you for your service."

"Thank you very much, but that's not necessary."

"Lots of things we do in this life aren't necessary, son. This is. I appreciate you standing up for your country—lots of people do but they don't say it enough. Stay safe! God bless, Marine!"

The cook spun around and headed back to the kitchen, the bottom of his apron slapping his legs.

Bobby waited for an opening in the stream of tractor trailers barreling past the on-ramp and gunned the car into a spot behind one with back and sides inscribed "KANE is Able."

*Which of them's the good guy, again?*

Bobby moved to the left lane to pass KANE but had to back off when it swerved in front of him without signaling. KANE passed a flatbed loaded with logs but labored to get past the truck in front of it, forcing Bobby to keep pace alongside the logs. He looked over at the logs, cinched to the truck bed by metal straps, held even tighter by metal teeth dug into their bark. Bobby looked at the rings at the cut end. Some were set close together—records of drought years. On other logs they were spaced wider, showing good growing years of plentiful water and no diseases. All dead now. Bobby remembered the Old Man marking the boys' growing years with pencil lines next to kitchen-door frames they'd had.

Bobby got off the highway at the exit for Green Gables restaurant and turned right onto a county hardtop. A mile past the house with a pink toilet on the lawn he made a left onto a dirt road running along Ratkowski's pond he and Nicky had fished way back, landing mostly pickerel, sometimes bass. After Nicky couldn't get a spinner from the throat of a beautiful bass and had to kill and eat it, he flattened the barbs on all of his hooks to give fish a better chance to spit the hook or for the hook to be easily slipped out without further damage. After that, Nicky would tell anyone else who brought up fishing that it wasn't a sport because to be a sport the consequences of losing have to be the same for everyone:

"If the fisherman loses, he goes home with an empty creel and mosquito bites and gets to lie about the big one that got away. If the fish loses, he dies."

———

As a kid, Bobby had watched an episode of *The Fugitive* where the main character—on the run after being falsely accused of his wife's murder—took a job at a lake renting boats and repairing motors. He befriended a boy, his mother, and, reluctantly, the mother's suitor, who often came to the lake with them. The man seemed an opportunist—the word ex-cop Ratkowski would use to describe somebody as a thief on the prowl.

The Fugitive liked the mom a lot but knew nothing could come of it because his lot in life was always to be running, always having to hide who he is.

In one scene, Bobby remembered the suitor is fishing in a lake and setting his catch down on the bank. Each time he laid a fish down, the kid would sneak in, pick up the gasping fish, and ease it back into the water. Eventually the suitor came running toward the kid, screaming just what the hell did he think he was doing, and raised his hand. The Fugitive's approach aborted the slap, and the kid ran away.

The Fugitive found the boy later, slumped against the hull of an overturned boat on the beach.

"I could hear the fish dying," the kid said through tears, drumming a twig against the boat, trying to distract himself to keep from crying harder. "They couldn't breathe. They were asking me to help them. They were saying they couldn't breathe in our air."

---

About a half mile up the hill from Ratkowski's was Bobby's family's land that had been passed down through several generations. No one except Nicky and Bobby had gone to it in years. Bobby parked next to the maple tree they'd dug up and carried from the woods as a sapling. He pulled the car fully into its shadow and smiled. *Ha! So big now it keeps the sun off the car. We saved it!*

Out loud, Bobby said, "I'll get the gun out of the trunk."

*How many times I gotta tell you, little brother? It's a "weapon." If you're wearing the uniform, you gotta get it right.*

Bobby opened the trunk, unzipped a tan canvas sheath, and slipped out the weapon. It was an M-700-40x sniper rifle, the model they say Chuck Mawhinney used to kill a record 103 Viet Cong in Nam, probably more, but they couldn't find enough guys to swear they'd seen him waste the other 216 he'd said he did in.

At the top of the slope, where he and Nicky had pitched a tent the first time they camped there, Bobby sank to his knees and plopped forward into the prone position.

He cradled the weapon across the crooks of both arms and crawled down the hill, propelling himself with elbows and knees, wriggling like a snake, chin almost scraping the ground, the way Nicky showed him they had to do in boot camp to stay low because live rounds supposedly were being fired just above their heads.

Bobby squirmed around the pokeweed's poisonous purple berries.

*Never, ever get suckered into thinking something is safe just because it looks pretty. Girls, too. Remember that. This is all part of the big-brother thing, me telling you stuff you gotta know. Lots of pretty things will kill you as soon as look at you. Man, you need me to keep you alive.*

Crawling, Bobby wondered what happened to the first guy to find out that the berries were poisonous. Did he die? Did he die knowing he saved people because they knew it was the berries that killed him? Did he go down as someone to remember or just a stupid dead guy?

Probably took a lot of people to die before the rest of them connected the dots and when they did they couldn't even remember the dead guy's name or a whole lot of people killed by things they thought were safe. The first person to die coulda been a kid, maybe some little girl running through the woods in a dress with flowers on it and thought they were pretty and would be good to eat. A good bet that somebody at her funeral was just pissed at the little girl for dying because now they had to get up at five in the morning to milk the damn cows.

Bobby's thoughts jumped to Robert McNamara on TV, wearing those I'm-smarter-than-you wire-rim glasses, hair slicked back like a carny guy, telling everyone how, as secretary of defense, he was winning the Vietnam War. Turned out he was a carny guy all along. He knew we weren't gonna win but still sent guys to die. Lied. Flat-out lied.

Then there was Jackie O, before the O, all prim, showing us the White House on TV. So many women wanting to be her. Of course she didn't take us downstairs to the pool house, where good ol' Jack'd knock off his pieces of tail.

The guy that offed Kennedy was a former Marine, Bobby remembered, and immediately felt guilty for remembering that.

Nicky would be angry with him for linking the guy to the Marines.

*You know, Bobby, it gets old you always ragging on the Marines. A lot of good guys—really good guys—had good motives, doing what they thought was right. You could say it wasn't a righteous fight—and turns out it wasn't—but they thought it was. They believed Semper Fi—believed in each other —and that's not easy to come by.*

Bobby rolled onto his back to dig out a round from his pocket—he'd need only one. He faced the sky for a second.

The sky all blue and pretty brought up the time when the TV played over and over the shot of that space shuttle exploding—live on Channel 2. Just before it blew, the father of that schoolteacher who was buckled into the spaceship had his neck way back, looking up, amazed at seeing the rocket, carrying his daughter, trying to outrun gravity.

"I'm not really surprised she's gonna be on that rocket," her old man said on TV a couple days before. "After all, we raised her to think big, to dare to stand out, to be exceptional. Maybe even a heroine—hero, they say these days."

Everyone was in on the father's tragedy before he was. Then everyone saw his eyes synchronize with his brain—his mouth still frozen open from being so proud of his daughter— that he'd just seen the rocket blow into smithereens, spewing pieces of his little girl across the blue sky.

If the daughter had made it past gravity before the explosion, would pieces of her orbit the earth forever? What was her name, the American hero?

Bobby scrunched into the ground, trying to get comfortable. He thought of Old Testament passages about grisly goings on he liked to read in church after he'd finished imagining Marie Castellano in her underwear beneath her choir robe. One favorite passage was: "Now therefore, kill every male among the little ones and kill every woman that hath known man by lying with him. But all of the women children that have not known man intimately keep alive for yourselves."

Bobby rolled onto his side, shoved the shell (he'd only need one) into his weapon and rolled back onto his stomach, stuck the butt firmly into his shoulder, and slowly raised the crosshairs above the target the way Nicky told him they were taught. He lowered it until Robert Strange McNamara's right eye was dead center.

A newt done up in Superfly orange froze a few feet from Bobby. They eyed each other, careful not to move until they knew which way the intruder would go.

Bobby used to be startled by the crack of the bullet's explosion, but it wasn't much different to him now than the puff-pop from the Red Ryder BB gun he got for his eleventh birthday the year they went to that lake in Vermont. The four of them paddled across the lake with their mother's great deviled eggs and cold chicken in a basket cradled on her lap. They picnicked behind a totem pole the Old Man insisted, with a grin as he pulled the canoe away from the water's edge, was put up by the Iroquois when they ruled that part of the world.

Breathe deep. Gently squeeze the trigger. Don't jerk it.

*Pop!*

Bobby got up, slung the weapon over his shoulder, and hup-hupped to the target.

McNamara's eye was shot out of the blown-up picture on the stake cross near a trembling aspen. Bobby whacked the cross with the butt of his weapon, sending the picture fluttering to the ground. He unzipped and streamed into the hole that had been McNamara's eye.

He walked up the rise toward his car. Over the stone wall he saw Terry, sitting on top of his big green and yellow John Deere, pulling a wagonload of hay and sucking on a Bud. Bobby returned a wave and a smile.

# A GOOD SHOOT

COUSIN EDUARDO, wearing gray shorts and a Boonie hat with a peace sign on one side and skull-and-crossbones on the other, looked over the second-floor railing at the tiny swimming pool in back of the Desert Song motel on the edge of downtown Las Vegas.

He saw something bobbing in the scummy water. A couple of hours earlier, he'd gone down to save a mouse about to drown. That one turned out to be a waterlogged cigar stub.

He turned and went into his room, pulled on a Grateful Dead T-shirt, ran fingers through thick black hair down to his neck, and slid into black flip-flops. Jenny would have insisted—actually foot-stomping demanded with tears in her eight-year-old eyes—that they save whatever it was in the pool. He smiled thinking of Jenny calling herself Florence Nightingale, whom she'd learned about from a television show, and organized her first rescue mission to save ants and other crawly things going too close to the edge of the town pool where they might drown.

"But, sweetie," he'd said, "sometimes that's part of life. Ants might drown, and we can't save everyone—everything. It's just the way it is. The way life is."

"No! No! That's not right, Eddie," she'd said, stomping her foot. "We have to do something. We have to try to save them. They deserve to live as much as we do."

So they built barriers from discarded sunscreen tubes, cigarette butts, bottle caps, and the like to divert them from the pool. Jenny would squeal with delight when an ant, spider, or any creature veered from the pool's precipice and headed—with her cheering them on—to the overflowing trash can next to the fence.

If they found a dead ant, or any other insect floating in the pool, they'd have a proper funeral, complete with eulogies like ones she'd seen on TV. She collected her mother's empty lip-gloss pots for coffins she'd bury beneath the playground's cottonwood tree. She'd stand over their graves and speak about families left behind and how the deceased were loved by so many other ants and spiders and everyone for their kindness. Then Cousin Eduardo, Jenny, and her mother, Algie, would go for ice cream as part of the wake. So it was perfectly natural, even respectful, Jenny would say, to have a double scoop of fudge ripple to celebrate a life.

Cousin Eduardo skipped down the motel steps, chewing an end of his mustache. When he got closer to the pool, he saw that floating in the scummy water was a browned piece of frond from the dying palm tree.

He went back upstairs and saw Ruby come out of her room at the end of the second-floor outdoor walkway.

As much as she could, given her stature that Marty once made the mistake of describing as "elfin-like," she flounced down the walkway in her latest thrift-shop find—a caftan deco-rated with red, green, and yellow jungle birds perched on branches. She carried a folded beach chair in one hand and in the other a bottle of Blue Nun by its neck. She set the bottle down next to the railing, unfolded the chair, took a plastic bathroom cup from a pocket, and plopped onto the chair. She poured four fingers of wine, stuck her legs between the bars of the railing, and admired them. She always drank wine, preferably Blue Nun.

"No pussy wine coolers," she'd told the crew when she moved into the Song after finally scoring disability checks for a nervous condition she'd heard about and convinced the disability people to approve.

"Drank a lotta this stuff back in my day at Oregon State," she'd told the gang when she first hooked up with them. "Woulda lasted longer, my old man didn't crap out and run like a thief with my tuition. Prick."

The guys mostly drank Lone Star beer except when they were flush and moved to Heineken. Marty—née Martin H. Schmidt, PhD, professor of Renaissance English literature, late of Smith College—drank only Johnnie Walker Black.

Marty, not much more than elfin himself ("a little turd of a bowling ball," Ruby'd called him, retaliating for his elfin crack), dragged a desk chair behind him on his way to the railing. He sported green plaid shorts, a tucked pink dress shirt, and a yellow-and-pink polka-dot bow tie, its tails dangling from his collar. Tortoiseshell reading glasses perched on top of his head.

From the other end of the walkway, Calvin, in a blue sweatsuit trimmed in white, flowed athlete-smooth, eating a peach. Calvin had bonded with Cousin Eduardo over being Marine Vietnam vets and brought Buttsie into the Song's crew after meeting him at a fundraiser for Marine veterans they'd gone to in the scruffy Rio hotel for the free food.

Calvin, at six foot two, was a very good heavyweight boxer with a great left hook, a man in a hurry, trying to make up for lost time in Vietnam and at jobs he'd thought he should like.

His immediate goal was to work his way onto a fight card at one of the way-off-Strip casinos—ones with tranny shows and all-you-can-eat gray-meat buffets—and hope a big-time promoter somehow noticed him.

Buttsie, thin as a bulimic model and bald with a red bushy beard, came out of his room, holding an opened can of Lone Star left over from the night before. He wore a cut off Marine fatigue shirt, matching camo pants, and tats on forearms so faded they looked like bruises. A red-and-black bandana was tied around his head.

The crew settled in front of the railing, waiting for the show to begin. A couple of months earlier, they'd assigned themselves the responsibility of critiquing celebrity impersonators presiding over speed-vows down on the patio behind the Chapel of Bliss cottage next door.

Out back, a pink '59 Caddy was permanently parked under a portico, its ceiling painted with cherubs, aiming arrows at the back seat where brides and grooms would sit holding hands and beers and be married.

Elvis would stand next to the driver's door, kind of harmonizing to "Love Me Tender" playing from a boom box set on the edge of the drive-up marriage window. If the good Elvis—the one with lifts in his shoes and a pitch-black rug draping his head—got a gig, Buttsie'd go deep and crackly to sing along with the King.

When the crew's favorite Cher showed up, they'd whoop and cheer, and Buttsie would spread his lips with pinky and forefinger and shriek a two-tone tribute. Cher'd look up at them, waving her hand side to side alongside a frozen home-coming-queen smile. For Wayne Newton, Marty would launch into a great falsetto of "I Saw Mommy Doing Santa Claus." Sometimes the gang would kind of get it together to sing other classics. Their favorite and loudest was "Rock Around the

Clock" with extra emphasis on "clock," for which they'd drop the "l."

That usually brought Duncan Busby, the Song's manager, waddling upstairs to plead they keep it down and clean.

Busby had been encouraging Cousin Eduardo to end his spree, running this time to three weeks, and go back to Algie and Jenny. Busby wanted to free up another room to rent hourly for his girls to accommodate the influx of sportswriters and TV support guys coming to town for a big fight who couldn't afford uptown hookers.

"I mean, C.E., Algie and Jenny are your only shot at, you know, a real life," Busby told him the day before. "They ain't gonna be waitin' for you forever, especially a looker like Algie with her, uh, outstanding equipment, even for this town."

Calvin slipped into a space next to Ruby and leaned against the railing. He winked at Marty and addressed Cousin Eduardo over Ruby's corkscrew black hair.

"So, C.E., tell everybody what you told me about how the word 'hooker' came to be. Kinda cool story."

Ruby glared at Calvin and mouthed, "Fuck you." Calvin dispensed his broad movie-star smile. Ruby smiled back, against her will. Buttsie snickered. Cousin Eduardo drained the last of his Lone Star.

"Don't think I didn't see that, Ruby," Cousin Eduardo said. "But in my quest to educate the masses I will ignore it to try to educate even you buncha clowns. Interesting bit how that all happened. Name'a hooker goes back to this general, name of Joe Hooker, in the Civil War. Of course, it's not what he wanted to be remembered for. But still."

Cousin Eduardo stuck his hand in the cooler for another beer.

They all shouted, "Timex: takes a licking and keeps on ticking!"

He'd always submerge the wrist in the cooler with the Timex watch on it and repeat the kicker to the old ad that depicted the watch being stressed—maybe taped to the bow of an ocean liner being smacked by tons of water—and then show it still ticking.

They'd all asked, but he'd only say the Timex was a prized keepsake from Vietnam.

Cousin Eduardo took a swig of beer and cleared his throat. "Think about it. You got the Civil War going and all, and a lotta guys're pretty horny so they gotta have some snatch or they'll be runnin' off, jumping farmers' wives and daughters and all."

"So what's wrong with that?" Buttsie said. "Them wives and daughters want it, too, ya know. Way'a nature."

Marty looked down and shook his head. Ruby sipped her wine. Calvin popped the peach pit into his mouth and licked his fingers.

"So, ol' Joey—he was a lousy general but not completely stupid," Cousin Eduardo said. "He had to find a way to get his guys some before troops'd be bustin' caps in his officers' asses 'cause the grunts're so horny and all."

Cousin Eduardo tugged the front of his Boonie lower on his forehead as the sun dipped.

"Of course, wantin' to put a hurtin' on scumbag officers, I understand," he said. "I mean, 'cause they are. You know. Scumbags. Trust me, I know. In the Civil War days and now. Some things never change."

"You got that right, brother," Calvin said, mumbling his words with the peach pit lumping his cheek.

"So ol' Joey gave passes to a bunch of *señoritas*, and they followed the troops, bringing their own tents and setting up for business, taking care of Joey Hooker's guys. Of course, you know Joey got first dibs on them whenever he wanted. So there we are. Hooker's girls. Hookers! Having your name go down in history even for that ain't bad, you think about it. I mean, we all should be remembered for something." He emptied his can and reached into the cooler for another.

"Timex: takes a licking and keeps on ticking!" they shouted in unison. Cousin Eduardo nodded and smiled.

"Think about alla the people use ol' Joey's name since then," Cousin Eduardo said. "At least his name's remembered. He's remembered for something. That's some kinda immortal. And he didn't get fragged."

"You know, C.E.," Marty said, sitting in his chair, tying his bow tie, "some historians dispute your version. They say that reference to women of the evening pre-dates the Civil War and that 'hooker' just means a woman of ill-repute—strumpets, they called them back then—who hooked clients' arms as they walked by."

"Who the fuck asked you, Marty?" Ruby said, withdrawing her legs from the bars of the railing to reach for her Blue Nun.

"I would have hoped, Miss Ruby, that a person exposed to the basics, however rudimentary, of an education would appreciate the need to be faithful to facts."

"Educate this, Marty." Ruby pointed her index finger at her lap.

"History should adhere to the strictest rules of accuracy, Ruby," Marty said. "So-called history, as told by the winners, of course, is rife with falsehoods often enough. Let us not perpetuate them. Sometimes a strumpet is just a strumpet."

"And you should know all about strumpets, professor," Ruby said. "All those little girls in that fancy college got you run outta town for diddlin' 'em."

"Anyway, C.E.," Marty said, "even if it's not an accurate rendition of history, it's a good story, well told. And, of course, there is the concept that many fictions bear more fidelity to facts than the so-called truth."

"You just can't get enough of yourself, huh, Marty?" Ruby said. "Those little girls jumped into your bed just to shut you the fuck up!"

Buttsie leaned over the railing and let loose a whistle in tribute to a woman in pink short-shorts and matching halter straining to contain Dolly Parton-size breasts that were just as real as Dolly's. She grinned at the ground. Her groom, wearing a T-shirt with the outline of a tuxedo jacket stenciled on front, looked up at the gang, jiggle-cupped his chest, and laughed.

Before anyone could tease out another story from Cousin Eduardo, Ruby blurted, "So, Calvin, when're you fighting again?"

Calvin disgorged the pit into his hand. "Next week in a smoker out of town."

"We should all go see you fight. You know, cheer you on and stuff," Ruby said.

"Can't do that, Rube. Smokers are private, you know, not licensed, even though guys from the athletic board come to eat and drink on the arm. Smokers are by invite only. Especially this one. It's big-time."

"Anyway, C.E.," Buttsie said, dipping into his bulging pocket, pulling out a handful of cigarette butts, examining them, picking one with lipstick rimming the end, and putting it between his lips, "what's the play with that statue with alla them arms and faces out front'a Caesars?"

Ruby picked up her cup and stuck out her middle finger at Buttsie as she raised it.

"Okay, wise guys," Cousin Eduardo said. "Don't think I didn't see that, Ruby. But I will persevere in the unlikely case some kinda knowledge'll sneak into your little brains."

Cousin Eduardo paused, looked down at the floor, patted his pockets, took out a piece of paper, and crouched and put the paper on the floor. An ant crawled onto it. He stood up, walked to a pot with a brown cactus in it, held the paper on top of the dirt, and gently shook off the ant. He walked back to the crew. Ruby slowly shook her head and smiled.

"Here's the free version about that statue," Cousin Eduardo said. "It's a shrine to the god Brahma outta Thigh-land and other places over there. Caesars put it up to make Asian types comfortable while losing their money. And, man, do they lose— a lot of 'em at baccarat, you know, that game they play in roped-off rooms, dealers in tuxedos and all. And that, children, is the end of the story. You want more, you gotta feed the Cousin Eduardo kitty."

After a couple in a wedding dress and a real tuxedo actually looking kind of classy went into the "Chapel of Love," the gang packed up to move into Marty's room. Cousin Eduardo took another hit of beer, executed a perfect about-face, and followed. Calvin peeled off to his room to get his bag before jogging to the gym. Ruby folded her chair, grabbed her Blue Nun in a choke hold, and headed to her room to spiff up before joining the gang at Marty's.

Styrofoam containers, ripped open last night, were on Marty's coffee table in front of the futon. Half an egg roll was in one of the boxes, its guts stuck to the bottom, a lump of hard rice pasted to it. There was a McDonald's wrapper open on the table smeared with dried ketchup and empty two-liter Pepsi bottles on each side of the table, looking like a 7-10 split.

Ruby came into the room, now wearing a yellow sundress and tan huarache sandals, plopped onto the futon, kicked off the sandals, and drew her legs beneath her, bunching her dress between her thighs. Cousin Eduardo sat on the opposite end of the futon, leaning over the table.

Ruby opened her big beach bag, on it a picture of a palm tree blowing in the wind against the backdrop of an aqua ocean, and began rummaging through it. She took out a red thong, matching bra, a strip of condoms, five tampons, and a pack of Juicy Fruit. She pulled out a small blue-flowered makeup bag and tossed everything else back.

"You know," Ruby said, her head down, setting up her rig on the table, "I'm still thinking about that gross statue in front of Caesars. I was up there last week, and I had to walk on the street to get past them. It's like they think they own the sidewalk. Fuckin' foreigners think who they are!"

"Now that's prejudice rearing its ugly head, Ruby," Marty said from a tattered armchair, lowering his dog-eared copy of *Beowulf* to look at her. "We may not understand their culture, but they deserve our respect to not label them with a racial slur. Let us hold onto our semblance of humanity, please. Sadly, that may be all we have at this point to recommend ourselves: semblance of."

"Get outta yourself once in a while, Doc," Ruby said. "It's gross. Just sittin' there, like, with a thousand arms, like an octopus with fingers looking to grab your ass. Four fuckin' faces. Belongs in a horror flick. Who prays to something looks like that?"

"This discourse addresses an existential question that is older than, uh, the Messiah himself," Marty said, putting his Johnnie on the side table and opening the drawer. He pulled out a Bible and riffled through pages. "Ah, we can always count on the Gideons to spread the Word," he said. "Here it is! Isaiah 44:9. I quote, 'All who make idols are nothing, and the things they treasure are worthless. Those who would speak up for them are blind; they are ignorant to their own shame.'"

"Yes! See what I mean?" Ruby said, cleaning her spoon off with the hem of her dress. "Shameless, worthless pieces of shit. They foulest the nest of our Lord."

"Good one, Ruby," Marty said. "From *The Book According to Ruby?*"

"Fuck you, you perv!"

"That statue means something to some people," Cousin Eduardo said, opening a toiletry bag to get at his setup. "Why the fuck you care what they believe in? At least they believe in something."

"Then keep it to yourself. I don't gotta see it," Ruby said.

"You see crosses around everyone's neck? You ever say anything about that, Ruby? All that in-your-face shit," Cousin Eduardo said. "They thinking they got a special ticket to heaven. Who's to say that ain't false too? Who's to say whatever we think we believe ain't a hustle we learned from hustlers, who learned it from hustlers, and so on and *et cetera*."

"Ahh. History as written by the winners, whose history is all we're left with. Uh, with which we are left," Marty said.

"You are so fuckin' in love with yourself, o defrocked professor," Ruby said. "That mighta worked on all those dumb-ass college girls, but you're with grown-ups now."

"Why hadn't I realized that?" Marty said, sticking the Bible back into the drawer, picking up his bottle of Johnnie from the floor, and covering three ice cubes.

"This is a Christian country, no place for a statue like that and people bowing to it," Ruby said. "Look at what Christians built here and around the world."

"And at what price, Miss Ruby? Onward, Christian soldiers?" Marty said. "Marching as to war? As if. As if. The war is still going on. Smoldering at times, maybe, but it's always there ready to roar with 'My way is the only way. My god is the only god. That's what makes me so special.' Surely our existence cannot be ephemeral as an ant's or, uh, a cow. Surely we're more special than that. Onward, soldiers!"

"Stay with me, Doc," Ruby said. "I'm talking about that pagan statue, not soldiers."

"Yeah, just sittin' there like it belongs." Buttsie pulled a folded tin foil packet from his pocket and carefully unwrapped it. "Sly, shit-eating smile on all its faces. Creepy." He sprinkled the powder onto the table and gathered it into a furrow with his dog tag. "Ain't never goin' to Caesars, they suck up to them people. Un-American. And to think we fought to save 'em."

"Fuckin' A!" Ruby said.

Buttsie stared at her breasts, still perky even after years of drugs and lousy nutrition, he'd said to Calvin. He took a cut off straw from behind his ear, bent down to his line of coke, and stuck the other end into a nostril. Ruby unfolded from the futon, pushed the Styrofoam containers to one side, and with the back of her hand swept the bottles to the floor.

"Not for nothing," she said, holding a lighter beneath her spoon. "You degenerate junkies got any manhood left between your legs, you go up to Caesars'n teach those Chinks a lesson. Someday, somebody with scrotes is gonna off 'em and no one'll give a rat's ass. Someone'll Uzi their asses. Serve 'em right, I say," she said, glaring at Cousin Eduardo. "Comin' here and praying to a fuckin' freak statue of a guy, girl—who knows what. Foreigners taking over. And you call yourselves men? Should be singin' in the Vienna Boys' Choir."

She shook her head and drew the liquid into her needle. She slid it under her skin. A few seconds later her head lolled against the back of the futon, a Mona Lisa smile on her face, saliva seeping from a corner of her mouth.

Cousin Eduardo fixed his own spoon and shot up. He usually didn't get too juiced at any one time, taking several hits during the day rather than one big one. That way he could focus—kind of—in pieces.

Still sitting, he bolted to attention.

"Gook? Chink? Slope? Who are we to talk about them like that?" he said, turning to Ruby, her head still slack against the back of the futon. He turned and stared through a hole in the lampshade at the blazing sun and burn spots on the shade that were planets.

"Leave 'em the fuck alone. What'd they ever do to you? To us?" he said, still staring through the hole. "That statue is for a lotta other people—from India, China, Thigh-land. You know, like a billion people in this world never even heard of some dead guy on a cross and pray to other stuff. They're still good people."

Marty poured himself more Johnnie. Ruby's eyes were glazed slits. Buttsie snorted up the coke and shook his head as it hit.

Cousin Eduardo turned to the group. "Respect all people. Respect flies. Respect worms. Respect gorillas. Yeah, and leeches. And, of course, ants—especially ants."

Cousin Eduardo stood up, found his equilibrium, spotted his Boonie crumpled on the floor, punched it open, pulled it onto his head, opened the door, and slammed it shut behind him.

He marched along the walkway toward the stairs, his shoulders tilted forward as if leaning into a strong wind. He passed the buzzing soda machine opposite the candy machine with the window cracked from Buttsie punching it when it wouldn't give up a Snickers. He skipped down the stairs to the parking lot.

"Open the trunk," he said to himself, as he reached his car.

He pulled out a long, narrow box from Sassy Sally's florist. Yeah! Bouquet of roses painted on it. Red on white, kinda an outline. Not a real-life painting. More an idea of what could be inside. Flowers and smiles. Box tells you to imagine what they look like and the look in the eyes of someone you give 'em to. Queen for a day. Prince Charming for a day. For a day. A couple of hours.

"Forward *maaaarrrch!* Your left, your left, your left, right, left!"

He marched out of the driveway, carrying the box over his shoulder, the Boonie's chin straps bouncing, keeping cadence. Past the Pepto-Bismol Caddy. A left up the sidewalk toward Caesars. Past Chapel of Bliss' eye-stabbing white with blue shutters. A white stretch limo sun-stroked in the driveway. Tires sagging. Waxed as much as you can to get something way past its time to get a little shine outta it. But still dead. Done. On the way out even as a memory. Crack on front fender filled in with Bondo. Painted over in white, whiter than the rest of the car.

"'A Whiter Shade of Pale,'" he said aloud to himself.

*How do you "skip a light fandango"? What the fuck is a light fandango? Song makes no sense, sticking to me like that leech in that jungle river. Watched him settle in on my arm, settin' up shop to suck on me. Had to just watch him suckin' my blood. Maybe he was a she.*

*How'd that other song go about being hustled to send your kids to Vietnam to fight for Uncle Sam?*

*. . . don't hesitate,*
*send 'em off before it's too late,*
*be the first to have your boy come home in a box.*

*Something like that. Us-in-a-box stuff for sure. Finally got to burn that leech off with a cigarette. Body fell into the river. Just doing his thing. Her thing? Not fair, you think about it. Just doing his thing. Her thing. Shoulda been a funeral and proper burial.*

*Group standing in front of the limo sucking on Buds. Cheering the "I do" line. "Fuckin' A!" one of 'em shouts.*

Laughing like they're at a comedy club primed to laugh at anything before they even get there.

Baby-blue flip-flop drops off the bride's foot, as she's hoisting herself outta the car. Looks of her, she's had a lotta practice climbing outta back seats.

She picks up the flip-flop, arranges it on the cement with her foot, and slides into it over grimy toe prints. Straightens up. Digs down the front of her T-shirt, pulls up her left bra cup. Pulls panties outta her crack. Tugs down shorts.

Groom keeps loud burp going. More laughs. Cans'a Bud, toasting it all. No one sees me. I'm just walkin' on by. Just a thing, walking on by. Yeah. Really is no-man's-land. No cars coming. Triple-time across the Strip! Hustle up!

"World's largest Souvenir Store!" next to a pawnshop. How do they know that? Probably a lie. Must be a bigger store somewhere. In India? China? They have souvenirs there? Probably not. They don't smile much. Past Helpful Herman's pawnshop. Yeah, helpful. Vulture, helping to rip you off. In the window a banjo, violin, watches, rings, purple frilly dress, dreamin' of prom night's twinkly lights and holding on tight to "Love Me Tender." Bongo drums hanging from a yellow rope, black patches in the middle of the skins, scraggly black lines running to the edges—left from pounding and sliding fingers, probably dead now. Lazy Larry's coffee shop—cactus in front, breathin' hard through dirty brown gravel. Lopsided 'cause of an empty spot from amputated arm. Does it still feel its missing arm?

Should be a song 'bout that.

"C'mon! You fuckin' lame-ass excuse of a Marine. Hoist the box onto your shoulder. Hup! Hup! Hup!"

Past Fashion Mall. Past Circus Circus set way back. Hot! Like walking across a desert.

"Dumb fuck! Where you think you are? Gotta push. Keep up the cadence. Hup! Hup! Hup!"

*"You slow. You stop! You stop, you're done! You lose, Marine. Maybe your life."*

*Comin' up on Treasure Island. Pirate ship still in the fake lagoon resting in front of the fake rocks of the fake volcano. Pirates chillin' somewhere. In coffee shops? Playin' golf? Humpin' girlfriends or not girlfriends?*

*Caesars property now.*

*"Hup! Hup! Hup!"*

*Over hill, over dale,*
*As we hit the dusty trail*
*And those caissons go rolling along . . .*

*Song goes way back.*

*Mrs. Henry waving that ruler she used to clip us with. Maybe that's where we got hooked on uniforms and heroes. That 4-F-fuck-fraud John Wayne put that shit in our minds. Made millions. Got lotsa poontang off'a being a fake war hero.*

Cousin Eduardo sees his destination come into view.

*Weird. Kinda cool, though. So peaceful. All arms and faces. One, two, three, four. Four faces. One, two, three, four, five, six, seven, eight. Eight arms.*

Strings of puffy colored stuff like carnations on steroids hang on a railing around the statue.

*Get behind it! Her! She's seen it all. Knows who we really are. Smile makes me wanna smile back. She's telling me—us— that she knows. Knows what we really need. She understands. Guard her for them. Guard them!*

*Yo, pray to whatever gets you through the night! Respect different. Respect. I fought you. You fought me. Respect.*

*Nights tough enough to get through on your own. Pray to whatever, whoever does it for you. Fuck I care? You got a right.*

*"Marine! I told you! Carry your weapon in your arms like a*

*baby, so you don't snag it on anything, you dumb fuck! Gimme fifty!"*

A weapon in a Sassy Sally's box meant for roses. Roses.

*Bunch'a them behind that castle in Central Park Algie showed me, we played hooky, went to that garden in the Bronx, then to see crazy-ass rollerbladers in Central Park. Great day. All-time great. Calzones and kisses. Bought her a bunch of red roses one time. Bought yellow ones for Jenny. Smiles and hugs. Goose bumps for me. Hero for a day.*

Cousin Eduardo climbs up and sits on the platform behind Brahma. He peeks out under one of her arms just above her thigh. *All those arms. Kinda awesome.*

*Take it out now. Show them what you got. Keep the bad guys away.*

*Couldn't always do that. Couldn't keep them away from Erickson our third day humpin' boonies hunting ears for beers. Once brought back seven ears. Woulda been eight, but Malickey so juiced he pumps five rounds into one'a the dead Gook's face. Couldn't find anything looked like his other ear.*

*Heard a round coming outta the grass. Caught Tomlison. He's screamin', "I'm hit! I'm hit! I'm hit!" Then squeaky voice floatin' outta the fog: "Soldie boys, soldie boys, lissen up—Dem thit nop mieng hum. Dem thit nop mieng hum. Dem thit nop mieng hum." Then she—a woman, for Chrissake!—she'd translate: "The tiger been brought his meat."*

*Then she cuts off Tomlison's balls. Cuts 'em off while he's fuckin' alive! Alive! He's screaming, beggin' for someone to shoot him. Couldn't even see him to shoot him. Like to think I'da helped if I coulda. Shoot him.*

*How do you forget stuff you wanna forget? Can't. Comes back when you don't expect, and every time it comes back with a "Fuck you—I own you!"*

Cousin Eduardo stands behind Brahma.

*Why're these people running away from Brahma? From me? Why?*

*Yo! I'm watching out for you! Not to worry! I got your back. Stay. Pray as long as you want. I'm here to help you do your thing.*

*I'm watchin' for the bad guys. Keep praying, you want. Can't hurt. Pray to her. No one gonna bother you. Got you covered. I'm watchin'. No one gonna bother you. Pray. Just pray. Pray for everybody. Pray! Pray! Pray! . . . Please! Please! Pray!*

*Slope. Gook. Dink. Didn't mean anything by it. Wasn't thinking. I'm sorry. Very sorry. I was really young and stupid, like they say.*

*Neon leaking on the sidewalks in front of Barbary Coast.*

*Kinda pretty. Blue and white different kinda neon. Flashing on the sidewalk of Barbary. A car? On the freakin' sidewalk? A car? Everybody running away awful fast.*

The Strip is Sunday-morning quiet. No party-hearties, toting margaritas you could drown in, no crooked-smile hustlers doing their things, no tourists' heads spinning to gawk at the miles of stoned neon still running up, down, and around casinos. Everything's just waiting to be clicked back into life.

Then a deep disembodied voice—God booming from the Mountain, over the Barbary Coast, floating across the street, to Brahma and to Cousin Eduardo. He shifts to look from another angle behind Brahma and sees a megaphone sticking out from behind a planter. Then more cops.

―――

"ALL UNITS! ALL UNITS! DIVERT TO THE STRIP! DIVERT TO THE STRIP! PERP WITH RIFLE BEHIND CHINK STATUE AT CAESARS. ALL UNITS! GO! GO

NOW! SET UP IN FRONT OF BARBARY COAST! GO! GO! GO!"

Claude hears the call over his police radio as he was grabbing the car keys to pick up Marla and her new tits. "Breasts, for Chrissake, Claude, breasts! Show some respect!"

Claude was the one who had to respond. The other sharpshooter-qualified cop had a day off and was out of range visiting his favorite whorehouse in Parumph, about an hour into the desert, where he gets a cop discount. Claude, who lives in Henderson, about a half hour from the Strip, jumped into his jeep and took off, lights flashing. He figured Marla could get a ride back from the hospital from someone—maybe Darlene, who doesn't start at Buckin' Fillies until ten.

Police cars had jumped the curb in front of Barbary, parking at angles flanking three huge planters on the sidewalk. Claude pulled in behind the cop cars, slipped out of his jeep, and ran, head low, carrying a long tan canvas bag. He knelt behind a planter filled with ruby and yellow marigolds, unzipped the bag, and took out his rifle, the model Chuck Mawhinney used to kill a confirmed Marine-record 103 Viet Cong. He claimed he wasted 216 in sixteen months. Wearing a bulletproof vest and a helmet, Claude peered around the planter, looking across the Strip for his target.

From the loudspeaker: "PUT THE WEAPON DOWN! NOW! PUT THE WEAPON DOWN! NOW!"

Strict new protocol had been implemented for confronting a shooter after a rookie cop—the public safety commissioner's nephew by marriage—shot and killed a tourist from Tulsa a year earlier, thinking a cop's wife was a hooker, complimented her on her breasts that were spilling out of her blouse on the moving walkway into Caesars. He asked her how much. The nephew had to wait six more months for his sergeant's stripes after the D.A. determined it was self-defense.

A minute later:

"PUT THE WEAPON DOWN! NOW! PUT THE WEAPON DOWN! NOW!"

Cousin Eduardo hears the command and grips his rifle tighter.

*How stupid do you think I am? You gonna sing to me, meat? I'll give the tiger meat. I'll fuckin' grease you and him, fuck with me. Dem thit nop mieng hum. Dem thit nop mieng hum. Dem thit nop mieng hum—The tiger been brought his meat. You want me to be 'nuther Tomlison? I'm keeping my balls, thank you. Ain't taking any more of your pep pills, Lieutenant Asshole! You ain't juicin' me to stay awake, thinking I'm Superman and kill Slopes and maybe me. Fuck you!*

Claude knew he had to hear two more warnings and that there would be a thorough inquiry into anything he did. He had to relax a little. Sometimes it helps to look through the scope somewhere else. That girl crouching behind the Caesars hedge in the blue halter. Tits—breasts—the size Marla's gettin' now—downsizing. Kinda perky. Nice! Who'da thought big ones could hurt her back and it would get old, all the guys staring at 'em? And to think they were her calling card when she first hit Vegas.

"PUT THE WEAPON DOWN! NOW! PUT THE WEAPON DOWN! NOW!"

Claude swings his rifle back to the target.

Cousin Eduardo watches and listens. *Yeah, right. Put the weapon down? What? I got a red 'S' on my forehead for stupid? These people got rights, too. Somebody's gotta stick up for 'em. I finally got it right. Do the right thing.*

*Atone, my son. Atone.*

"*Dem thit nop mieng hum. Dem thit nop mieng hum. Dem thit nop mieng hum.*"

*"Just wave the weapon at 'em if anyone bothers 'em. Stutter-step 'em, make 'em think."*

"PUT THE WEAPON DOWN! NOW! PUT THE WEAPON DOWN! NOW!"

An ant crawls onto Cousin Eduardo's forearm he'd braced against the back of one of Brahma's arms. He shifts his arm onto the ledge between her arms and leans his head close to it so he can see better and gently nudges the ant toward safety.

*Pop!*

Cousin Eduardo's head jerks back and disappears.

Claude says to himself, "Dead center of his forehead. Dead center. Took only one. Way it should be. Just like in Nam. Took just one. Just one. Way it's supposed to be.

"A good shoot."

# PROM DRESS

"*OOOH-WHEE*, GIRL! WORK THAT *BOOOO-TEEEE*!" Lily Chou squealed three octaves above her normal voice.

High school friends, Lily and Esme were in Pretty Lady in Little Saigon, in Westminster, California—an inland, mid-state town with many Vietnamese refugees—where Esme was trying on prom dresses. Lily allowed herself to be genuinely enthusiastic about helping Esme find the right dress, after Lily finally had accepted that no way her mother would allow her to go to something called a prom, especially not with a round-eyes like Esme's date, Brendan. On top of that, her mother said, scrunching her face, he has red hair.

Esme had started coughing the day before to set up being too sick to work at Touch of Asia restaurant, owned by Phuoc Huu, who couldn't care less if customers caught whatever Esme might be spreading. After all, when food spilled onto the floor, he'd maybe rinse it off before putting it back on a plate. But coughing could be heard and that wouldn't do. So he told Esme to take off the next day.

"Red be fly on you, bring out you 'do, all wavy and all and

them long, uh, deer kinda eyes too," Lily said, imitating the Black girls who, when they were in the mood, let the Asian girls sit at the lunch table next to them.

Lily got up from her chair in front of the platform in Pretty Lady, where Esme was preening in front of three angled mirrors, and folded her arms.

"But no room for nuthin' else," Lily said, "even thong be showing theyself. No way them schap-a-rones be letting you shake that out, girl!"

"Yeah, kind of outrageous," Esme said, looking over her shoulder and wiggling her hips. "But how cool to mess with that uptight bitch Miss Gaffney and Coach Jefferies, like they're some kind of dress cops. Like everyone doesn't know they're doing it."

When Phuoc Huu first complimented Esme on her tall, voluptuous figure and encouraged her to swish her way across the room to serve customers, he used "derriere," a word he'd learned from the French when they ran Vietnam before Communist troops overwhelmed them at Dien Bien Phu in 1954. After the Americans swarmed ashore a little more than a decade later, Phuoc Huu picked up more English when it was inevitable they'd be the next occupiers. "Ass" soon became his go-to show of American cool. Once he even mentioned taking up golf.

Phuoc Huu promoted Esme to hostess so her figure would be on display longer, striding across the large dining room, often in an elegant soft-blue *ao doi*, panels of its tunic swaying over her long legs, snug in white trousers. Esme knew the attraction she was. Husbands, boyfriends, whatever would slip her extra tips—often accompanied by phone numbers—to keep their fantasies alive about this exotic girl with large breasts and "legs all the way to China," one diner told his wife and daughter.

Esme saved her "husband" tips for the jar hidden in her closet. She'd use the money to find her father some day. All she knew about him was that he was an American G.I.—a Marine— who maybe had married her mother in Saigon, as it was called back in the day before the Americans were kicked out of the country.

In a small box under her bed, she kept a faded Polaroid picture of her mother in a flowered *ao dai*, a tall, handsome African man next to her, his arm around her waist. The head nun at Good Shepherd orphanage near Da Nang, midway up the Vietnam coast, had given her the laminated photo when she aged out at thirteen. The photo literally never left Esme. She taped it to her leg, where it stayed through the nearly two years she spent living and begging with dozens of other mixed-race outcasts in Reunification Park in Ho Chi Minh City, renamed from Saigon after the Communists won the war, following "Uncle" Ho's blueprint.

"Shake ass when walk room," Phuoc Huu told her when he made her hostess, effectively demoting his wife to supervising the kitchen. "Men like. They pay check. Come back see you ass in *ao dai*."

Esme wanted to tell him that "ass" was crass and sounded silly coming from him. But if she ever brought it up, he'd twist it to her talking about her body and then, of course, that she was coming on to him.

He even bought Esme a scarlet *ao dai* with white trousers beneath the long tunic so when, as Phuoc Huu instructed, she quickly turned around after seating customers, the panels would whip around, like tendrils of fire lapping at her legs.

"And use accent—but only little. Americans want only little foreign. Remember, it just A Touch of Asia." He'd rejected making it A Touch of Vietnam, because that name teased out too many raw American emotions.

Ironic, that name. Phuoc Huu was constantly touching her when he thought his wife wasn't looking. He'd slide his hand off the side of the host's stand to graze her derriere and wink, as if it was a secret she was a part of. His wife allowed him to pretend it was a secret because she knew husbands need to think they have secrets.

One late afternoon, a family came into the restaurant with two girls in school uniforms. In one of his rare comments about the war, Phuoc Huu gestured toward the girls and said to Esme, "Millions of Vietnamese die. Americans easy forget that. They no know that from school here."

Esme didn't respond but knew he was right. She'd only learned about U.S. soldiers' deaths—a fraction of the Vietnamese left dead.

Esme didn't care about Phuoc Huu, his wife, or their two daughters—all part of a business arrangement to get her to California, America. Soon—not soon enough for her—she'd be on her own with time and money to look for her father, hopefully still alive and wanting to be found.

Truth be told, Esme liked displaying herself as she walked across the room—sometimes longer strides for slinkiness, sometimes short steps to wiggle her derriere. Often, during her performances, she'd glance at the room's three-panel divider, between the tables and the waiting area. The scene painted on it was framed by bamboo. It was an Asian Norman Rockwell's Eden-lush scene of jasmine vines, blue sky dappled with puffy clouds, lolling over loamy fields, with rice paddies and soft mountains in the distance.

Maybe that was how Vietnam looked to her long-ago ancestors before it became a killing ground for so many countries through the years trying to claim the long, narrow country spooning the South China Sea. Esme, though, knew only a place pockmarked with American bomb craters, charred remains of villages, and stories of bloated carcasses of water buffalo slaughtered in rice paddies after whooping soldiers emptied their guns into them for fun.

Esme hadn't told anyone that Phuoc Huu and his wife, Binh, were not her aunt and uncle. Many of the children—dubbed Amerasians by U.S. bureaucrats—were the offspring of Black soldiers and as such were ostracized and worse. Vietnamese called them *Bui Doi* ("dust of life")—literally trash to be thrown out. Eventually, as North and South Vietnam were reunited and slowly tried to enter world markets, the presence of *Bui Doi* embarrassed Vietnam and the United States alike. The desperate children included dozens living in Reunification Park. The deal with Phuoc Huu and Esme locked her and his family into a pact of mutual destruction—deportation—if any of them revealed they were not related.

———

Esme, still called by her Vietnamese name, Ngoc, back then, had known since she was thirteen at Good Shepherd that men were captivated by her. She knew which ones wanted to just slam into her, which men wanted her to want them, which men wanted her to notice them with kind eyes, which men just wanted to look at her and sigh. She knew it, too, from the eyes of the priest, his blue and red nose veins looking like secondary roads on a map. He would come every month, look her budding body up and down, and stroke her thigh when he chose her, beginning when she was eleven, to sit next to him at supper.

Crucifixes hung on all four walls of the girls' dormitory. The one on the wall closest to Ngoc's bunk was the biggest, and had a plaster Jesus glued to it, drops of raised red plaster blood frozen on the sides of his face, wrists, and feet. A seam ran down the middle of his face and torso, through his covered genitals, splitting him in half.

Ngoc would stare from her top bunk at the chipped paint on the ceiling. The small, almost round spots were planets, and the swaths of flaking paint were the Milky Way, which held her fate when they were formed, even before Buddha, who was way older than Jesus, she'd told girls at "Good Shepherd" who never questioned the nuns' take that Jesus and his father was the only way.

She had learned about Buddha when her grandmother took her home for short, furtive visits each year for Tet, the new year.

Ngoc watched her grandmother sit before a statue of Buddha and burn incense, as a reminder of the need for virtue of thought and deed. The light of the flame, she told her granddaughter, is to remind that knowledge is light. Ngoc learned that flowers, while beautiful and joyous, will fade and die, that everything changes, nothing stays the same. Except knowledge, which you must always strive for. During Tet, her grandmother would, of course, burn special fake money for her ancestors, who would receive the good will and in turn bring the living good luck, prosperity, and blessings.

Heathen practices, the nuns said.

Ngoc figured she should hedge her bet on getting spiritual help to have a better chance of a Christian God hearing her if she said her prayers in English, even in her head. The nuns always spoke English and insisted their charges learn it. After all, nuns say they're Jesus' wives, so they would know best how to please him.

"Jesus, I drink your blood. I eat your flesh. Why doesn't Mama come back for me? I pray you to bring her back. I am good girl. Please hear me!"

———

"So, have you pretty ladies decided on a dress?" the saleswoman asked as she approached Lily and Esme, who held the three dresses Esme had tried on draped over her arm. "I think you have several flattering options."

Esme glanced at her watch. "I'm sorry, but we're late for another appointment. We'll be back, though, later today to make a decision."

The saleswoman snatched the dresses from Esme, brushed them free of nothing, and walked away, pushing her shoulders into perfect posture.

Esme and Lily left the store onto the scorching sidewalk, simultaneously putting on sunglasses and wide-brimmed straw hats and setting out to walk the twenty minutes to Bernie's, a popular diner with kids from school. They'd never been to Bernie's, but on this special day they'd pretend they belonged.

They waited for a traffic light to change.

"So how did Brendan ask you?" Lily said, dropping her earlier Black-girl-speak. "Did he send you a note or what?"

The light changed, stopping a yellow convertible with four guys in it. Esme and Lily crossed in front of them.

"Hey, Brown Sugar," a guy with stringy blond hair over his ears shouted at Esme. "Love your ass!"

Esme and Lily did not look at the car. As they passed it, Esme raised her left arm over her head and extended her middle finger.

"Bitches!" shouted the guy.

"Yeah," one of the guys in the back seat yelled. "Chink bitches!"

"Don't look at them," Esme told Lily and kept her arm and finger extended until they reached the other side of the wide street.

"What were we talking about?" Esme said as they stepped onto the curb. "Oh, Brendan. He just stopped me at my locker and asked if I'd go with him. I mean, it took a while for him to get it out, and he was looking at the floor until he asked and then stared at me with those puppy eyes, waiting for me to say something. To play with him, I made him repeat it, saying I hadn't heard him. Then I told him I'd think about it."

"You are a bitch!"

"Yeah, I guess," Esme said, adjusting the brim of her hat to block the sun as they turned into it. "He got all squinty-eyed and red in the ears. If I didn't like him, I woulda kept it up to see him squirm. But I said I was just kidding and that I'd go with him."

"Why'd you say yes right away? I mean, you knew Ricky was gonna ask you. That's what Sam said. Brendan's kinda cute and all, but he's not in Ricky's league, you know."

"Depends what league you're talking about. But you wanna know the biggest reason I said yes? 'Cause Brendan never looked at my boobs when he asked me. Not once. Ricky never takes his eyes off them, like they're dessert. I guess more like appetizers."

They came through Bernie's back door and luckily found a booth against a wall, beneath a poster from *Saturday Night Fever*—John Travolta, frozen mid-gyration in a white leisure suit and wide-collared black shirt open to mid-chest. On the opposite wall was a psychedelic portrait—of Elvis in splashes of red, green, and yellow.

A waitress brought menus and water. They ordered Cokes and cheeseburger deluxes.

Lily took a long sip of her Coke.

"You know, I was thinking, watching you sexy it all around at the store, that you look like you're, uh, you know, experienced with your body, you know."

"C'mon, Lil, just say it. Just ask. Am I a virgin?"

Lily lifted the top of her burger bun and plucked off the four bread-and-butter pickles on top of the cheese and put them onto her plate.

"Okay. Are you?" Lily said, cutting her burger into precise fourths.

Esme smiled. She took a slice of onion from her cheeseburger and put it aside. "That depends on the definition of virgin. It's complicated."

"Huh? You either are or you aren't."

Esme smiled. "It counts what you think about it when you're doing it. Does it mean anything? Why are you doing it? You can not be a virgin technically but still be a virgin."

Lily slapped her forehead. "Oh, I get it. Sure. Like a little pregnant. Of course."

"Let's get off the subject," Esme said, replacing the top of her bun and pressing it hard onto the cheeseburger.

"But I wanna know what it's like. Did you do it back in Vietnam when you were Ngoc? Did it hurt? Do you get to like it? My mom says it's just something you have to do that comes with being married, like it or not."

"I was just playing with you, Lily," Esme said, lifting the burger with both hands. "I'm still feeling my inner slut from wiggling it all out in those dresses."

"Don't blow it off, Es," Lily said, squeezing a lemon into her Coke and stirring it with a straw.

Esme chuckled and bit into her burger.

"Seriously, Es, I wanna know what it's like and how you know when to, you know, do it and what to do. I mean exactly."

"I'm not blowing you off, Lily," Esme said, chuckling again. "Interesting word choice. I'm no expert. I can't tell you when or how to do it. You gotta figure it out for yourself. Like, what's best for you. The thing is to know why you're doing it and not deceive yourself about your reasons."

"Huh?" Lily paused from carefully folding a paper napkin smaller and smaller.

"Well, I mean, finally doing it stays with you forever. I mean the first time. So if you have a bad time, I think it might mess it up for you for a long time. Maybe forever, if you take it too seriously."

"Were you, uh, are you messed up about it? Did you lose it when you were Ngoc or when you were Esme?"

Esme looked at Lily over her bun. "What's to lose? It's all way, way dumb. You know, all the stuff about virginity for women. What about guys? They get to brag they're not virgins. Kinda spreading the seed kind of thing, I guess—everyone thinking it's natural for them—you know, it's what the world needs to keep going. Guys use that as an excuse to use us whether they know it or not."

"Huh? What're you—" Lily stopped as Tommy Anglinotti, the starting halfback, short and compact with a mound of curly black hair, plopped onto Esme's side of the booth and then, looking across the room at his posse, exaggeratedly wiggled against her to get room. Esme moved over and Tommy moved with her, his thigh against hers.

"That may be a big thrill for you with all the little girls that put up with you," Esme said, turning to look at Tommy, "but you don't back off, I'll break this ketchup bottle over your dumb-ass head."

Tommy's neck turned pink just below his ears. "That's why they call you a stuck-up bitch! Who knows what I could catch from a Slant like you!"

Esme reached for the ketchup bottle. Tommy quickly slid out of the booth. Safely beyond Esme's reach, he set himself back to swaggering mode and walked back to his friends, who watched the episode, sniggering in a booth on the other side of the room below a poster for *American Graffiti*.

"Close your mouth, Lily," Esme said, smiling while opening the ketchup bottle and replenishing the dipping puddle on her plate.

"That'll make us real popular," Lily said. "Why'd you do that?"

"You let them touch you at all without permission, they'll think things, Lily. Don't forget that. Even if they pretend it's all innocent and all. It never is. And if you let it slide, you gotta get something for it."

"But still, Es, you didn't have to say that in front of his friends and all."

"That's exactly why I had to. C'mon! Now, where were we?" Esme looked at Tommy's friends. She smiled and slowly shook her head at them.

"C'mon, Es, stop it! Now you're playing with them. I asked you if you're messed up about, uh, doing it and, like, when did you? Why the big secret, anyway?"

Esme speared a couple of fries with her fork and held them aloft, swaying them in the air. "No secret and no, I'm not messed up about it. Not that I know, anyway." She decapitated the fries, leaving their halves on her fork. "As far as I'm concerned, it's just a thing—a thing you sometimes want to do, sometimes don't want to do, but you do it anyway. It's the most intimate thing a woman can do—and sometimes just a thing and no big deal."

"But what if you pick the wrong guy and it means something to you but nothing at all to him except like a conquest or something."

"Well, after all, it is a conquest thing for guys—almost always—and chances are you will pick the wrong guy for your first time."

"So tell me!" Lily said, taking the straw out of her Coke and draining the last of it. "C'mon! When did you do it the first time? Was it back in Vietnam?"

"Okay, why not?" Esme said with a shrug. "I'm not ashamed of it. Actually kinda proud of some of it. Surviving it, I guess."

Esme sat up straighter and stared at the boys on the other side of the room loudly slurping their sodas. They looked down at their table.

"I don't have a short version of the story. I gotta tell it all or nothing. It's kinda weird that every time I tell the story, I remember more of what happened, and sometimes it makes me feel scared how I got through it all. But kinda proud, I guess."

"I wanna know," Lily said, putting down her burger, plucking a fry from Esme's plate and dipping it in Esme's ketchup pool, "but I don't wanna make you sad. You know what I mean?"

Esme pushed her hair behind her right ear and looked up at Travolta. "I was trying to get out of Vietnam 'cause I wasn't even a second-class person there. I mean, if I'm not light-skinned, I'm dirt to be thrown away 'cause white is pure, and so I was, uh, dirty, just a worthless thing with my skin and all. And, of course, that made my mom a whore—worse, a whore for American devils, who raped and killed us, sometimes just for fun, like the water buffalos, dogs, and everything else they killed. Not all of them, I guess, but still."

She paused to dip the stub of a fry into the ketchup and popped it into her mouth.

"My mom couldn't keep me 'cause even her friends thought I was disgusting, and that was dangerous for both of us. So she put me in an orphanage when I was little."

"So you did it in the orphanage?" Lily said, licking ketchup from her fingers.

"Of course not. Well, maybe not 'of course not' but, no, I didn't. I knew I didn't want to be hidden away all of my life, be afraid and hate the way I look, so I was trying to figure out how to get away to California, America."

"But, wait, back up," Lily said. "What was it like in the orphanage?"

"Okay, maybe that's how to begin," Esme said, taking a bite out of her burger and sipping her soda. "But you gotta let me tell it my way. I'll give you some highlights, I guess you'd call them. Or maybe lowlights. Actually, kinda Cliff's Notes of it 'cause I blanked out some of the stuff, you know, stuff a shrink would say I repressed in my brain. Sank it deep-like."

"Bad stuff, like, at the orphanage with those creepy nuns?"

"The orphanage wasn't all that bad, considering what it would have been like living in my village, me kinda a freak, a dirty freak and all. The nuns were mostly nice even though they forced us to pray every day—actually, twice a day. One of the nuns was always staring at us with eyes kinda fierce and shiny-like." Esme squinted. "You know, like she was singing alleluias in the chapel and thinking glorious thoughts. I remember she yelled at Hanh for not putting her shoes together two nights in a row and asked if Hanh wanted her panties taken down to be paddled."

"So was it all just prayers and avoiding that nun? I mean, what did you do all day?"

"Mostly we made sun hats and bamboo baskets and cut up old tires to make flip-flops the nuns would sell. But I remember once we had an actual party. The nuns got a rock band of American Air Force guys from Da Nang to play for us," Esme said, grinning. "I heard the nuns say they were kinda worried that the men would, you know, have tight pants and all. I didn't know what they meant then. They showed up in a truck and a jeep with guys with guns and straps of bullets across their chests. We all were looking at their pants. They weren't all that tight, but, you know"—she raised her eyebrows—"you could tell they weren't girls."

Esme told about the men unloading cases of Fanta orange soda and Mountain Dew, big bags of M&Ms, cartons of potato chips, and silver-domed trays the men set in the strip of shade next to the chapel side of the building. They lit Sterno cans underneath the trays and ladled strips of gray meat into the biggest tray. Mounds of mashed potatoes and dark-green string beans from giant cans were heaped into other trays.

"The band was way loud, and the guitar player walked back and forth in front of the rest of the band, like, you know, a rooster showing off his stuff. When the band took a break, I got in line for food next to the guitar player. I was, you know, scared, but I was gonna for sure talk to him."

She shook her head.

"I just had to talk to him. I remember my dumb-ass opening line: 'Pleased to me meet you.'"

"Now, that's funny, Es!"

"Yeah, but he was nice about it even though he looked kinda weird with a mustache that looked like a streak of oil on top of his lip, and he had on these red sunglasses. But he took off the glasses, smiled, and winked. He had sad, kind eyes."

Esme squinted in recalling how she spoke to Fischer that day.

"It is a pleasure to meet you, pretty lady," he said and winked.

"What for you name, please?" she'd asked, leaning back to stare up at him.

"I'm Sergeant Fischer—Fish. Mark. What's your name?"

"I name Esme." It was the first time she'd said it out loud to anyone.

"I got it from a book I found in the market," she told Lily. "I brought it back to my room and hid it in a pocket I'd cut in my mattress, 'cause the nuns didn't allow us to have books they didn't see first. I asked one of the nuns what squalor meant. It sounded a lot like the way my grandmother lived after the Americans came and went."

After Ngoc heard the name "Esme" slide from the music sergeant's lips like a breeze slipping through the bamboo tree outside her window, she was convinced it would be her name from then on.

"That sure is a pretty name for a pretty girl," he'd said, all smiley.

"I couldn't help it. I just stood there grinning as wide as . . . I don't know, as wide as, well, really, really wide."

Esme stopped speaking and cut into a piece of carrot cake with a tiny orange cream carrot on top of the white icing.

"So there I am, standing next to that big soldier, grinning like a crazy person. Sergeant Fish reached down and kinda rubbed my hair—uh, there's a word for it, I think—and smiled. I couldn't stop the grin from spreading. I looked at the ground and smiled so wide I thought my mouth would break."

"What else did he touch?"

"C'mon, Lily, nothing else. It wasn't like that."

Lily scooped a spoonful of maple walnut ice cream from a tall, thick fluted glass.

"Okay, if you say so. So how did you get from the orphanage to here?"

"So, one day this commander in charge of who got to go south to Saigon to try to get out of the country was in the market where I worked some days and winked at me. He told me he could get papers for me to get a visa to leave. He stunk of perfume and his teeth were black like a burnt tree stump from chewing betel nuts."

"Betel nuts? Sounds gross," Lily said.

"Lots of people chewed on them back there. They kinda keep you revved up, you know. You get kinda high on them."

"Boy, you people are strange, you know?" Lily said.

"Yep, and your kind are all normal, huh? Like breaking bones in your feet to keep them small. Real normal, Lil. Real normal."

Lily shook her head. "So this commander guy?"

"He said he could help me, and I should be nice to him," Esme said, lifting off the layer of icing with a knife. She licked the knife and ran her tongue around in her mouth.

"He told me to meet him one night in the middle of the curve on the far side of China Beach. I knew where it was 'cause my grandmother had told me that's where American soldiers partied and to stay away from it because the Americans were like the French and all of them, you know, grabbed whatever they wanted.

"I agreed to meet him. It was the only way. You can guess the rest, I suppose," Esme said, shrugging her shoulders. "He said I had to do it with him before he gave me the papers. So I did."

"Wait a minute, Es!" Lily said, frantically waving her hands in front of Esme. "You can't just say, 'So I did,' and leave out the details. What was it like? Did it hurt? Was it gross being stuck by him? C'mon! Spill!"

"How can I describe it? You have to find out on your own. It's different for everyone, I think. Some people take to it right away. Some never do."

"C'mon, Es. Don't be playin'."

"Well, it hurt. It was like someone was trying to stick sandpaper under my skin over and over, kinda a rhythm, he had. I smiled at him and moaned and then yelled, 'Yes! Yes! Yes!' like I heard men like to hear, you know, so they think they're so good and generous to us to make us feel so good. He grunted one last time and slid off me and stayed on his back on the sand for a long time, looking up at the stars. Then he said he didn't have the papers but would the next night."

"And you believed him?"

"What choice did I have? I had to get out of the country. They were sending people who looked like me to work camps and worse. I wanted to be flown away, but it cost a lot to get the right papers, and you had to be in the right place at the right time and all.

"Part of the new law was that they'd let you and your relatives out of the country if you could prove they were yours. So I needed papers to prove I existed, kind of, in the eyes of the government. Some people without papers packed themselves into bad boats to get away and a lot of them sank and people drowned just as they reached deep water. So, I wanted to fly out.

"I met Phuoc Huu in the park. He had money from the two restaurants he owned in Uncle Ho's City. He tried to pay me as little as possible for me to say he was my uncle. But when I walked away from him, he chased after me. I tripled the price and when he hesitated, I walked away again, this time losing him as he tried to follow me. I knew he was desperate, like he was a target for something bad to happen to him because he'd named one of his restaurants American Sam's and made a lot of money offa U.S. soldiers."

She took another forkful of cake and sipped her soda. "I let him find me the next day and he paid up."

"That's it? Doesn't sound that bad. I mean, you had to get out of the country. Anyone would have done that. And the rest is history, you coming here, going to school and all. Sounds like one o' those success stories—poor girl comes to America, works hard, and is okay in the end."

"I guess, but there's a kinda twist to the story I never told anyone else and shouldn't, but sometimes it's like I have this thing pressing against my head in the back and I think I should tell what happened to feel better, kinda be relieved. Maybe to figure out if it's all that nasty. What I did."

Lily raised her left shoulder. "So?"

"You promise? Swear you won't tell anyone?"

"Of course. Yes."

"I'm serious, Lily. I'm very serious."

"I just told you. What else do you want from me? If you don't want to tell me, if you don't trust me, then forget it."

"I need to tell someone."

"Okay, okay, then tell me! I mean, how bad can it be? You're making it sound really bad."

"I'm not saying it's bad. It doesn't have to be automatically bad, but most people would think it is."

"I'm not gonna beg, Es. C'mon, just tell it."

"Okay, here goes. I was waiting for the commander under this bamboo tree the next night when he said he'd have the papers. I even made a kind of bed in the sand. Like, I dug a kind of trench around it and piled up sand so it'd look like a fluffy bed.

"So I see him coming down the beach, skipping away from the waves like a little kid. He's smoking a cigarette and he sees me, and he takes another puff and shoots it up into the air. I can still see it somersaulting like something dying until it hit the water and drowned.

"I asked him if he had the papers, and he said they had been delayed again. He unties his belt and then he's, like, shaking his hips like bugs're all over him. Anyway, his pants fall down to the sand.

"I asked him when he would have the papers. He just laughed and couldn't stop, like someone told him a great joke.

"I took off my pants and my bra and shook my boobs out

and bounced them around for him, and of course his thing is getting bigger, you know? Well, of course, you don't know. Maybe you like girls and—"

"I like boys, Es, I do. I just don't know how I'm gonna do it. I don't want to wait too long, but—"

"I was kidding you, Lil, just kidding. Anyway, he gets on top and pushes into me, and I almost couldn't find it in the sand."

"Find what?"

"Oh, yeah, ha! I forgot an important thing. I was squirming around underneath him trying to reach my knife my friend Tranh had made for me from bamboo when we lived in the park. It was beautiful! He was beautiful. A green vine curled around the handle with a lotus flower on top."

"The commander, Es, the commander."

"He thinks I'm squirming around excited, like, by him and want it again."

Lily's mouth was open.

"He gets on top, and I stick Tranh's knife into his back. I mean, I hated him. Really hated him. Hate, kinda beyond him, you know? So I stuck the knife into his back but couldn't push it that far into him. But it musta hurt him 'cause he flipped off of me. I'm pretty strong and all, but he was a man so he was still stronger than me. I was scared—he was screaming so much— that he'd get back on top of me and strangle me. He was on his stomach on the sand. I yanked out the knife and he rolled over and was trying to get up. So I sat on top of him and kept sticking him over and over with the knife. Stick it in! Pull it out! Stick it in! Pull it out! I stuck it in his throat. All the way in until he couldn't scream any more 'cause the blood was squirting out of his throat like the drinking fountain at school."

Lily's face contorted as if she was about to scream or vomit.

"His eyes bugged out, and he put his hands up to his neck.

The knife was sticking almost through to the back. All I could see was the lotus flower and blood pouring through his fingers. He was gargling with his own blood. He took one more breath, but kinda a weak one, then he didn't move. Nothing moved. His eyes were frozen wide open."

"Holy shit! Holy shit! Holy shit! I mean, you killed some-one. Murdered someone! Holy shit! Holy shit! Holy shit! I mean, like, holy fuckin' shit! You murdered somebody!"

"Yeah, I did," Esme said with a smile, sucking up the last of her Coke, sounding like she was clearing sinuses. She glanced over at the boys' table and smiled, wide.

"So if I'm supposed to feel bad about it, I don't. I'd do it again only make sure he died, like, a lot slower."

"Holy shit! Holy shit! I don't believe it!" Lily said, rapidly shaking her head.

"Believe it, Lily. And he had the papers in his pocket. I won!"

———

"Oh, you're back," the Pretty Lady saleswoman said. "We're closing soon, so there's no time to try on even more dresses."

"That's okay. I've made up my mind. I'll take the blue one, please. It doesn't show too much of my boobs. I don't want to give anyone any ideas."

# STETSON

DEACON RICHIE MUNSON stands in front of the glass doors of his Blood of Jesus storefront church off East Mesquite Avenue on the edge of downtown Old Las Vegas. A painted red heart on one door is dripping blood. On the other door is a white cross with Richie's name on the crossbar in an old-English font he'd seen on a British biscuit tin in a Caesars gift shop.

Richie's wearing a white open-collar dress shirt and a bolo tie strung with a green stone he says is rough-cut genuine jade. The tightly curled brim of his white Stetson is tilted high on his forehead. Spit-shined toes of black cowboy boots poke from black jeans. He flashes TV-perfect teeth, for which he'd just made the last $225 payment, courtesy of last Sunday's record take for his new Jesus/Devil bit.

"Welcome!" Richie shouts at small clusters of people gathered on the sidewalk in front of the church. They're waiting for him to open the doors for the three p.m. service for Cousin Eduardo Pedro Rosario, who two days earlier was shot dead in what the Las Vegas *Review* called "suicide by cop."

Richie is drowned out by mufflers popping like strings of firecrackers. Three Honda Civic lowriders—black with orange flames running over the hoods—coast into the curb. The drivers pump fists out of windows and laugh at the cringes they'd drawn from those waiting on the sidewalk. They rev their engines again. Cough. Crackle! Pop!

The drivers get out of their cars, amble around to the passenger side, lean against doors, fold arms, and glare at Richie. After staring for about half a minute, they saunter back, get into their cars, and slowly pull away, pausing mid-shift to spout off mufflers.

Richie understands the Mexicans' message: he needs to make them whole. Before Richie had made his church a modest financial success, he'd stiffed more than a few people, including the Mexicans, with his can't-miss schemes that missed by a lot. Richie looks up from the sidewalk at the groups in front of his church.

"As I was about to say, welcome one and all to our humble place of worship where Jesus is always the headliner—for everything. Everywhere. He will feed our souls from his endless, free buffet of love and hope."

Richie had thought the buffet line might be too much. Brenda winced when he tried it out on her. But, being superstitious by nature, he won't change it because for two Sundays after showcasing his new sermon—with him alternating the voices of God and the Devil arguing—brought in nearly twice the usual number of rumpled dollars and casino chips tossed into his collection basket.

Richie walks from group to group, shaking hands with those who hadn't stuck their hands in their pockets or shuffled away from him.

Buttsie, next to Calvin, is straightening up after finding a half-smoked cigarette on the sidewalk. He adds it to his stash in a bulging pocket of his Marine camo pants. He's wearing a matching sleeveless vest that's fraying at the armpits over a black T-shirt. He'd pinned to his vest just beneath his name tag the Purple Heart he got in Vietnam that Herman of Helpful Herman's pawn shop loaned back to him for the day.

Ruby swishes down the sidewalk in a light-blue sundress splashed with yellow roses and blue high-tops trimmed in white. Her short dark hair is wet and slicked back. Her shoulders are erect, looking like she's practicing good posture. Her chin is snub-high and she lifts it higher as she approaches Buttsie and Marty. She's still angry they'd dipped into her stash and left her nodding off on Marty's futon the whole night after they'd heard about Cousin Eduardo from Terry when he came back from a drug run on Fremont Street, downtown.

"They killed someone called Cousin Eduardo," Terry said, joining the crew on the second-floor walkway of the Desert Song motel across the Strip from Adult-Arama. He popped the tab on a can of Lone Star. "They said he lived here. They called him 'cousin' like everyone knew him. Weird."

"Not weird, new guy," Ruby'd said, giving her best "fuck you" stare. "Everyone knew him and liked him. For the record, you couldn'ta carried his jock."

On the sidewalk in front of the church, Ruby twists around Buttsie, Calvin, and Marty to get to the building next to the church. She leans against it, her right leg behind her braced against the wall, her dress riding to mid-thigh. Calvin, wearing gray pants, black polo shirt, and chocolate jacket with a Marine Corps pin on the lapel, glides boxer-smooth toward her.

"Hey, pretty lady," he says.

"Fuck you, boxing boy! I'm not anybody's lady. What? They dropped your ass in from 1956 to here? Lady? Jesus!"

"C'mon, Rube, you know you love me. No one else you'd like climbing into your crib. Admit it."

"Into the '60s with 'crib.' In your dreams," she says, reining in the start of a smile, killing dimples trying to sink into her cheeks.

Lazy Larry, in his trademark gray cowboy hat with an inch-high sweat stain circling the crown, walks toward the church, slapping his flip-flops on the sidewalk.

Larry had a love-hate relationship with Cousin Eduardo and his posse—alternately giving them free coffee and throwing them out of his threadbare coffee shop, which he insists on calling a bistro, when they were too scuzzy even for him.

A dark-haired woman in black pumps, black pants, and matching blouse walks down the sidewalk toward the church. She's holding the hand of a girl about eight in black pants and navy T-shirt with a grinning Minnie Mouse on the front in a yellow circle.

"Uh, Carlos, I gather that's the deceased's widow?" Richie says, head-pointing. "The woman who booked the church asked if it would be disrespectful if her daughter wore that shirt."

Carlos looks at Algie and Jenny and back to Richie. "They weren't married, Richie, but might as well have been. They were as much of a family as any family. Not without issues, of course. But he loved little Jenny with a passion. Gave her that shirt before they were supposed to go to Disneyland one time, but he went chasing his ride and didn't come home for two weeks."

"Now, that's channeling Jesus, wearing the shirt in forgiveness," Richie says.

"No! Richie! That's a good kid channeling her love, showing character we all should have. She kept loving someone who disappointed her. Jesus had nothing the fuck to do with it."

"What am I gonna do with you, Carlito?" Richie says with

a pained smile. "You will find the way—the Word—my friend. You will. Jesus will come for you."

"Uh, sure. Whatever gets you through the night and to the bank, Richie."

"Notice that I choose to ignore your disparaging remarks. I choose to suffer slings and arrows rather than return a slight." Richie centers the rock on his bolo tie. "I choose empathy. I choose love."

"Yo, Deacon! You know who you're talking to? C'mon. Remember. I was the guy boosted TVs with you back in the day when Hey-soos was your go-to dealer."

"For the record," Richie says, pushing his shoulders back, "I don't think it's respectful to name anyone after the Lord. And I have implored the good Lord for forgiveness for me and us for our transgressions back then."

"Implore away, Richie." Carlos shrugs. "For yourself. Don't include me. I only need my own forgiveness."

"Moving along, Carlos. When she booked the service over the phone she told me her name—sounded like Algae, like stuff growing in that pool in that unfortunate complex you live in. But that couldn't be her name, correct? I forget."

"It's Elgidia. Algie. She's nice. A straight-up woman, you know, a different breed guys like us know," Carlos says, fingering the top of his tie and tightening it. "She kept Cousin Eduardo straight for longer patches of time than anyone could've. He adored both of them, but let them down a lot. Himself, too."

"She's a fine-looking woman, I gotta say," Richie says, watching Algie and Jenny getting closer. "Very fine, indeed."

"Don't go there, Richie. Especially not now, for fuck's sake!"

"C'mon, Carlito. I still have the eyes Almighty God blessed me with."

He watches Algie accept hugs and cheek kisses on the way to the church door.

"I'm just admiring his work. I like that she wears a cross around her neck. And you gotta notice her, uh, formidable figure, even through the dark clothes," he says, raising his eyebrows. "Statuesque, even for this town. And that wavy black hair and those high cheekbones. Praise the Lord! You gotta appreciate it—man of the cloth or not."

Carlos narrows his eyes at Richie. "Yeah, and you wanna take her 'cloth' off in the name of the Lord, huh, Richie? Just like Hey-soos would, huh? She's good people, Richie. Don't go shootin' fish in a barrel. Keep it in your pants, for once, for Chrissake."

"Carlos, that's pretty harsh," Richie says, shaking his head and looking at the sidewalk. "And putting the Lord's name in such a sentence is blasphemy. I'm always celebrating God and his son and Christian values. I'm just admiring God's work at its best. C'mon, you know me."

"Yeah, Richie," Carlos says, looking hard first at Richie's left eye and then the other. "I do. I really do. We all do."

———

That morning Richie had been standing in front of the living room mirror adjusting his Stetson, setting the brim for different looks, staring at the ceiling, wide-eyed in what he thought was spiritual awe, and then squinting, eyes narrowed—Clint Eastwood assessing an outlaw before he draws and kills him.

"The service is for that guy the cops killed that was behind that false-god statue, sitting outside Caesars!" he shouted to Brenda, who was at the bathroom mirror, the door open while she dabbed makeup onto her face.

Brenda was in her second week as a real estate agent, after

spending two years working at Maria's brothel in Pahrump, about an hour's drive from Vegas. Richie had been her longtime customer every Sunday night.

"The guy was waving a rifle at anyone who approached that disgusting statue—not a bad idea, really," Richie said, pulling his bolo tie from a hook, "to keep people away from such a heathen symbol."

He walked back to the kitchen island and poured another cup of coffee.

"It's a statue of something called Brahma," he said, walking toward the bathroom door. "Another example of casino greed, putting it there to suck up to foreigners wanting us to believe in a god that looks like an abomination. Disgusting!"

"Why would he do something like that?" Brenda said, moving her head closer to the mirror to apply eyeliner. "He must have been very upset to do what he did. It's sad to imagine what problems he had to drive him to do that. It's so, so sad."

"Sad? He could have killed innocent people. Evil has to be destroyed, for Chrissake. And, not for nothing, all these foreigners bringing their money here to impose their heathen beliefs on us should be a crime no matter what they say about embracing our so-called multicultural society."

He took a bite out of a cruller he'd taken from a cardboard box on the counter.

"This, thankfully, is still a righteous Christian country, and we gotta fight to keep it that way," he said, his words garbled through a mouthful of cruller. "We don't want their false gods. No, sir."

Richie went to the living room mirror again and adjusted his Stetson. He nodded approval and grabbed his coffee cup from the kitchen counter, sipped, and took a bite out of Brenda's honey-glazed doughnut. He walked back to the bathroom and leaned against the door frame, watching Brenda swipe blush onto her cheeks.

"I really would have wanted to do the funeral earlier," Richie said. "But no way those people get up before noon. Whaddya think?" he asked, moving to stand behind Brenda so she could see him in the mirror. "The hat still a good look? I think it has a few more miles on it 'til Gentleman Cowboy has his sale. If the sale's decent, I'm thinking of getting a black one, too."

He turned his head to profile. "It could work with the white one. I mean, I wear the black hat when I'm preaching about the Devil and sins we have to guard against and then pop the white one on when we're hitting a buncha alleluias. That could be inspiring, you know, visually show 'em good and evil. Better than playing a freakin' guitar and singing 'Kumbaya' like Tommy does at his joint, where I hear the take is down. Larry told me that. He admitted that he sometimes goes to Tommy's to sit next to that trapeze girl from Circus Circus. You remember, the one he brought to dinner that night. Remember? Body sculpted by the gods?"

Brenda brought her head back a few inches from the mirror and fluttered her eyes. "So there are other gods, Reverend?" she said, digging through her bag.

"It's an expression, Brenda, for Chrissake! To make a point."

"Gee, I'm glad you straightened me out."

"The hat, though. Whaddya think?" he asked, taking a step forward, giving Brenda a full view of him.

"Yeah, it looks fine," Brenda pulled an eyelash curler from her bag, "if that's the look you're going for—cowboy preacher and all. But I gotta tell you it kinda reminds me of that Texas saying 'all hat, no cattle.'"

"Nice, Brenda. Nice. Don't give up your day job, such as it is."

"Fuck you, Elmer Gantry!"

"You used to."

"Well, maybe that's where it should be—a used-to-be thing," she said.

"Think about what you're saying, Brend."

"I, for one, think before I speak, Richie," she said, crimping eyelashes on her left eye. She latched the curler onto lashes on her other eye and squeezed. She fluttered her eyelashes in the mirror. "You asked my opinion, and I told you. The hat is fine for your purposes, Richie. No real cowboys in this town anyway."

"What's that mean?"

"Whatever you think it means, Deacon."

She opened her lips a little to put on coral lipstick. "You know, Richie," she said, standing back from the mirror and smoothing the blouse around the waist of her skirt, "before I go off to show this big-commission house, you could have said I'm smokin' today."

She turned to look at herself in profile and sucked in her stomach.

"You only say I look good when you want some. You know, all women like to hear that they look good—hot even—and not as an attempt at some kind of foreplay."

"Egos that need to be constantly fed are spiritually lacking, even dangerous, Brend."

"Is the pot calling the kettle black?"

"You know, a little support, like, encouragement, for my endeavors would be nice," he said, turning away from her and going back to the island. "Boy, do you forget things, when it suits you. Remember when I was there to listen to you when you were thinking of getting out of the life?"

"Sheesh! You think you have a lifetime chit on me because you were being a decent human being, listening to me trying to make a big decision," she said, whirling from the sink and marching past him. "When do you mark it 'paid'?"

She stopped at the island and turned to face him. "Gets old, you know. I at least have a straight job. Off the hustle."

"Say what you mean, Brenda. You needed. I gave. The Christian way, for fuck's sake. I need support, Brenda, not shots."

"Whatever, Reverend," she said, backhanding the air. "We'll deal with this another time. Just don't forget, Donna and, uh, what's-his-name are coming in tonight. What is his name? I keep forgetting it. Must be a, you know, one of those, uh, subliminal things, like I really don't accept him so I forget his name."

She took a tan lightweight shawl from the hook next to the door. "I wish she'd forget him and . . . aww, forget it! She wants to marry him, I have to stand by her."

She paused and turned back to Richie. "Oh—Frank something. He'll probably give you a good tip for marrying them, you know, if she talks him out of getting married at one of those cheesy Elvis places. Anyway, he's very lucky to marry someone like her. She coulda had her pick."

"You know," Richie said, putting his cup in the sink, "a guy was in last night and told me I'm the best Bobby Darin he ever heard. Said I was better than Bobby himself and I'm too good to be just a lounge act buried inside Caesars mall." Richie loosened his belt and re-tucked his shirt. "How long is your special friend in for? I'm debuting my Elton covers Tuesday that Bobby woulda done, he lasted long enough. A'course, there's Bobby's standards—'Mack the Knife' always brings the house down. Donna and what's-his-name could come with you."

Brenda stood in front of a tiny mirror hanging next to the

front door and fluffed her hair. "I'll ask but, you know, they don't get to Vegas that often and they want to see big-time shows."

"Nice, Brenda. Real nice."

"What?" She turned away from the mirror to look at him. "You want me to lie to you? Pretend you're playing the MGM? Talk about egos. Gotta go. House is in Pahrump."

"Old stomping grounds, huh? Nostalgic?"

"Fuck you, Richie!" She walked toward him, pushing her hair behind her ears and jutting out her chin. "Yeah, Pahrump as in 'hump'—Whorehouse Central, Poontang Palace! You can't get off without me describing what I did there. I'm not ashamed of it. It was honest work."

She came closer to him and scrunched her face, as if she smelled something foul. "I gave something of value for a fee. A nice time for a price, I gave. What do you give?" She spun away, then turned back to stare at him. "I'll tell you what you give—dumbass hopes about loving Jesus, who'll take care of you. Got cancer? Get down on your knees and pray to Jesus. He lets you die? It's part of God's plan. Then it's 'Here's my contribution bucket to show how much you love Jesus.'"

"You're a piece of work, you know that, Brenda? A cold, blasphemous piece of work. And to think I thought Jesus and I could help you. The word of God is about saving yourself with his help. Like I helped you."

"Wow! Jesus and you in the same sentence. Think about that. And not so, by the way. The next time you want to rub my face in it, think about how we met. Remember, you had to pay for it. So how cool were you?"

"And you selling it. And you should think about me for once, Brenda, how it feels always wondering which guys know you, like, uh, biblically. How many are there out there?"

"That's on you, Deacon. Get over it. Get over yourself," she said. "This from a guy hustling people into believing in God, when you don't even."

"There's believing and there's *believing*, Brenda. Besides, I don't need to believe. I just give 'em what they want. I'm what gets them through the night. You think all those priests grabbing all those little weenies believe in what they're preaching? You oughta reflect on what—who—you are, Brenda."

She spun around to face him, her eyes slits. "Who I am? What I am?" She turned her back on him and headed toward the door. Over her shoulder she said, "Don't be here when I get back. Ask Jesus for a room."

She snatched her keys from the pink of an upturned conch shell next to the front door and slammed it on her way out.

———

Algie takes a seat on the right side of the church—as far as she can get from the huge, gleaming metal cross dangling from the ceiling over twenty gray metal chairs. Richie had made the cross out of ancient chrome bumpers from the junkyard he'd inherited from his grandfather, also named Richie.

Richie Senior won the junkyard in a Texas Hold'em game in a back room at the Flame, a bar and steak house tucked away in Old Las Vegas. Richie Senior had teamed up with his girlfriend—a world-class card counter—the night before a big fight to break an accountant from Des Moines, who was not betting with his own money.

Former welterweight contender Carlos "The Cannibal" Seguro sits next to Elgidia in the first row next to Jenny, who's staring up at the bumper cross. Algie's wearing a thin black shawl with gray fringe over her shoulders that doesn't cover all of her décolletage.

"Algie, Algie. I'm so sorry. He loved you both so much,"

Carlos says, putting his hand on top of hers in her lap. "Always talked about both of you. Devoted."

"Sometimes, Carlos. Sometimes."

"Yes, of course. Sometimes. But that other side of him wasn't him, you know. I can't believe he meant any harm. He was shouting for people to pray, for Chrissake! That gun wasn't even loaded. They didn't have to shoot him. What happened to negotiations? Cops thought they were some kind of Rambos."

"Yes," she says, looking up from her lap and turning toward Carlos, her eyes filling up. "But, Carlito, he was waving a rifle at people and was too stoned to be rational."

"That wasn't Eduardo, Algie. He was a good guy doing what he thought he should do. I think making up for something."

"Well, it got him killed, didn't it?" she says, freeing her hand from his and pulling her shawl over her shoulders.

"When we were kids, he was so happy," Carlos says, staring at the coffin. "I remember he wanted to be a magician. Always performing for us. I remember the day he thought he could fly and took off from his stoop. Busted himself up. He wanted to be a Spanish Houdini, he'd say even in high school. Escapologist, he called it. 'Some people have it,' he'd say, 'and I have it. Watch this!' he'd say with that grin you had to grin back at. Vietnam broke his soul. Put a big hole in it."

"Something did," Algie says, staring up at the junkyard cross. "Was it broken all along? Could we have done more to try to patch it up? That will always haunt me, Carlos. We all knew it was broken and kinda lost, you know? I—we—loved him. We tried to give him that when we could, when he'd accept it. Thank you, Carlos, for his casket and the flowers."

Richie presses a button on a boom box. The Marine Corps hymn starts up. Buttsie unpins his Purple Heart and lays it on the coffin. Calvin comes over and stands next to Buttsie. They salute Cousin Eduardo's coffin. A track plays "I'll Fly Away"—the old hymn that asks people to remember someone gently flying away in death.

Elgidia sits alone, ramrod-straight, twisting a handkerchief in her lap as Cousin Eduardo's coffin is wheeled out through the doors. Tears run down her cheeks, leaving scraggly gray lines. She doesn't move to stop them.

Richie sits next to her and asks if he can buy her a cup of coffee at Lazy Larry's.

"That's very kind of you, Deacon, but I, uh, don't think . . . I mean, Eduardo and all," she says, looking down at her hands.

"I certainly understand the need to mourn," Richie says, putting his hand on top of Algie's in her lap. "But it doesn't have to be alone. I want you to know I'm here for you. Anytime, any place."

Elgidia slumps her shoulders and sighs. Then she raises her head, pushes back her shoulders, takes a deep breath, and turns to Richie. She sighs again, slightly shaking her head.

"You know, it's lonely, kinda empty to not even have to worry about Eduardo anymore. You know, wondering how to help him, make him feel the love for him."

"That's the problem with loving—it hurts so much when you can't show it anymore to the person you loved," Richie says, lifting her hand and putting his other hand beneath hers. "But the love you felt and gave is out there. You put it out there. You put love into the world. Don't hold back any of it."

Elgidia looks up at the bumper cross, dabs a tissue at her eyes, and sits up straighter. "Well, yes, actually, I think that would be nice. Coffee. That's kind of you, Deacon."

"Call me Richie, please."

"By the way, uh, Richie, I like your cowboy hat. A Stetson? White for the good guy, huh?"

# AMERICAN DREAM

ESME STANDS next to a blond woman dangling a mic along her thigh. The two of them stand in front of a three-story Gothic building, flanked by a large American flag on one side and California's on the other—each drooping in the morning stillness before the heat comes. Esme wears a white oversized man's shirt, sleeves folded back to her elbows over faded, stylishly ripped jeans. Her thick brown hair is drawn into a ponytail. Large round yellow-framed sunglasses glow from her brown face. In one motion, she shrugs a green backpack onto the crook of her arm and sets it down in front of her.

Amanda Pennington, KCBS's lifestyle reporter, turns her back to Esme to look into a mirror held up to her face by a big-bellied guy in khaki shorts, multi-stained white T-shirt, and a blue Dodgers cap. She brushes errant strands of frosted blond hair from her face, moves closer to the mirror, and smiles broadly, baring her teeth and examining them. She runs her tongue over her lips. Esme folds her arms, shifts her weight to one leg, and purses her lips. She looks to the right of the mirror guy at someone counting down from five. At zero he points to Amanda, who swivels her head back to Esme.

"I'm standing outside Thomas Jefferson High School—TJ as they say around here," she says, quarter-turning toward the building, sweeping her arm to its smudged twin towers, and moves closer to Esme. "Next to me is Esme Nguyen, in her senior year."

Esme is looking to the right of the camera at the countdown guy. She nods and pushes her sunglasses on top of her head. Amanda turns to the camera as it zooms in on her.

"Esme has been on an incredible journey that has taken her from being warehoused in a Vietnamese orphanage as a despised reminder of the Vietnam War to a California high school where she is carrying a straight-A average and getting ready to go to prom. Esme graciously has agreed to speak with us about her incredible journey from there to here. Esme, it's a little late, but welcome to America," Amanda says, pushing her hair behind her ear.

"Thank you, Amanda," Esme says, squinting in the sun. She lowers the sunglasses over her eyes.

"When you were in a Vietnamese orphanage just a few short years ago, did you ever think you'd be on American TV and getting ready to go to prom?"

Amanda puts the mic to Esme's mouth. Esme tugs her shirt down, stands straighter, stares into the camera, and says, "Of course not. It was enough to not be thrown out in the garbage like many babies who look like me."

"That seems a bit strong, Esme. I mean, into the garbage? Surely you don't mean that literally."

Esme pushes her sunglasses back onto the top of her head and takes a step toward the camera. "That's what they wanted to do and did to lots of babies who looked like me. They even had a name for us—*Bui Doi*—that basically means 'trash to be thrown out.'"

"That's horrible. You must be so glad to have put that in the past." Amanda wrinkles her brow.

"Sometimes that's tough to put in the past. Sometimes people won't let me put it in the past."

"Talk to me about that, Esme. Are you implying you're still subjected to discrimination? A pretty girl like you?"

"Well, you know, pretty or not doesn't really have anything to do with it."

"Would you elaborate on that for us?"

Esme looks down, sighs, raises her head, and stares into the camera again.

"Well, I mean that for some people, you know, I'll always be on the outside looking in. I mean if you don't, uh, you know, have round eyes and white skin. Not that some people haven't been nice, but still."

Amanda quickly brings the mic back to her lips. "Still? What do you mean?"

"Well, it's not really their fault, it's the way they're brought up, I guess. You know, people who mostly only see me as different, so I'm kinda, like, strange to them. They, uh, stare and say stuff," she says, turning to Amanda, caught by the camera looking the other way, adjusting her earpiece as Esme was speaking.

Amanda quickly turns to Esme. "What do you mean by 'stuff,' Esme?"

"Well, I mean, some guys called me 'Chink Chick' and 'Rice-a-Roni' the other day."

The camera zooms in on Amanda, as she deepens furrows in her forehead. "I'm sorry you had to hear things like that. But I'm sure those people are in the minority."

"Maybe."

Amanda tilts her head in understanding, maybe sympathy. "I suppose it's difficult for anyone to walk in your shoes, but surely you appreciate your place now," she says, quickly adding, "I mean, how far you've come."

"Oh, yes. But sometimes I wonder why I had to come so far. You know, like what did I ever do in the first place to have to, you know, come so far?"

"Can you tell me what you mean, exactly?"

Esme pulls down her sunglasses and looks into the sky. "I'm not sure I should. I don't want to stir things up, please."

"I'm quite sure you wouldn't be stirring things up. After all, it's been a long time since the war ended so unfortunately. And we recognized we owed you a debt. And to show that, we brought you here, and you immediately became an American citizen. Isn't that true?"

Esme pushes the sunglasses on top of her head. "Yes," she says, tilting her head quizzically and looking up at Amanda.

"And isn't it also true that now you're living the American dream?"

"Well, I guess. But there are lots of dreams, not just American ones. I have to go now. Thank you." Esme brings her sunglasses back down over her eyes. She dips her legs, picks up her backpack, and slings it over her shoulder. She turns and walks away.

"And there you have it. A young high school student, wondering if she can fit into America. This is Amanda Pennington reporting and reminding everyone that today we're under a high smog alert. So stay inside if you can."

———

"Brendan!"

Brendan is in his bedroom reviewing film negatives through

a photographer's loupe in one eye. He winces at his mother's shriek, and the loupe falls onto his desk and rolls onto the floor. He picks up the loupe and marches down the hall to his mother's bedroom, where she's dressing for dinner out with his father.

She's standing in the doorway in a pale-pink slip.

"What?" he asks. "You didn't have to yell so loud, like it was an emergency."

"Did you know," she says, putting her hands on her hips, "that your little prom date was on TV? Do you know you're planning to take someone to the prom who says she doesn't believe in the American dream? Huh, Brendan?" Then loudly, "Huh! Answer me! Someone who denigrates our country?"

"Mom! I saw it! You don't have to scream about it. She wasn't putting down the country or anything. She just said there are other dreams, too."

His mother turns from him and goes across the bedroom to her open walk-in closet. She slides dresses one by one along a rack, pausing briefly to consider each one before whisking it aside.

"She's living the American dream, for crying out loud!" she says from the closet. "And she should pray she's worthy to be here to take part in our dream. Our great dream! She shouldn't be saying there are other dreams." She closes the door halfway.

Brendan looks through the door's opening as she reaches for a dress, her slip straining against her hips.

"What's a better dream than ours?" she says, gently scrunching the dress, putting her head through the neck and over her shoulders, and wiggling to help it cascade down her body. "And everyone can live it. She should be grateful to us and to our country for taking her in. Even from Vietnam."

"Maybe we should be happy she's here, too," Brendan says, looking through the opening. "We're all from immigrants, Mr.

Prescott said, and we're supposed to welcome people like it says on the Statue of Liberty. Besides, this country left her behind when we ran away from Vietnam."

"We did not run away! Our politicians did! I will not have such unpatriotic thoughts expressed in this house, young man!" she says, walking out of the closet into the bedroom, holding up the front of her dress. "Come zip up Mommy's dress."

As Brendan approaches, she turns her back to him and straightens her shoulders. He pinches together the sides of the zipper in the middle of her back. She squirms her shoulders back farther as he zips the dress over her bra strap and attaches the safety hook.

"Thank you, Brendie, sweetie," she says and sits on a stool in front of her dressing table. "You know, we have to love our country as our brave men did. They loved it so much they died for it. Gave their lives for us."

"A lot of them really didn't have much choice, though," Brendan says, sitting on the bed behind her. "The draft and all. Why wasn't Dad drafted for Vietnam?"

"We were married and I was pregnant with you. It was a double exemption." She opens a small plastic case, plucks out a brush, and hovers it over an array of colors in little pods. "Your father had responsibilities to his family, and he had a bright future, on his way to being a positive contributor to society. He is an educated man."

She dabs her brush onto "Midnight Surprise" and strokes it onto her eyelids. She gets up from her stool and sits on the bed next to Brendan.

"You know, sweetie," she says, tapping his knee, "we should be very wary of anyone trying to tear down the best country in the world. Think about what we have and look at all those other countries where people are starving and living on streets."

"Mom, people live under bridges in Los Angeles too," he

says, putting the loupe into his eye, lying back on the bed, and looking up at the light. "I saw them. We went on a class trip with our cameras to do street photography, but it felt kinda like taking pictures of the animals in the zoo. So I put my camera away."

"Really, Brendan? It was part of your schoolwork, and you're supposed to get an A in that class. And we got you that new camera for it."

She goes back to her dressing table, picks up a perfume bottle, sprays the air, and walks through the mist.

"Understand, Brendie, that you—none of us—had anything to do with them choosing to live that way. One of the great things about this country is all of the choices we have. Some people just don't make the right choices."

She gets up from her dressing table, goes to the closet, emerges with three boxes of shoes, and puts them at the foot of her bed.

"Help me pick out shoes for tonight."

Brendan looks at the boxes on the floor and shakes his head.

"Mom, not all those people under the bridges had choices. You know, fathers that ran away, people who died on them, no money or jobs. That's what Mr. Prescott said. For a lot of them —us too—it's just the luck of the sperm."

"Brendan! Such a potty mouth! Just disgusting!" she says, shaking her head violently. "Is that what they're teaching you in school? I told your father we shouldn't have sent you to public school. But, no. He thought you needed to get out into the real world. As if we don't live in the real world. And just what is Mr. Prescott teaching? He's an English teacher, not a philosopher! And now you're consorting with this girl who doesn't appreciate this country. Who knows what that could lead to."

"Mom, I'm just taking her to the prom."

"Actions have consequences, my dear," she says, smiling tightly. "We don't always know what they will be and you have to be careful to do what is expected of you. That's how a civilized society works."

She opens her closet door to look at herself in the full mirror. She pushes her hair behind an ear and fastens a barrette to it. She frowns and unclips it. She puts on a necklace with a gold heart. She takes it off and tries one with a diamond set in a gold circle. She decides on one with a teardrop emerald and smiles.

"Brendie, dear, I understand this new girl might be considered pretty—in a different sort of way. A foreigner's way. I can't deny that. But what do you really know about her? How much do you know about her family? From the looks of her, they're not from around here."

"Who cares where they're from, Mom. I'm not taking her family to the prom."

"Don't get smart-alecky with me. You know what I mean. Don't pretend you don't. Your father will be here any minute, so I should go downstairs. You know how he gets if I'm not ready to walk out the door."

She picks up a black clutch flecked with silver threads from her dressing table. They walk to the stairs, his mother leading.

Down in the living room there are two love seats on either side of the fireplace, a distressed wooden cocktail table between them. She opens French doors into the dining room and walks to the bar cart. She takes a rocks glass from a shelf and goes through swinging doors to the kitchen. She returns to the bar cart and splashes scotch over ice.

"Think about it, Brendie, foreigners are not like us," she says, walking to the love seat. "They have different values, they have all those different religions, I guess you could call them.

You know, you don't spend your life wading in rice paddies and then all of a sudden say you're civilized."

She squirms farther into the love seat. "You know something else? They don't love America and don't believe in God. They pray to a strange-looking statue of a fat thing, sitting with his legs crossed, looking smug."

"That's Buddha, Mom. Sort of their god, or maybe it's their Jesus, Mr. Prescott said. I don't remember."

His mother snorts and sips her drink.

"Well, this is America. We have Jesus, who is beautiful to see and think about. And that's what we believe in. If you don't agree, then just maybe you shouldn't be here where we love our country and what we stand for."

"We read in old newspapers Mr. Prescott brought in that back in the Vietnam War days people were telling people who didn't support the war that they didn't love America. They said, you know, 'America, love it or leave it.'"

"What's so bad about that? Of course we should love America. And why would you stay here if you don't love it? Actually, you shouldn't stay."

She walks into the kitchen, puts cubes into her glass, and walks back to the cart and pours more scotch.

"Learning about different religions tells us about other cultures, Mr. Prescott says, and how civilization came to be."

"Mr. Prescott, again. What's he doing talking about ancient history, about the war? And religion and this Buddha? He's an English teacher. He should stick to English."

His mother stands, walks to the front windows, parts the curtains, and looks out. She gulps the last of her drink, jiggles the ice in the empty glass, and holds it up to Brendan, who takes it back to the bar cart and pours more scotch.

"By the way, how did your prom date—Esme, right?—get her name? She doesn't look like an Esme. Kind of a strange name for a girl who looks like her." She takes a long sip of her drink.

"It was Ngoc then. She changed it," he says, carefully stacking coasters on the cocktail table, "because she liked the way it sounded. She got the name from a book she read, I think."

"Well, you just don't fit in because of a name. Being American is more than your name. How do you spell her real name, again? Some people have such strange names."

He pronounces it again.

"You can't even guess at it phonetically. Those people are so different. You're too young to know about what actually went on during the Vietnam War, but those people—her people—would ambush and kill our boys. Just kill our boys without warning," she says, eyes wide. "I remember seeing on TV where people called Viet Cong used these sticks coated with poop and our boys stepped on them and got infected. How fair is that? That's just cruel."

She takes a long sip of her scotch.

"She didn't do that. She ran away from the Viet Cong. Besides, they were protecting their country, and it was war. That's what Mr. Prescott said."

"That sounds like something a Communist would say. Mr. Prescott this, Mr. Prescott that. He doesn't sound very American, from what I'm hearing. Is he Jewish?"

"Mom! It's called free speech. I can say whatever I want. Just can't say I want to shoot the president or yell 'fire!' in the movies. It says so in the Constitution."

"There is a time and a place for free speech, Brendan. Who are this girl's parents?"

"She only knows her mother. She doesn't know what happened to her after she left Vietnam. Esme lives with her aunt and uncle."

"And she has a real accent, doesn't she?"

"Of course she does. She was born in Vietnam and learned that language first."

His mother quickly swivels her head to face him. "Don't 'of course' me, young man."

She grabs her drink and walks to an easy chair, closer to the front door, and sits.

"Is she trying to lose her accent? She has to fit into our country. Foreigners these days don't even try to fit in. They keep to themselves with their foreign ways and don't even try to speak Amer— English."

"Esme speaks good English, with a cute accent," Brendan says with a smile. "She says she has a knack for languages."

"She doesn't seem very modest. Young women should be modest in everything. And accents aren't cute."

"She *is* modest, Mom. She was just saying she likes languages."

"What about her father? Where is he? Who is he?"

"She's never met him. She thinks he might live in Las Vegas, and she's saving money to go there to see if he's there."

"Las Vegas! They prey on weaknesses of the flesh there," she says, reaching into her cleavage to pull up her bra.

"Anyway, she's working all kinds of extra hours to save up to go there. He was in Vietnam. Her mother and her father got married there. Her mother and her—"

"Her mother and she. You know better."

"Her mother and she. They came here without anything. The government flew them to California, and she lived in a kinda tent city and they helped them find an apartment and jobs. She's a citizen 'cause her father is American."

"You're telling me she's going to meet her father for the first time at her age? Was she born out of wedlock?"

"I don't know. It never came up."

"Well, you should make it come up. Being married to have a child is sacred. The way Jesus—yes, Jesus—said it should be."

She rolls her tongue over her lips.

"But she was in an orphanage, Mom. She didn't have a family then."

"That's exactly my point. This country reveres and exists on families and family values. Christian values. People without them don't contribute. Not in a good way. In fact, they tear it down."

"Mom!" he says, throwing up his hands. "She's not tearing down anything! She's just trying to get along. She's funny, too. She can imitate all kinds of accents."

She holds out her glass to him. "Just a little bit more, sweetie. I don't need ice."

"Esme makes me think about things, too," he says on his way to the cart. "She was telling me how surprised she was by all the things you could buy in the supermarket—how we have so many things of the same kind. She thought that was weird."

"Weird? Where does she get off saying that?"

"She didn't mean anything by it," he says and hands her the drink. "Just her impressions. So different than Vietnam, she says."

"I should hope so. This is America! A democracy! Choices are what make this country great."

"I'm just sayin'."

"Finish your words. Don't sound like you're on a street corner and don't know better."

"I'm just say-*INGGG* that it makes me think when someone looks at things, you know, different."

"Differently! Grammar, please."

"She asked why we need to have so many cereals? And rice? She said it was confusing and she didn't know what kind to buy. She bought the one with the name Uncle Ben's because uncle in her country is a trusted person."

"You don't get to come into this country and start criticizing it and giving your opinions. You become a true American, maybe, and then maybe you can talk about America."

"She *is* an American citizen. As much as we are. Her father is an American."

"There are citizens and there are citizens. Some are more American than others. Some love their country more. Those people who didn't like the war made riots. And the Blacks rioting and burning things. They made your father and I detour that night we—"

"Uh, Mom. I think it's 'father and me.'"

"Now that's rude! Especially rude to correct your mother like that."

"You always say speaking proper English is important 'cause it tells people what kind of family you come from."

"We know what kind of family we come from, young man! And it's not one where the child corrects his parents. You will not be allowed to use the car for the prom if you insist on taking that girl. I will not lend a hand to this folly of yours. Seems it's up to me to protect this family's standards."

A car horn honks twice. She shoots up from her chair, wobbling before stabilizing herself.

"I don't care if I get the car!" Brendan shouts. "I'll find a way. You're prejudiced, that's what you are."

"That's it! You're grounded for a month. I will not have such disrespect in my house."

"It's my house, too!"

"You just live here. We set the rules. You follow them. End of discussion."

She takes a quick sip of her drink, plops the glass onto the table, and rushes to the door.

At five o'clock on prom night, Esme puts on white trousers and slips Tranh's sky-blue *ao dai* from its hanger in the back of her closet.

She's never worn Tranh's dress outside her room. Lotus blossoms curl from the waist across the front of the long tunic and up to her left shoulder. She walks across the small room, the long panels of the *ao dai* twitching around her legs, snug in white trousers.

She walks back, takes off the *ao dai,* and lays it gently onto her bed. She takes the pale-blue prom dress from its velvet hanger and places it on the bed next to the *ao dai* Tranh gave her when he told her he wouldn't be going to America, California, with her.

He'd made the dress at his grandfather's shop near the huge U.S. base at Da Nang, on the South China Sea, that serviced U.S. forces during the Vietnam War.

"I would be so different in America, California," he said that afternoon as they sat on a bench in Reunification Park in Ho Chi Minh City, where Tranh and Esme had camped for months with dozens of other abandoned children, trying to survive by begging in the streets. And when they'd see foreigners, especially those carrying cameras, they'd circle them, asking to be photographed, hoping somehow their American fathers would see them and come back to rescue them.

"It wouldn't be just the way I'd look in California, America. I won't know when to be afraid there, you know, who to be afraid of. Here I can work making clothes in my uncle's shop where not many people will see me. I know what to expect here, what to watch out for."

She had told her best friend, Lily, about Tranh and that she wondered how he was, what life was like now in Saigon, as she always would call it. She told Lily she was sad that she couldn't remember details of Tranh's face.

At nine o'clock—two hours after Brendan was supposed to pick her up—Esme unzips her prom dress, wriggles out of it, and takes a pair of scissors from the kitchen drawer. Starting at the sweetheart neckline, she cuts the dress in half. Then into fourths. Then eighths. She keeps cutting.

She gets down on her hands and knees, sweeps the blue and white scraps into a pile, and puts them into a trash bag.

She walks across the parking lot, pushes up the lid of the Dempsey Dumpster, turns the bag upside down, shakes it, and watches pieces of her prom dress float into the darkness that smells of rotting food.

# THE ELEMENTS

BOBBY PARKED in the overflow lot of McNeil's funeral home, where Nicky's casket had been a few years earlier. He walked down the hill and across the street to the Dew Drop Inn and its low-key vibe: have a few pops, watch a game, tell some jokes, but keep them clean if women are around and don't hit on them too hard.

It took awhile, but Bobby felt comfortable stopping at the Dew now because there were fewer awkward condolences about his big brother, Nicky, not coming home from Vietnam.

He pulled open the dark-wood door, a green shamrock painted on it, and stopped at the jukebox just past the door. He slid in quarters and pressed buttons, selecting Dave Brubeck's "Take Five," a couple of Lambert, Hendricks, and Ross' perky harmonies, and, of course, Bunny Berrigan's old-time "I Can't Get Started with You." Playing that one was kind of an homage to Grandma Cora and Granddad Edward, who used to play it on their phonograph Saturday nights back in the family's best days.

On the wall to the right of the juke was a yellowed *Daily*

*News* photo of Staten Islander Bobby Thomson, hitting his famous home run way back in '51, an arrow tracking its flight. There was a headshot of Hank Majeski, another Island guy, who'd played third base for the Chicago White Sox. He was a solid player, but everyone on the Island forgot about him after Thomson became a hero.

That brought to mind the picture Bobby had in his wallet of the Old Man, Nicky, and Hank in the visiting dugout at Yankee Stadium, Nicky between them, grinning and holding a bat in front of him, balancing it straight up on the dugout floor. It came up to his neck.

Bobby had to stay home that day because the Old Man said he was too young to really enjoy the game. He said he'd take just him the next year. Nicky told Bobby how cool it was that Hank, whom the Old Man knew from around the Island, told the guard to unhook the gate, and Nicky and the Old Man walked onto the field and down the dugout steps like celebrities.

Also on the wall was a stock photo of Yogi Berra, squatting with his fist up alongside his catcher's mitt. Bobby knew it was a fake pose because in a real game having his hand out like that would be an invitation for broken fingers. But most people didn't seem to know or care about it being fake. To them, Yogi just looked cool in Yankees pinstripes. The old picture gallery included one of Marilyn Monroe, flashing her panties over that subway vent that drove DiMaggio crazy because it showed a lot of what he thought was only his to see. They divorced after nine months. DiMaggio sent roses to her grave for twenty years. Next to Marilyn was a smoke-yellowed newspaper, showing Lyndon Johnson, hand raised, taking the oath of office aboard Air Force One, Jackie standing next to him in that pink suit, stained by her husband's blood, her dark eyes wide open, staring into space. The Camelot fable to come.

Bobby hung up his jacket on the rack next to the juke and perched on a stool. He told Jimbo he'd have a whiskey sour on the rocks—Nicky's favorite—and settled in as Bunny's trumpet began its climb to clear-throated lament.

Giggles and shrieks of delight leaked through French doors separating the bar from the banquet room, its wavy panes, kaleidoscopes of twirling bodies, and swishing hair. Jimbo shook his head and grinned. "It's a bridal shower for the Antonucci kid—the one packing torpedoes could sink a battleship."

The music in the banquet room wound down and several women straggled through the doors to get coats from the rack. Through the back bar's mirror, Bobby saw Tara walk into the room, wearing a pale-yellow sweater above a gray tweed skirt, clinging to her still-shapely figure Bobby first admired when he went to high school basketball games to see her jump and gyrate in that short cheerleader's skirt.

Bobby swiveled on his stool. "You're not gonna say hi, Tara?"

"Bobby! What're you doing here?" Her grin morphed into that half-dare-maybe-I'm-a-bad-girl smile. "Looking to meet a girl? Want me to introduce you to someone?"

She took her coat from a hook, wobbling as she missed the sleeve.

"Nah. I'm just getting out of the house," he said, holding her coat, which gave off a whiff of mothballs. "You know, my mother and Nicky and all. All of those Nicky memories she keeps talking about. Not that I don't have them, too."

He guided the other sleeve onto her arm. "I'm not really up for meeting anyone. Besides, I have a National Guard meeting early tomorrow."

She looked down and slowly shook her head. "I wish Nicky had done that—the Guard," she said as Bobby pulled up her coat. "He didn't have to go. Why didn't I tell him that? But he looked so cute in that uniform, and he knew it, you know. Me, too. King of the Hill! Marine! Best of the best! 'I gotta go get me some Viet Cong,' he'd say."

She stumbled as she wrapped a scarf around her neck.

"Where'd it all get us? Any of us? Huh? Where'd it get your big brother? Gone. Gone forever. Evaporated. And me, a widow at twenty-three. Twenty-three!"

She blinked away wet eyes.

"Who would have thought we'd be where we are, huh, Bobby?" she said, slinging her purse over her shoulder. "We all made up such dreams for ourselves. Huh? Look at me. The widow Trocadero. You pay a price for daydreams, Bobby. Ya know?"

"I know. Sometimes I think I was kinda part of the dream—big brother hero and all, thinking some of it would rub off on me. Even the part about a pretty girl," he said with a soft smile.

"A widow girl, Bobby."

Bobby pulled his shirt cuff down, grabbed back at it with his fingers, and began wiping away tears rolling down her cheeks. Tara wobbled into his chest.

"Lemme drive you home, Tara. Gotta keep you in one piece."

She pulled herself back from Bobby and snuffled. "I'm fine. Just had a sidecar, that's all. Maybe a couple sips of Sandy's Seven and Seven."

"Wait a second." He walked back to the bar, gulped the last of his drink, took his change, and left a couple of dollars. "C'mon. Don't be stubborn. My job is to make sure you're okay."

"C'mon yourself, baby brother. I need to watch over you! Who else is gonna, huh? We have to watch out for each other."

They got into Nicky's red Olds convertible Bobby still kept.

A thin layer of frost glistened on the hood under the parking lot's light. It was ear-stingy cold. Bobby started the engine to warm it up before turning on the heater. They sat still to not move cold air. They didn't speak, just watched puffs of breaths leak from their mouths and evaporate as soon as they saw them. It was cozy beneath the canvas top, as if they were in a tent, protected from the elements, but still close to them.

"Don't take this the wrong way, Tara. But come over here and we can snuggle. You know, our body heat and all."

Tara slid over to Bobby and burrowed her head into his neck, brushing her lips against him. Bobby wasn't sure if it was a kiss. He stroked her hair.

He smelled sweet Chanel No. 5 perfume—the scent Nicky had first given her. And mothballs.

# DAUGHTERS

GEORGIE WAS on his usual stool at Ray Ray's hunched over a ball and a short beer when he heard the back door slam and saw Big Joe bulling down the dark, narrow hallway leading to the bar, his bulk silhouetted by a faint light bulb.

He burst into the barroom a flash of kelly-green sport jacket, tan pants, yellow shirt, and an almost-matching handkerchief fluffing from a breast pocket. A bricklayer turned liquor salesman, now promoted to manager of insurance adjusters, he'd treated himself to the new outfit he just got out of layaway from Kennedy's Gentlemen's Shoppe up the Avenue.

Sam watched Joe's grand entrance through the back bar's mirror and said to the Dempsey brothers—swearing in turn at their bad luck in a game of Liar's Poker—"This fuckin' guy," and jerked his head at Joe. "Look at him! Thinks who he is."

The bar was packed with guys in work shirts, dungarees, chinos, one in a mailman's uniform, and one rent-a-cop, all celebrating Friday by diligently working on getting buzzed before wives and girlfriends began calling. Georgie, at the far end of the bar from Joe, was in a green T-shirt with his name in cracked gold lettering over his left pec, dungarees speckled with dried cement. He still wore a crew cut, flecked now with gray. Overall, he came close to leading-man looks with high cheekbones, blue eyes, and a chin that just missed being square, tilted slightly center-left.

Georgie put his shot and short-beer glasses into the well for Ray Ray to pour another. Behind him, a long window ran the width of the bar, overlooking the curb where the bus let off the Catholic schoolgirls every afternoon at 4:12.

Georgie sipped from a new ball of Carstairs and took a bigger hit from his short beer. He was only an inch or so shorter than Joe at six foot one but more solid from wrestling his cement truck all those years.

In high school, Georgie had been touted as having a good shot at snagging a full ride to college to play football, but his father ran off with Georgie's aunt—his mother's sister—and Georgie had to quit the team to work after school. Meanwhile, Joe became the local hero for blocking an attempted field goal to win the big Thanksgiving Day game that Georgie watched from the stands. To Joe's delight, for a couple of years after his heroics, he was called "Big Joe." But the name didn't stick.

Georgie and Joe hadn't spoken much over the years when they'd see each other at Ray Ray's—mostly "How're you doing?" or "Hey." One exception was the day Georgie bought a round for the bar to celebrate his wife's pregnancy. Joe congratulated Georgie and bought him back a drink. Joe told him he'd be facing a lot of nights without much sleep. Georgie smiled at that prospect.

Their other conversation took place a year or so before that, when Joe asked Georgie if he wanted to make a few bucks on the side, pouring leftover cement from his truck for an extension on his brother-in-law's house.

"I'll pass," Georgie said. "I work legit—no skim. You want cement, call the office."

"Boy, it must be nice not to need a few extra bucks, cash. Didn't know driving a cement truck paid so good."

That Friday afternoon when Joe showed off his new outfit, he was displaying his six feet three inches and considerable girth, leaning against the partition that separated the bar from the dining area—tables topped with checked tablecloths and stubby candles stuck down throats of wine bottles. Joe loudly told Harold he was gonna throw a big shindig for his daughter to celebrate her engagement to a guy who lived on the country club's grounds.

"A pool and everything, the guy's got."

He told Ray Ray to buy the bar a round on him.

"You got it, big guy," Ray Ray said, making his way down behind the bar with the permanent limp he got from breaking his leg in three places, running away from cops when he was an apprentice car thief twenty years earlier. He put downturned shot glasses in front of those still working on drinks—markers they were owed one on Joe.

The guys congratulated Joe, tipping glasses his way, and he tilted back. Georgie righted the shot-glass marker and slid it down the bar toward Joe, who flicked his eyes at it and scowled. Joe was lifting his glass to take a hit when Barry, in a Knights of Columbus softball jersey, shouted, "Man, Big Joe! Your daughter's marrying up—way up! Way, way the fuck up! She must have some kinda magic."

The noise in the room stopped like a plug had been pulled. Nat King Cole's "Lazy-Hazy-Crazy Days of Summer," which had been background noise, now bounced loudly off the back bar. Joe paused his glass mid-chest, collapsed his smile, and stared at Barry.

He carefully fingered back into place strands of glossy

black hair that had wilted onto his forehead from his carefully combed coif. Still staring at Barry, Joe chugged the rest of his beer and thudded the glass onto the bar. He kept his eyes locked onto Barry's and drew himself straight. Barry stared back. Joe turned and took a few steps toward Barry, stopped and grinned, tiny dimples sinking into his chubby face. Then he turned back to the bar and waited for Ray Ray to pour him another Rheingold. He sipped, leaving a foam mustache, licked it off, and bellowed down the bar.

"Eat your heart out! The magic's being a Dolan! My little girl wins! Big-time! Big-fuckin'-time! Here's to my little girl!" he shouted, raising his glass. "Fuckin' A!"

"Yeah!"

"Fuckin' A!"

"Ah *salute!*"

"Yeah!" guys shouted—a collective effort to pump air back into the room to protect their buzzes.

Georgie paused, raised his head, and before the noise got back up to speed with Nat singing again about hot dogs, pretzels, and beer, shouted, "Living the dream, huh, Joe? Guess you think you got it all by the balls, huh?"

"You know it, cement man," Joe said, glaring back.

Just as it had been rising, the chatter stalled again. Joe picked up his refill and, juicing the tension, swaggered down the bar toward Georgie. He put his glass on the bar next to Georgie, then laid his forearms on the lip of the bar, lowering his head level with Georgie's and turning to him as if sharing a secret. The strands of hair flopped back onto his forehead.

"You know, Georgie, I wish it for your daughter too. I really do. You know, you bring 'em up right, who knows what they can be."

With an apparent peace huddle taking place, the noise gathered again for another run up the scale, and soon Nat was just background nostalgia for the days nobody there had ever lived in the first place.

"Your daughter's a lot younger than mine, right?" Joe said. "Your time'll come. It's a great, great feeling knowing you raised her right and get to send her off for the rest of her life. I'm just so fuckin' grateful I get to see it."

Georgie shifted in his stool and reached for his shot glass. "My daughter's—"

"Hold that thought, Georgie!" Joe said over his shoulder, checking his watch as he turned away and headed toward the men's room. "Gotta see a man about a horse before the show."

Georgie finished his shot and ordered a double.

"Hey, Georgie, how're you doing?" said Moses Francis Patrick Aloysius O'Brien, who on Friday nights would find a way several times to invoke his full name and explain who all he was named after before Ray Ray poured him into his car at closing time. Mo climbed onto the stool next to Georgie. Richie, Mo's friend and supervisor at the city's Parks Department— Staten Island's Clove Lakes region—sat on the other side of Mo.

"Mo, Richie, how're they hangin'?" Georgie said. "Ray Ray! A couple of beers for our plant doctors."

"Appreciate it," Mo said.

Richie raised his glass in thanks to Georgie. They sipped.

"You know, I been meaning to ask," Georgie said, "seeing as how you're experts on Mother Nature and all—how to grow hydrangeas. I mean, not that I got any to grow now, but I might put new ones in my backyard—uh, my ex-wife's backyard now. She really likes them. Tried to grow a couple of them a few years ago, but they never took."

He tossed down the rest of his shot. "Each year I waited for them to bloom, but nothing," Georgie said, shaking his head and pushing the shot glass to the edge of the bar's well for a refill.

"You mean Hydrangea Macrophylla, native to Japan," Richie said, straightening up on his stool.

"See? That's why he's a gardener," Mo said, offering a turned-up palm toward Richie, "and I'm still a laborer. I just don't know my Latin. Foreign languages are tough. I took the test a couple of times but I just don't know my Latin," he said, shaking his head. "You gotta know Latin 'cause they ask the Latin for all the stuff we plant."

"Whatever they're called," Georgie said, hunching his shoulders over his ball and beer, "I wanted big puffy flowers, even blue ones, maybe. All I got were dead sticks and my wife riding me about being a lousy gardener, can't even make hydrangeas grow."

"They don't just grow on their own," Richie said and sipped his beer. "You gotta fertilize them right—not too acidic, not too alkaline. And ya gotta kind of love 'em too, to be corny about it."

"See? Richie knows his chemistry too," Mo said, spreading a Ritz cracker with cheese from the Wispride crock Ray Ray put out on Fridays and Saturdays.

"They gotta have the right soil, and they love shade but of course not too much," Richie said, "so you gotta figure out how the sun hits your yard. You gotta set it up to have a good shot at surviving. People think we just dig a hole and throw plants in and they grow. Not so. You gotta baby 'em, make sure they got everything they need to survive."

He gulped the rest of his beer.

"You know, a backyard has mini climates, so what'll grow in one place won't make it just a few feet away. By the way, it's a nice touch if you add Dicentra, commonly known as Bleeding Hearts, 'cause their flowers are shaped like hearts."

Richie took a cracker Mo offered that he'd slathered with cheese. He shoved it into his mouth whole and chomped.

"But in the end, everything's a crapshoot. Like life." He swallowed hard, forcing the cracker down. "You know. Things are looking up, you dig a good hole, fertilize it, feed it right, and then, *bam!* You get sucker-punched and it all turns to shit. Just like that"—he snapped his fingers—"and you gotta wait a whole year to start over again, if your heart's into it. But when we get it right," he said, reaching for a cracker, "it's really nice to see them take, ya know? Like you created something. A life."

"I guess," Georgie said, tossing down his shot.

"Got a parent-teacher thing tonight," Mo said and drained his beer. He threw a half-dozen green Tic-Tacs into his mouth, crunched them, breathed into his cupped hand, sniffed, and tossed in more.

"Yeah, gotta show," Georgie said. "Guess it's kinda strange to know your kid has a whole other life outside the one you see at home. Huh?"

"You got that right," Mo said, spinning off his stool.

Joe came out of the men's room, grabbed a new beer Ray Ray had waiting for him, and hustled down the bar, checking his fly on the way. He shot his wrist out from the cuff of his jacket, glanced at his watch, and forked up his collar.

"Just in time. Like clockwork," he said as the bus pulled into the curb. He set his beer on the low windowsill behind Georgie, leaned on it with stiff arms, and looked out, like a teacher hovering over his desk, monitoring pupils during a test. The Catholic schoolgirls spilled from the bus in short black-and-green tartan skirts, high white socks, and pale-green blouses. They gathered on the sidewalk for a few seconds before setting out down the block, prancing past the window.

"Look at that one," Joe said to the window. "Nice now"—he shook his head—"but developed too soon, so she's on track to fade early, like everything's gonna go south before long. Looks purebred Eye-talian. They get great bodies early and that's when we get suckered. But then it's not too long before they start to go downhill. Now, the one in the middle," he said, head pointing, "the one with Irish cream in her face, legs up to her ears. Great shiny long black hair—great combo of Guinea and Mick."

Most of the guys had heard Joe's take on the girls before and ignored him.

Joe pursed his lips, slowly turning his head from side to side in admiration, and grinned.

"Little tits she's got now, but they'll be punching out her shirt soon. She's a sleeper. Gonna be a keeper. Hey, I'm a poet and don't know it!" he said, grinning at the window.

He gulped half his beer and smacked his lips, as if he'd been parched from watching the scampering, laughing girls.

"C'mon, Georgie," he said. "Take a look. See what I mean. I know about these things. I know potential when I see it. She's gonna have a rack and legs to go with. Just takes time."

Georgie turned around on his stool and faced Joe's back.

"What's up with you?" Georgie said, turning his palms up. "That's some kinda perv talk. She's somebody's daughter. And you with a daughter? How'd you like it if someone said that about your daughter? 'Tits'? 'A rack'?"

Joe turned his head a quarter turn, keeping his eyes sideways on the girls.

"They'd be speaking the truth, my man. Besides, no crime looking." Joe turned back to look straight out the window. "You stop looking, you're dead, Georgie. Last time I looked you weren't all the way dead yet."

Georgie turned back to the bar, shaking his head.

"She's gonna have all the goodies, that one," Joe said, craning to see her as she disappeared from view.

Shaking his head in appreciation, he picked up his beer, turned from the window, and sat on a stool next to Georgie that Juvie had vacated to challenge the winner at the puck bowling machine next to the juke.

"You know, it's a privilege, maybe a kinda duty to appreciate a life taking shape. You know, uh, appreciate that the life you created keeps growing and keeps going after you don't. You know what I'm saying here, Georgie?" Joe said, raising himself straight, looking down at his yellow handkerchief, carefully plucking it to stand up a fraction of an inch higher.

"I dunno. You been saying lots of shit, Joe."

Joe leaned back down, his face even with Georgie's. "I'm saying true stuff whether you wanna hear it or not."

Georgie slowly sipped from his shot glass. "Maybe. But there's a way to say it and a way to say it, Joe."

"Well, I gotta say there's times," Joe said, "you know, when you just wanna stop it all, freeze time so you can keep them a little longer before you gotta let 'em, you know, go. But you already know that, Georgie," he said, straightening up.

"Yeah, it's tough to let go," Georgie said. "Really tough."

Georgie finished off his shot and raised his hand for Ray Ray to pour another and sideways-wagged his forefinger for a round for both of them on him.

"How many years we been seeing each other here but never really talked?" Joe said. "Years go by."

"Yeah, been a few," Georgie said, carefully aligning his shot glasses dead center on the coaster.

"So how's your daughter, anyway, Georgie? I don't hear you talking about her."

Georgie sipped from his shot and then the beer. "She's fine. Her name's Sally. I read to her every night, I do. I like doing that. Puts her to sleep and eases me into the night too. I don't like to talk about her here."

"Your call. Sally's a nice name. Kinda, you know, perky."

Joe slid from the stool and walked toward his cousin Sal down the bar, fishing peanuts out of a bowl. "Later, my man," Joe said to Georgie over his shoulder.

Farther down the bar, Fireman Mikey gnawed a pickled pig's foot. He put it down, wiped his mouth, and shouted to Joe, asking whether Joe's daughter had to sign a "prenup, you know, with all the money on the guy's side and all."

"Nah," Joe said, "it's more like he had to sign her prenup before he'd, you know, get her to welcome him with open arms or, uh, open anything else, you catch my drift."

Mikey dropped his chin, trying to bury a smile. Guys on both sides of him guffawed, along with Joe. Over the next few minutes, Georgie threw down two more balls and beers. Then he spun off his stool and headed toward the back door, the narrow hallway framing his broad shoulders. He bounced off the wall, swearing as he righted himself.

He had an hour left on his shift before he was due to return the truck, its red and blue stars on the fat white barrel still spinning slowly in the parking lot, so the last of the cement wouldn't harden before he got back to the yard to flush it. His dispatcher built in free time on Fridays for Georgie as a bone for thirteen years of driving.

Georgie had called Tara when he got to Ray Ray's and told her to meet him in the lot, if she still wanted a ride in the truck. The last time they'd been together in his Impala she told him she'd always wondered what it would be like sitting in the cab up high, with the big barrel spinning stars behind her.

Georgie had dated Tara years ago for about six months. One night at a movie, when they were trying to lose themselves in the story, Tara went to the women's room just as the plot was reaching its climax. Afterward, they walked to his car, awkwardly not holding hands. She said, her head down, that she had finally gotten her period. They were quiet for a long time and broke up the next week.

Years after her husband had bought the farm in Vietnam, they ran into each other in Baranco's Diner on a Sunday morning when she was sitting in a booth and he was at the counter. They rekindled something that Georgie was grateful for—more grateful maybe than Tara was.

But they liked being with each other. It had become easy between them the second time around. Georgie quiet, moody sometimes, Tara more outgoing and more considerate than he'd remembered.

He'd told Ray Ray that he didn't really like her cartoon-red hair, but it seemed to go with her out-there personality he really liked. He thought it was good for him. She was much more spontaneous, and she got a kick out of the littlest things. He liked it when she laughed—when she really got into it, she absolutely roared.

"Nicky's so-called friends, they literally spit at me, for Chrissake," she'd told Georgie, "for just walking down the street with my cousin. I was a slut, dirtying Nicky's memory," she said, bugging her eyes. "You know, I was supposed to never have a boyfriend again, or for sure never a husband. Nothing."

She shook her head, her red hair swirling. "Those so-called friends of his wanted I should wear black the rest of my life."

Wet-eyed, she turned toward Georgie. "We were married three freakin' months, Georgie!" she said, staring at him. "You know what I mean?"

She blinked rapidly several times and turned to look out the window.

Georgie slapped the white steering wheel of the midnight-blue Impala. "They were losers then and still are, Tara. Just losers," he said. "Don't spend any time thinking about what they were thinking or saying. A lot of it was because they ducked the war and Nicky didn't and got killed for it. They thought they were making up for that by calling you out, showing how devoted they were to Nicky."

Georgie and Tara bonded over having daughters. She told him she wasn't very close to her daughter, blaming it on her not having a father and so Tara had to be the lone disciplinarian. But she was still proud of her girl, she said. Unbelievable, really, watching her grow. Georgie opened up about his daughter, his eyes filling. Tara looked into them like no one ever had and listened to it all, stroked his arm, nodded, teared up, and sighed.

———

Tara was sitting on the truck's step in the parking lot when Georgie came out. She wore the sassy red skirt Georgie liked that almost matched her new hair color that the box had promised would be luxuriously, believably dark red. Tara told Teressa she thought it would look like Maureen O'Hara's in *The Quiet Man*, her father's all-time favorite movie.

Tara's large dark eyes were set off by thick black mascara. Her mouth was framed by two sets of parentheses, and she almost had a little cleft in her chin that was more square than rounded. Her nose was straight with a slight flare to the nostrils. All told, she was sexy in a mature woman's been-around-the-block way. The kind of woman boys, and men for that matter, fantasize about teaching them things.

"Georgie Porgy," she said, greeting him, her smile slipping into those parentheses.

"Hey," Georgie said, walking to the driver's side. Tara smiled and went to the other side, theatrically swaying her hips.

Georgie missed the step on his first attempt, but on the second try his foot took hold and he grabbed the hand grip next to the door and hoisted himself. Tara had clambered into the passenger's side with ease and was waiting for him.

He settled into the cab and, after missing first gear, clutched again and found it. He lumbered the truck out of the parking lot onto the Avenue. They passed Frankie's Everything store with kites, balloons, erector sets, and a pyramid of Barbie dolls peering at them from behind their cellophane windows.

They cruised past the Chase bank that, a long time ago, had turned down Georgie's father for a loan because he'd had cancer.

"I really still want to rip up that bank and punch out the manager," Georgie told Tara. "But then I realized, 'Duh,' they aren't there to help people like they pretend. Dummy, I was. It's all part of the profit game. I guess part of growing up is realizing that. No way my old man woulda paid off the loan. But they didn't know that then. Truth is, I still wanna rip off that manager's face. Just because."

Every so often Georgie would walk slowly past the bank's big plate-glass window, hawk out a huge loogie on it, and stand there watching it ooze down the glass. He always hoped someone—maybe that manager—would come out and yell at him. But his linebacker's body kept them all inside, heads down. Tara told Georgie as they approached the bank that her first job was there as assistant to the assistant manager.

"They were nice to me," she said, "once I made clear what was off limits. You know, my boss's frisky hands and all. Really frisky."

"You never told me that," Georgie said, turning to her. "I'da known, I'da cleaned that guy's clock. Big-time! Putting his hands on you."

"That's sweet, Georgie Poo. Real sweet. But I handled it. Had to handle lots of things over the years, you know?"

They drove by Stein's hardware, Jerry's liquor store, and

the Carvel stand on the corner with pictures of cones dripping chocolate down mountains of vanilla and pictures of cakes topped by burning candles with unnatural-looking yellow flames. Half a block farther, Pete Holister, who'd been in Vietnam all those years ago, was coming out of Muchie's sporting-goods store, leaning on a cane. His son, smiling and carrying a new baseball bat on his shoulder, was about ten feet ahead of him. He turned around toward his father and stopped to let him catch up.

Tara smiled at her reflection in the store windows, the truck spinning its stars and her with her arm sticking out the window. She had aimed the small vent window at her face, and hot wind fluffed her red hair, making it look like wisps of flames hit with a burst of oxygen. They looped around the Lutheran church that was mostly below ground because they'd run out of money to build it higher. He told Tara he often checked to see whether they'd finally got around to putting a cross on top. They hadn't.

They turned back onto Broadway, past Baranco's Diner and the tiny park—dingy now with a broken seesaw—named after her dead husband, and up about a mile to Manor Road, past the old war memorial obelisk.

All those years after the war, one of the plaques still was blank, waiting for the names of guys dead in Vietnam. The Parks Department said they were working on it.

A little bit farther, they had flickering glimpses through breaks of tall hedges of Victorian homes with turrets and wrap-around porches. Tara stared out the truck's window at the houses.

"You know, my wife liked to look at those houses and dream," Georgie said. "Me? I didn't give them a second thought. I mean, what's that gonna do for you, dreaming and pretending you're not what you are, where you are, and where you're gonna stay."

"That's kinda depressing, you know, Georgie."

"Yeah, I guess," he said, blasting his horn at a driver who turned without signaling. "Sometimes what's real is depressing if you let yourself think about yourself too much. I mean, I guess some people gotta think they don't belong in the world they're in so they can deal with the world they're in."

Tara slid over to Georgie, kissed him, and patted his cheek. Georgie smiled a tight, shy smile.

They took a left past Silvestrie's gas station, owned by his father's friend Sal, who'd let Georgie stash his bike out back when he was in grade school. Georgie's father told him that the slips of paper Georgie had seen stuck in a log were bets Sal picked up every day. *Nobody talks about it,* his father said, *but Sal is a bookie.* His description of a bookie's business turned into a math lesson. That was a month before he checked out of Georgie's life.

On their way back down the Avenue, Georgie just missed hitting a parked car. Farther down the street, he admired a classic aqua-and-cream Chevy too long while it was stopped, signaling a left turn in front of him. He had to swerve to avoid crushing it and just missed another car coming head-on. They drove past Baranco's again and Angie's and Teressa's Beauty Salon, their names in pink swirls on a sign over the door.

Tara cozied up to Georgie, putting her hand on his thigh. Her head slipped below the dashboard onto Georgie's lap. Distracted, he drifted into a right turn onto Church Street and hit the accelerator instead of the brake.

The truck exploded the plate-glass front window of the new ShopRite due to open that Monday, sending a stack of Charmin flying onto checkout counters and squashing a pyramid of pumpkins before Georgie found the brake and stopped just short of a stack of Rice-A-Roni boxes. Tara lay against the passenger door whimpering, her legs splayed.

Georgie's forehead was on the steering wheel, blood running down his face. The truck's stars were slowly spinning behind them.

The cop car's siren growled to a stop on the side of the ambulance, its red lights flashing as two attendants unloaded a stretcher.

One of the cops gingerly walking through the mess of glass, pumpkins, and Charmin was Billy Perosi, who had been second-string guard behind Georgie before he had to quit. Billy stood on the truck's step peering into the cab.

"Get the fuck outta my face, Joe!" Georgie shouted at Billy. "Big Joe, my ass! You're just the fat man in the circus now. Leave me the fuck alone!"

"Now this is funny, Georgie. Really funny," Billy said, shaking his head. "You, your dick loafing out, and not knowing where you are and who you're talking to. And we got Tara in her favorite position. You know I gotta take you in, you smellin' the way you do. Maybe they'll let you bring some of that Charmin to lockup. I hear there's never enough toilet paper in the clink."

Georgie looked up from the steering wheel, rapidly blinking his eyes. "Fuck you, Joe," Georgie said. "Big Joe. Big asshole!"

Georgie drew himself up straight and passed his hand down his face, leaving red stripes, looking like war paint, his blue eyes shining through the blood.

"I gotta right! I gotta right!" Georgie said, failing to suppress a burp. "I gotta daughter, too. Fuck you! Her name's Sally. Sally! Sally! Sally! Her name's Sally! Always near me. Kermit the Frog on her bed. Cinderella-pink walls they call 'em, yellow sheets, hearts on 'em. We love going into the woods with Winnie the Pooh. And we really like the story about the girl spider and her pig friend and all. Gotta feed the mind, too. Every night. Every freakin' night I'm reading to her."

"Georgie, what the fuck you talkin' about? Again, and not for nothin', you stink, like really, really stink, from all of the booze!"

"Fuck you, Joe. Fuck you! Fuck them! Fuck alla you! I gotta right! I gotta right! 'Just a fetus,' they said. Fuck you! She's mine! No law against keeping her in formaldehyde! I gotta daughter! Fuck you, Joe! Fuck you!"

# JUST A DOG

"ROAD TRIP! FOR THE AGES!" Nicky had written to Bobby from Da Nang, the huge U.S. base on the South China Sea in central Vietnam. "It'll be 'Look out! Lock up your women—Nicky and Bobby Troc are on the loose!'" Nicky said they'd drive from the big Marine Corps base near San Diego where Nicky probably would be stationed after his tour.

"We'll go through the Mojave Desert to Vegas and take a couple of side trips. I'll take you to Pahrump not far from Vegas where whorehouses are legal, and I'll give you tips on what to do. We'll hit Death Valley too, because it's there."

———

It took Bobby years after Nicky didn't come home, but he finally flew to San Diego and rented a red convertible, the color of Nicky's cherished Oldsmobile Bobby still had, and pointed it toward Vegas.

Just outside Baker, California, about a hundred miles west of Vegas, he saw a huge "EAT" sign with "Oasis Lounge" below and clinking cocktail glasses. A blinking red arrow pointed to a building behind a gas station. He filled up and drove around the service bay to the restaurant.

The skull of a Bighorn sheep—regally curved horns sweeping behind—hung above two thick wood doors. Next to the door stood a wooden Indian, yellow and black war paint smeared down his face. Around his neck were several strands of snap-together colored plastic necklaces like those tossed around at Mardi Gras.

The doors opened into a foyer with a doorway straight to the dining room. In the middle of the room, an elderly couple sat holding hands across the table, heads down in prayer. Against the far wall, a toddler sat in a highchair, a pink bow clinging from hopeful wisps of blond hair. The mom was holding a French fry in front of the kid's mouth. The father, wearing a baseball cap, looked up at the baby, sipped his beer, and dug back into his steak.

To the right, a corridor led to glass doors to the Oasis Lounge. Inside, about twenty feet from the door, was a big fake horse with a ratty mane perched on a platform, mid-buck, eyes flashing devil-red. Above the bar were pictures of smiling guys in cowboy hats and trucker caps, raising beer bottles for the camera. They'd made "The Bronco Busters Wall of Fame" for staying on "Buckin' Bruce" five times in a row.

Bobby took a stool at the end of the bar. He took two coasters from the well and put one in front of him and one in front of the empty stool next to him. The bartender, well into a third-trimester paunch, broke off a conversation with a guy at the far end and made his way to Bobby. Gray hairs curled over the edges of his black rug. He took away the coaster in front of the empty stool and put it back on the stack in the well. Bobby ordered a whiskey sour on the rocks—Nicky's favorite cocktail.

Three stools down, a guy sat in front of a draft beer and a

cheeseburger deluxe, oozing ketchup from the sides. Another guy, lanky, was two stools away on Bobby's other side, a can of Coors in front of him. He wore a tightly curled black Stetson cowboy hat with a red feather arcing from the hatband. The hat was tilted up on top of a thatch of sandy hair, matching a bushy handlebar mustache. His jeans were perfectly faded. He finished the look with tooled mahogany cowboy boots hooked onto a rung of his stool.

Bobby wore a vintage black New York Giants cap with an intertwined orange "NY," khaki chinos, and a navy polo shirt—no polo player. He turned to the empty stool next to him, put a coaster back in front of it, and whispered, "This guy looking so pretty, you think he's gonna break into 'Oklahoma' for us?"

Cowboy Hat, perplexed, stared at Bobby, shook his head, and picked up his beer.

"Fuckin' A," Cowboy Hat said as the bartender slid open the lid of a cooler beneath the bar. "Caught that mutt with my fender doin' 'bout eighty. Timed it just right. Was good for a forty-yard field goal."

The bartender shook his head, slightly smiled, and put a coaster in front of Bobby and took away the one he'd put down in front of the empty stool. He walked to mid-bar to make the sour. Bobby put the coaster back in front of the empty stool.

The bartender made a show of shaking and pouring the sour, topping it off with the two cherries Bobby had asked for. He put the sour in front of Bobby and took away the coaster from in front of the empty stool. The sour was too sweet and without a head. Definitely not like Ray Ray's—where the thick head lasted and there was always extra in the chrome shaker. In those days, they used real egg whites and real lemon juice.

The bartender came back and fished out a bottle of beer from the cooler. He looked at the coaster in front of the empty stool.

"What's with the coaster, friend?" the bartender said.

"Saving the seat."

"Knock yourself out," the bartender said, walking away.

"Yep, mutt never knew what hit him," Cowboy Hat said, ending his story as the bartender receded.

Bobby shifted the stubby glass with the bad whiskey sour on the Coors coaster until it was dead center. He winked at the empty stool and turned back to Cowboy Hat.

"Sounds like you could have flipped, chasing him going that fast."

"Don't drive one of those fag SUVs. Ford 350. Extended cab. Heavy-duty tow package. Balanced perfect. Ain't going nowhere it hits something."

"Buy my friend what he's drinking," Bobby said to the bartender.

"Don't mind if I do. Appreciate it. Name's Bert. Where you headed?"

Bobby looked at the empty chair next to him and winked. Then he turned to Bert, who held his can aloft in toast to Bobby. Bobby raised his glass back.

"Bobby here. Going to Vegas. There a problem with stray dogs around here, Bert?"

"Not really. One less now, though."

"Guess so. At least he doesn't have to worry about surviving out there anymore. Too bad he never had a real shot at a good life."

"Just a fuckin' dog." Bert sipped his beer.

"A life snuffed just like that. You never know what's gonna get you and when, huh?"

Bert sniggered.

Bobby turned to the empty stool and raised his eyebrows. He whispered, "Check out this guy, bragging about it. Big man, ending a life just because he can."

Bert stared at Bobby, slightly pulled his head back, slightly shook it, and shrugged.

"Where're you headed?" Bobby asked.

"Uh, gonna wind up in Vegas, after a couple of stops." Bert eyed Bobby tentatively. "Like to hang out at the hotel where a big fight's gonna be. Free pussy, you catch one of them fight groupies right."

"Tell me," Bobby said, "any detours I should take to get a feel for the desert other than from the highway?"

"Tell the truth, don't really know. Don't pay much attention to it long as I been living here. Bunch of sand with fuckin' hills sticking up, you ask me."

Bert tilted back his head, drained his Coors, and put the can into the well for another. He took off his cowboy hat, smoothed his hair, carefully put it back on, tilting it just so, and turned again toward Bobby. "Have one on me."

Bobby took the coaster in front of the empty stool and put it back on the stack of them in the well.

"Thanks, my friend, reached my limit." Bobby spun off the stool. "Gotta go. *Adios.*"

On the way out, Bobby turned his head to the side and whispered, "Shoulda let the turd buy me a drink, play with him a little more."

He went to the parking lot and brought his car to the side of the restaurant so he could see when Bert came out the front door. He took a newspaper clipping from his wallet.

It was from the *New York Times*—an editorial about Robert McNamara's book that the former secretary of state wrote—a feeble mea culpa, describing how difficult it had been for him making all of those decisions in the early years of the Vietnam War. He forgave himself because his decisions were made during "the fog of war."

McNamara had titled his book *In Retrospect.* The big

reveal was that McNamara admitted he knew seven years before the war ended that the U.S. would not win the war. But he continued to lie, saying America would prevail, and poured increasing numbers of death-destined troops into Vietnam to show off his perseverance.

Bobby had been at Ray Ray's with Tool a couple of days after McNamara's book came out and he was on TV hawking it.

"This fucking guy admitted he lied about winning the war and killed Nicky and how many thousands of our guys? Fifty-eight thousand two hundred and twenty, Tool, and you just missed making it one more."

Tool raised his beer in toast to Joanne Dolan, sitting at the end of the bar with Jimmy Garafano. She looked down at her glass and smiled.

"What? I'm talking to myself here, Tool?"

"Sorry, Bobby. Yeah, a lot of guys never got to get old and, you know, to score their fair share o' chicks. Lookit Joanne with that dirtbag. She's mine, I just know it. I mean, no competition."

"*In Retrospect?* What? In retrospect?" Bobby said. "Sounds like a guy thinking he shoulda used a wedge instead of a nine-iron. In fucking retrospect? In retrospect? You lying piece of shit! You just admitted our guys died for nothing. Nada! Zilch! Bupkes! And you, you fuck, you killed them."

"Yeah, he did," Tool said, sliding his glass to the edge of the bar for a refill.

———

Bobby sat, waiting for Bert.

With his hand covering the *Times*'s clipping against the

steering wheel, Bobby recited word for word the best part of the editorial, aimed at McNamara.

*"Surely he must in every quiet and prosperous moment hear the ceaseless whispers of those poor boys in the infantry, dying in the tall grass, platoon by platoon, for no purpose. What he took from them cannot be repaid by prime-time apology and stale tears, three decades late."*

Where the fuck was the writer of the editorial when those kinds of words might have saved some guys? He was drinking in Elaine's on the Upper East Side, sucking on congratulations for such pretty words. He was yukking it up with all of the pretty people with exemptions—phony shin splints, fallen arches, flat feet, Daddy paying for graduate school, knocking up someone.

Bert came out about fifteen minutes later and cock-walked the brick path around the building to the parking lot. He eased out of the driveway and hit second gear hard, popping the clutch, squealing tires, sending up puffs of blue smoke. Bobby thought of the smoke signal sent up the chimney when a new pope had successfully worked the room to get elected.

Bert's Ford pickup was the same candy-apple red Nicky had painted that old Schwinn bike Curly had given him. In turn, after Nicky bought the Olds, he gave the bike to Bobby for his birthday back when Bobby wanted to be just like his big brother. Before Vietnam. All these years later, Bobby still has the bike, hanging on a wall of his apartment. He dusts it every day he's home and Turtle Waxes it once a month.

Bobby tailed Bert on a packed sand road, heading toward a big hill, where there weren't any houses or trailers and the sand was speckled with just a few scraggly bushes. Tumbleweeds? What's a tumbleweed anyway, besides the obvious?

From the radio, a kind of wailing electronic gong gave notice to listen up.

"Born in the USA." Bobby used to go to Binghamton Mets games with Jimmy. In the seventh-inning stretch, everyone roared the refrain, singing along with Bruce, beer cups pumping the air, suds sloshing onto the kids—mothers and fathers laughing at that one.

"Everyone thinks it's a patriotic song," Bobby had told Jimmy. "They go by the name of the song and its refrain 'cause they need it to be tough, they need to be proud of something, need to scream about it and believe what they want and not what the words actually mean. The fans were all 'USA! USA! USA!' thinking, 'Send all those Spics back to Mexico and the 'Roes to Africa. 'Let's go Mets! Let's go Mets!'"

Bobby stayed about a mile behind Bert, his truck a spot of red slipping along the sides of tawny hills. Bobby scanned the desert. The only thing he could see except bushes—tumbleweeds taking a break from tumbling?—and little hills was another sandy road off in the distance, winding toward a small cinder-block building in front of a tall antenna, looking like something from an erector set. Probably a signal-booster for one of those radio stations whose main income is from the God hustlers: "Buy this beautiful, simulated, leather-bound Bible and experience the word of God in the luxury it deserves for three easy payments of $19.99, plus shipping."

Bobby closed in. When the gap between them had shortened to about a hundred yards, Bobby started hitting the horn. Bert checked his rearview three times before pulling over. Bobby stopped about twenty feet behind him.

He took his reproduction double-action Colt .45 pistol from under the front seat, opened the door, and got out, carrying it behind his right thigh. He wanted Bert on the side of the truck that would shield them from anyone coming up the road, unlikely as that was.

Bert got out and walked around the back of his truck to the

passenger side. "Hey, good buddy," Bert said, as he recognized Bobby. "What's the matter?"

"Looks like a leak."

Bert squatted to look, and Bobby walked closer until he was right behind him. "Tell you what, you low-life scumbag, you do anything but get up very slow with your hands plastered to your side, it'll be the last thing you ever do."

Bobby brought the Colt from behind his thigh and pulled the hammer back. *Click.* (A much better sound of scary than a single-action, which is just pull the trigger and *bam!* Bobby figured the "click" before the hammer dropped gave more time to be scared.)

"What the fuck! What's going on?"

*Play with him. Make him realize on his own that he just might be heading for a world of hurt.*

*Give him time—to get really scared, maybe think that gophers and sheep and birds and coyotes are gonna rip apart his toes and arms to get at the good meat and delighted ants and lizards'll be lapping up his still-warm blood.*

"That's one of the problems. You don't even know what you did, what you are."

Bert turned around, his back against the truck, and slowly straightened. He was assessing his options.

Bobby put the gun on Bert's knee and let it sit there for a few seconds. Then he pulled the trigger. Bert collapsed, screaming, twisting and rolling around, pounding the sand as if fire ants were crawling up his ass.

Bobby smiled. "You don't shut up," he shouted, "I'm gonna put another one in your other knee!"

Bert turned down the screams to grunts and whimpers.

*Click.* Pause.

Bert's eyes opened wide, terrified. Pleased, Bobby shot him in the other knee.

"That's for the dog you killed and didn't give a second thought to."

Bert screamed, "A dog? A fuckin' dog?"

"Yeah, a dog. A dog that didn't deserve you. A dog who should be alive instead of you!"

Bobby stood over Bert and told him to lie as still as possible so he could tie tourniquets on his legs.

"Only chance you got now. Roll over on your back and stop screaming, or I'll put one in your head."

Bert brought the screams down again to squeals, rapidly sucking in air and pushing it out, whooshing like a woman trying to get past the pain of childbirth, and rolled onto his back, his eyes fixed on Bobby's dark eyes. Bert's were green. Mr. Mannenberg said that only two percent of people in the world have green eyes.

Bobby unzipped and streamed into the wounds.

Bert thrashed around, violently shaking his head like he was in the Olympics thrashing event. Bobby shook out the last drop and slowly zipped up.

*Click.* Pause.

He shot him in the groin. Blood and bits of flesh—maybe pieces of his dick—splattered onto Bert's tooled boots.

Bobby gently cleared his throat, hummed in falsetto, moving slowly down the scale to get the pitch he wanted. The words were just there. Just popped into his head like they'd always been there. Waiting.

*You thought you was cool,*
*Now you a fool.*
*Here you lyin' doin' your dyin'.'*
*Ain't nobody cryin'*
*You be runnin' outta life.*
*Soon someone else be fuckin' your wife.*

Bobby pulled his shoulders back and stood at attention. He looked down at Bert, splayed on the sand, his eyes open. Bobby smiled. A turkey vulture riding air currents circled above him. Bobby executed a perfect about-face the way Nicky had taught him and walked back along the road he'd come down. A tumbleweed scooted across it. The turkey vulture tightened his circle on his way to Bert.

# RETRO

ESME LIES ON THE BED, watching the lava lamp on the dresser, a pink blob floating inside, rising to the top, splitting into two, flattening against the top and disappearing. It reminds her of a monitor in a doctor's office revealing a fetus.

She remembers the retro club where they met last night, and the strobes—white, pink, yellow, and blue—flash-freezing dancers, arms and legs akimbo in throes of something.

Esme and Lily had just finished their first year at Fresno State, and Lily pleaded that they celebrate by going to the club with their fake IDs. It would be good for both of them to get out, Lily said. She left with the first guy who bought her a drink.

Esme made her way through the crowd at the bar to get a drink. A tall guy wearing a blue satiny shirt open below his chest pushed through the crowd behind her and wedged himself next to her.

"I saw your girlfriend split with that guy, who needed a drool bib the way he was looking at you," the guy said. "I guess he knew he didn't have a shot at you, so he settled."

"Cute. But drool isn't," Esme said.

She wore a sparkly black shirt and a short red pleated skirt that clung to her thighs and hips—a kind of retro look itself. She had thought about doing her hair in ringlets like lovelorn chorus girls wore in the old-time movies she liked to watch, but decided she didn't want to be that retro. No one would get it.

"I'm Chad. Mind if I look at you? I'll try not to drool, even though there are lots of nice things that make me want to."

"Things?"

"Yeah, things," he said, smiling. "You know, nice things that you have that most girls don't."

He pushed their glasses toward the bartender for refills, a twenty-dollar bill protruding between his fingers. "Really, you should get to know me. I have nice things, too."

"If you have to brag about them, they're probably nothing special. I'll pass. I hate to be a disappointed . . . girl," she said, brushing aside his arm and waving a twenty at the bartender.

"Bitch," Chad said, a rainbow of strobes slapping his back as he walked away.

He was replaced by an almost-handsome guy with a long face, shy smile, streaked blond hair in a ponytail, and half-moon clusters of acne scars high on both cheekbones. He wore a bright-white shirt that soaked up the colors of the strobes splashing him. He said his name was Michael and that he was tired and about to leave, but saw her and wanted to say hello. He seemed normal, and Esme wanted normal. She called herself Beatrice.

They drank champagne from flutes in his neat chrome-and-glass living room.

"I wish my dad could have seen all of this," he said, sweeping his arm across the room and its view of lights in the valley.

Esme nodded and smiled softly. "I'm sure he'd be very

proud of you. Fathers are very proud of sons from the day they're born," Esme said, looking straight ahead at the view. She turned and looked up at him. "Daughters have to wait longer. Sometimes they run out of time."

"I guess. I never thought of it that way," he said, pushing back wisps of hair from his ponytail. "Is that what happened to you?"

She took his hand and walked them to the bedroom, where he turned on the lava lamp.

"It was my dad's. The only thing I wanted of his after he died."

It had been fine with him in his wide water bed, letting the waves sync their rhythms. He was attentive and didn't suggest anything. Anything at all.

Now, lying awake in bed listening to the first birds of the morning, she remembers having her dream again: her hair being tousled the way she'd heard some fathers do to gently wake daughters. But she knows it's useless to try to go back to the dream. The dream has evaporated and she can't summon it at will. Each time she's afraid will be the last time.

She lowers her eyes from the lamp, the blobs slowly turning and disappearing. She sees a trail between bathroom and bed of her cream sandals, sparkly black shirt, and red skirt, its pleats looking like a collapsed fan. Closer to the bed is her black bra lying on top of red panties.

She turns her head to the right and looks over the ridge of his body beneath the sheet and through sliding glass doors to the pool and its early-morning cataract sheen. A robin is perched on the back of a pool chair. It flies away, flashing an edge of a wing in the pool. It's replaced almost immediately by another robin.

She can't be in the house a minute longer.

She eases out of bed, careful to make nothing more than a

ripple. She shakes her hair loose and runs her fingers through it. She backtracks the strewn clothes, stopping along the way to pick them up as quietly as possible. Dressed, sandals dangling by their straps from a finger, she unplugs the lava lamp, stopping the floating blob mid-rise. She gathers the cord and wraps her hand around the lamp. She uses the powder room next to the front door.

She had insisted on following him to his place in her ancient, sun-bleached red hatchback she'd parked down the street from the club to avoid a valet charge. She opens the hatch, takes out a towel, and swaddles the lamp. She gently sets it onto the passenger seat, tucks it in, and drives away.

# SMOKER

AN HOUR before the limousines arrived, Charley Cuba opened the trunk of his car and unloaded the following supplies into a black gym bag with a white Nike swoosh on its side: two red boxing gloves, plaster of paris, a painter's mixing stick, plastic bucket, hand-wrapping tape, box cutter, red matte lipstick, and needle and thread. He slipped through the back door of the Valley of Fire National Park's Education/Visitors' Center, about fifty miles northeast of Las Vegas.

Tommy Macklin sat on a gurney in a storage room. He wore black boxing shorts, black shoes, and a black robe draped over his shoulders, a bright-yellow lightning bolt on the back. Across from him on a table was a stuffed coyote in a plastic case next to a tall, scrawny stuffed bird on a pedestal, its beak frozen open. Macklin read the label: "The Greater Roadrunner, native to the Mojave Desert, is so quick and cunning it can grab a rattlesnake for dinner mid-rattle."

Macklin, out of Tulsa, had worked on oil rigs and driven long-haul trucks throughout the Southwest. He billed himself as a 16-2 boxer, his record cobbled together from tough-man contests at carnivals and county fairs throughout the West, where he was known as a skilled heavyweight—true enough when he was in shape and motivated.

Cuba was getting Macklin ready to face the final fighter of Clarence "The Chief" Clearwater's "Smoker"—the name dating back to the early 1900s, when illegal boxing matches were held in basements, back rooms, backyards, and the halls of Knights of Columbus, American Legion, Moose, and the like. Fighters back then mostly were Black and unpaid. Coins were tossed into the ring after fights, sending the fighters scrambling on all fours to scoop them up. Some smokers featured blind-folded fighters, flailing around the ring, swinging wildly, trying to find and hit opponents. All, of course, to the delight of laughing White fans.

Clearwater's plan was to send a fresh Macklin in for the last fight of the night, presumably against Calvin Jackson, whom, the consensus had it, would likely survive all of his fights in the smoker and win the right to fight for the heavy-weight championship of the world. The Chief and Cuba were betting 50K on the side that a fresh Macklin with loaded gloves would destroy Calvin.

Macklin twisted his head and rolled his shoulders to loosen up when Cuba came in.

"Hey," Cuba said. "You know the deal, right? You never saw me."

"Yeah," Macklin said, sliding off the table to throw lazy jabs and uppercuts into the air. Then he hopped back onto the table.

Cuba, who'd done three years in prison for loading a boxer's gloves in a bout that left a fighter in a coma and then dead, put water into the bucket, mixed in the plaster of paris, and dunked hand-wrapping tape into it. After a few minutes, with the tape sufficiently soaked, Cuba wrapped Macklin's hands. The tape would harden, providing—along with the thinned gloves—lethal punching power.

"Just sit there, don't move your hands," Cuba said, as he walked to a table and set the gloves down next to a jar of three tiny iguanas drowned in a formaldehyde concoction. He cut small slits in the palms inside each glove and pulled out horse-hair and foam padding, then stitched up the slits and rubbed lipstick over them.

————

Calvin, with Buttsie driving a beat-up blue Impala with a dented white hood, had pulled into the parking lot two hours earlier. Getting out of the car, Calvin spotted what looked like the top of a tall white hood peeking over the edge of the building's flat roof. He did a double take, slowly shook his head at himself for the fear handed down over generations, and walked around the side, where he saw five smaller tents with similar pointy tops. The largest tent would be the site of the Chief's biggest smoker to date.

Clearwater, who claimed Native American Paiute blood through his great-grandmother (it would come out a few years later that she grew up a Shaughnessy in the Bronx), was the biggest boxing promoter in Vegas, and therefore in the world. His audience for the invitation-only smoker included Vegas power brokers whose support he needed to buy Paiute land for a new casino complex close to the brothels in Pahrump, about sixty miles out of Vegas. It was a limo ride away known to many of his VIP guests, including a federal judge, two state judges, a U.S. senator, who was a former POW in Vietnam, Vegas' police chief, and its mayor—all, of course, given ringside seats and comps to visit the "Indian maidens" in tents out back.

———

Three weeks earlier, Clearwater had summoned Calvin to his home in a gated development in Henderson, a Vegas suburb about fifteen miles off the Strip.

A week had passed since Calvin had committed a huge boxing sin—knocking out Clearwater's fighter Ivan "The Terrible" Rodriguez in a sparring session, just two weeks before Rodriguez was scheduled to fight an elimination bout for the right to fight for the heavyweight championship of the world. Boxing's protocol is that a boxer cannot fight for a minimum of thirty days, often longer, after being knocked out.

Calvin sat opposite Clearwater in a matching white leather love seat, at right angles to a fireplace, a glass coffee table between them. "Clair de Lune" played from a white player-piano behind Clearwater. He went to the piano, turned down the volume, leaned against the piano, folded his arms, and glowered at Calvin.

"I must state the obvious, my pugilist friend: knocking out Señor Rodriguez less than three weeks before his big bout was not your most intelligent decision and could lead to dire consequences for you."

Clearwater was still practicing his voice coach's lessons, trying to soften his New York accent and make him sound like a sophisticated businessman—or the way he thought they sounded. Clearwater had played tapes over and over of politicians and CEOs he'd recorded from television to improve his speech.

He unfolded his arms, flipped his black dyed braids from behind his back to dangle down his chest, and pointed a finger at Calvin.

"You have a choice. It is either to become the headlined combatant in my upcoming sub-rosa pugilistic event or endure the not-painless fracturing of your kneecaps. If you survive the eight bouts of my competition, comporting yourself with élan and intestinal fortitude, I will allow you to have the biggest opportunity you will ever have in your less-than-successful life to date. To wit: if you impress, I will place you in the championship contest in Señor Rodriguez's stead. The rewards for that are considerably more than your actions deserve."

"How much do I get for winning your smoker?" Calvin said, easing back into the love seat and staring at Clearwater, who had moved to the love seat opposite Calvin. "And I need it in writing."

"Excuse me. What in writing? You 'need'?"

"My deal," Calvin said, leaning back and crossing his legs.

"What do you get? In writing? Your deal? Now that would be humorous if it were not so delusional. Clearly you fail to comprehend your negotiation leverage here is less than zero," Clearwater said, tilting his head and raising his eyebrows.

Clearwater shifted to the edge of the love seat and glared at Calvin. "Can you even begin to fathom how much compensation was lost to me by your intemperate actions? Think for a moment of the expenses for advertising, training, and myriad financial commitments linked to the promotion. And, of course, there is the bruise to my reputation for employing a sparring partner who would do what you did."

He stroked his braids and squinted at Calvin.

"Let me be perfectly transparent. Yes," he said, nodding, "I am under certain scheduling strictures to announce another elimination contest as soon as possible. And I wish to secure the weekend when Cinco de Mayo will be celebrated here as usual with gusto by our south-of-the-border friends. And with you on the card, there will be even more of our Spanish *amigos* attending, hoping to see you ingloriously defeated for what you did to their fellow Hispanic."

Clearwater sat back, opened a cigar humidifier, made a selection, clipped the end off, flared the other end with a gold lighter, and rapidly sucked until it smoldered properly. He leaned back into the love seat and put his feet up on a white leather footrest.

"If you thwart my new plans, I will absorb my losses and turn to one of the many gladiators in this town waiting for a chance to rise through the ranks. Thereafter, it will be a matter of when—not if—your kneecaps will pay for your actions."

Clearwater stuck the cigar into his mouth, rose, went to the piano, and pressed buttons to the side of the keyboard. He returned to his love seat, leaned back, put his feet on the stool, and puffed away, looking at the ceiling.

"Ah," he said, closing his eyes as the opening aria of "The Goldberg Variations" began. "I so love this piece. You have approximately five minutes before the conclusion of the aria to render your decision."

Signaling silence, he turned his palm up at Calvin and closed his eyes. Calvin thumbed through an *Architectural Digest*. When the music stopped, Clearwater opened his eyes and looked at Calvin with raised eyebrows.

"I accept," Calvin said, tossing the magazine onto the table. He rose from the love seat and walked toward the front door. "You know where to find me."

———

Calvin walked behind the reception center's building to one of the tents half hidden behind an outcrop of boulders. Inside were four gurneys parked along one of the long walls. A row of dressing cubicles was against the opposite wall. He undressed, stepped into his thick leather cup-harness and red and green trunks, marked as always with "NGOC" in gold letters across a white waistband. He laced up black boxing shoes, hopped onto a gurney, and draped around his shoulders a kelly-green robe with the Marine Corps logo on back.

His trainer, Luis Ortiz, came into the tent. Calvin shucked off the robe, slid from the table, and began shadow-boxing in front of a full-length mirror. He threw mostly left hooks, the big weapon that had taken him to a 12-1 pro record, built in desert towns around Vegas, small clubs in L.A., and several in Tijuana —once on three consecutive nights.

The stream of limousines, Jaguars, Cadillacs, and a couple of Ferraris dropped guests in front of the visitors' center. Young women, moonlighting from the Tropicana's topless Folies Bergère, lined the walkway leading to the doors.

They were decked out in fringed leather buckskin halters and matching miniskirts. Each Folies Bergère "Indian maiden" had a single feather jutting from the back of her head. They produced wondrous smiles and flutes of champagne.

Inside, tables filled the large main room, heaped with platters of oysters, caviar, shrimp, and smoked salmon. On a long table on the other side of the room were crab croquettes, sliders of filet mignon, pulled pork, and chicken barbecue. A separate table had two more Indian maidens behind it, serving Dom Perignon, prize-winning wines, and spirits for any taste.

Another lovely wound through the crowd offering a list of the various proposition bets for the night. She also discreetly handed to single male guests another slip of paper with a time grid showing slots available later in the smaller tents out back with companions dubbed "Serendipity," "Scheherazade," and "Cleopatra."

After an hour of eating, drinking, and ogling, a boxing bell rang several times. Guests were asked to enter the main tent, where tiny spotlights pinballed around the sides of the tent and across the sand floor. After the crowd had been seated, the lights were turned off, and a single spotlight popped on, piercing the smoke to illuminate Michelle Butler, standing in the middle of the ring. She held a microphone along her thigh below the hem of her trademark red, white, and blue cheerleader outfit.

Michelle had become a celebrity at big fights for her gravelly voice, small but voluptuous figure, and signature jump. She'd begin it by squatting and then bursting into the air, body arching, skirt billowing, flashing brightly colored panties.

"Gentlemen, and, of course, ladies," she said, emphasizing "ladies" with a lopsided, conspiratorial grin, "welcome to the inaugural 'Night of Blood and Guts'—a nonstop, fight-'til-you-drop demonstration of intestinal fortitude brought to you courtesy of Marcus 'The Chief' Clearwater and the Paiute Nation.

"It is a winner-take-all night. If one man wins all of his fights, he will have demonstrated skill to go on to contend for the heavyweight championship of the world. If no one emerges without a defeat, well, we would have had a fun night to remember," she said, dropping a handkerchief, bending down to retrieve it, her skirt riding up, revealing red panties.

The crowd erupted in hoots, whistles, and laughter.

One of the proposition bets at Michelle's fights was on which color panties she'd reveal when she jumped before the last fight of the night.

Earlier in her career, when her popularity first took hold at licensed bouts, a Reuters photographer, buzzed from free pre-fight booze, had organized a ringside photographers' pool. The winner would be the one who got the best shot of whatever was revealed when her skirt flared above her waist before the main event. Extra points for topographical details.

"I get ten percent. My idea." He'd just bought a condo in Edgewater, New Jersey that he couldn't afford and was always on the hustle for money. His expense reports were worthy of a Pulitzer Prize for fiction.

Michelle put up her hand, asking for quiet.

"There are no knockdown rules," she said, wiggling her butt first at one corner and then at the other, to the crowd's delight.

"These gladiators are fighting for their professional lives. Some will be signed to promotional contracts with possibilities of big-time money even if they lose, as long as they demonstrate potential. The less-talented losers will go on to careers parking cars. Make no mistake, these are desperate men, taking desperate measures.

"While you enjoy your beverages and company, please take a moment to consult your fight cards. Our beautiful ladies will make their way through the room to take your wagers and orders for refreshments.

"Oh," she said with a goofy grin, "one of the props is about these." She lifted her skirt to show her panties—bringing thunderous cheers and laughter—and then dug into a Hermes bag at her feet. "Will I be wearing this color later? Or one of these?" she asked, pulling out and draping on her fingers blue, red, yellow, green, and fuchsia panties.

"The contests will begin in one-half hour. Good luck to all," she said, wiggling to the ropes, where a guy in a red tux with a matching rhinestone-studded bow tie lifted the middle rope and pushed his foot down on the one under it for her to slip between. Standing on the apron, she turned around, grabbed the top rope, and stuck out her butt, wiggling it at the audience.

*Cheers! Woofs! Snorts!*

A half hour later, with blue cigar smoke floating over the room, the lights went off again. A few muffled giggles were heard in the darkness. The theme from *Rocky* rose to rock-concert volume, accompanied by those tiny lights again, frantically racing around the tent until they were cut in favor of wider spotlights, falling on a row of shirtless men standing in the ring, boxing gloves dangling at their sides—boxers in a police lineup.

Michelle introduced each fighter. One by one they stepped forward to a round of polite applause, then back again. After they'd all been introduced, the ring went dark for a few seconds before the spotlights burst on again, hitting two fighters, hoods up, entering the tent from opposite sides, shuffling toward the ring, throwing short punches into the air. The *Rocky* theme rose again. They approached the steps to the ring, Michelle standing in the middle, arms extended.

"And we begin the evening, ladies and gentlemen. Introducing in the blue corner, all the way from Manchester, England, hoping to establish a career in the colonies, is Jack 'The Ripper' Spotswood!" she shouted. "He enters this contest with a 10-4 record with four knockouts and is fighting at 16.8 stone—that's 235 pounds for the colonials among us.

"And introducing in the red corner, our American hero—Vietnam-veteran Marine Corps sergeant with a record of twelve victories against only one questionable defeat. Ten of his victories were by knockout. He is fighting at 210 pounds—fourteen-stone-nine. He is the odds-on favorite to emerge undefeated tonight. I bring you Calvin 'The Fighting Leatherneck' *Jaaaaacksooooon!*"

———

Calvin raises his arms to modest applause, turns to each side of the ring, and bows.

Spotswood has Calvin by twenty-five pounds, and Calvin needs to find out early if he knows how to use that advantage.

When the bell rings, Spotswood plods to mid-ring, standing straight up, his left held rigidly straight in front of him and his right up against his chest like one of those pictures of bare-knuckled fighters from the 1800s. Classically British. Classically stupid.

Calvin moves toward the flatfooted Spotswood and throws a jab, splitting his gloves, landing square on his nose. Spotswood slips to his left to reset his rigor-mortis stance. Calvin steps in again. Spotswood backs up. Calvin throws a lazy jab—a slap, really—to distract him and comes over the top with a right, followed with a left hook. Down. Crumpled.

Spotswood rolls onto his back, shields his eyes from the ceiling lights, brushes his right glove over his nose, checking for blood. There isn't any. He stays down. His corner throws in the towel. One down, seven to go.

Calvin sits on a stool in his corner. Luis wipes his face and smears Vaseline over his eyes.

He holds a bottle of water for Calvin to sip, massages his shoulders, then pulls on his arms, flapping them to loosen them. After three minutes of rest, Michelle introduces Calvin's next opponent.

The bell clangs and the guy runs across the ring and throws a flurry of windmill punches with no specific target in mind. Calvin throws a couple of jabs, but mostly stays at a distance. After a half round of flailing, the opponent isn't raising his fat arms as high.

With his opponent winded—breathing through his mouth instead of his nose—Calvin moves in. He lands a textbook left hook and a right cross. The guy goes down, gets up and goes down again from the same combination. It takes three trips to the canvas before the ref waves off the fight. The guy's corner couldn't throw in the towel because they'd left after the second knockdown for the visitors' center to see if there was any free liquor and food left.

Calvin's next three opponents have much more skill than their predecessors. They move adroitly around the ring. It takes Calvin a total of twelve rounds to dispatch them, the last after four knockdowns and a broken nose, following Calvin's beautifully executed head butt that opens up a flood of blood over and into his opponent's eye.

Calvin's legs are starting to go. He needs to end the fight as quickly as possible.

At the next opening bell, Calvin rushes across the ring, snorting and grunting, wild-eyed, nostrils flaring, head shaking as if in the throes of a fit. The guy pauses.

Calvin fakes a right, lands a left hook and a follow-up elbow to the neck. Calvin spins the guy around to block the referee's view, dips, and throws an uppercut under the guy's cup. Those in the crowd who could see the low blow roar. The guy folds at the waist. Calvin finishes him off with a clubbing right at sixty-three seconds of the first round.

The next two fights are easy and short—two and three rounds. Calvin dispatches one guy with a lead right, followed by a left jab, and then a right cross torqued perfectly by his hips and legs. The other guy, obviously not prepared for the speed of Calvin's jab, takes five of them consecutively. When he retreats, Calvin steps on his foot and hits him with a left hook, spins the guy off balance, and lands a hard right behind his ear. From the canvas, his opponent pleads, *"No mas. No mas."*

After Calvin's seventh fight, Michelle climbs into the ring. "And now, ladies and gentlemen, the final contest. Here is Tommy 'The Tulsa Tornado' Macklin. Will he end our Marine's dream? Or does our Marine hero have enough left to turn the Tornado into a summer breeze?"

Stealing the intro line from the great referee Mills Lane,

Michelle screams, "Let's get it *aaaaaaaahhhhhhonnnnnn!*" and fires herself into the air—green panties sparkling through the blue haze. The crowd goes wild.

Calvin and Macklin spend the first round cat-and-mousing, throwing range-finder jabs and feinting to gauge reflexes. At the end of the round, Calvin's legs are wobbling like a drunk's as he goes to his corner.

"What's that Marine doing in Dress Whites sitting over there?" Calvin asks Luis. "He got a pass from the colonel? Dress Whites at a fight?"

"What're you talkin' about? C'mon, get your head straight," Luis says. "That's a broad with a white hat. What the fuck?"

Luis puts a sponge on top of Calvin's head, sluicing water over his face.

"There's Nicky. Laughing at me."

Luis slaps Calvin. "Stop talkin' shit. Get your head outta your ass!"

At the bell to start the second round, Macklin springs from his stool. Calvin gets up slowly. Macklin bobs and weaves his way inside, catching Calvin with an overhand right. Calvin's nose appears broken. He shakes his head and opens his mouth to breathe deeply, his black mouthpiece looking like he has rotten teeth. Luis is shouting at Calvin to shut his damn mouth. It's dangerous to breathe through the mouth because there's more of a chance for a broken jaw. Also, breathing through the nose delivers more oxygen to the blood.

Calvin shuts his mouth. *Boom!* Macklin hits him again with a right cross off a jab and follows with a combination left-right-left, staggering him. He covers up against the ropes as Macklin tattoos him with body and head shots, including a couple of elbows to the head. Calvin throws a flurry of punches as cover to slip along the rope to get out of the corner.

The bell ends the round. Calvin wobbles to his corner.

"This guy can hit," he mumbles to Luis. "Never been hit this hard in my life. Sledgehammer it feels like."

"Forget that! Beat him to the punch and slide away! C'mon! Get it together!"

Round three starts. Calvin tries to get a good angle, but Macklin sidesteps him, turning him into the corner. Calvin throws a flurry of not-very-hard punches but manages to slide along the ropes to get out of the corner.

Macklin chases Calvin, who pivots, takes two steps toward Macklin, bobs left, and comes up throwing a hook, pausing Macklin's advance. Macklin shakes his head "no" that he wasn't hurt. He misses with a left and lands a glancing right, ending with an elbow to Calvin's neck.

The crowd roars.

Somehow Calvin stays on his feet and grabs onto Macklin. The referee separates them and warns Calvin for holding.

Calvin catches Macklin coming toward him without hesitation and hits Macklin with a forearm to the neck and a clubbing right, staggering him. He covers up, slips away to mid-ring, and waves Calvin toward him. Calvin takes the bait and advances.

*Bam!*

Calvin's on his back. He gets up. When the referee motions the fight to continue, Calvin grabs Macklin. The ref separates them and again tells Calvin to stop holding. Macklin comes in again.

Emboldened by the warning to Calvin, Macklin hits him well below the belt. It mostly lands on the top of his cup. Calvin bends over as if he's hurt. The ref calls time and points to Macklin to move to the far corner. Calvin is on one knee, not forgetting to grimace while resting. He looks at the crowd. His gaze lingers on the face of a young woman in the third row. He nods and smiles around his mouthpiece. He thinks she nods in acknowledgment. Maybe. He gets up slowly and makes his way to the ropes and leans on them, baring his black mouthpiece and wincing.

After about four of the allowed five minutes to recover, Calvin signals he's ready to resume the fight. Macklin comes in for the kill flatfooted, thinking all he needs is one punch to end it, not worried about a Calvin counter. Calvin quarter-turns away from Macklin, dips, spins back, and catapults a right with everything he has. The punch lands full-on. Macklin staggers backward and goes down.

*Out!* Done! The crowd erupts. Calvin wobbles to a neutral corner and drops onto a knee. The noise is deafening. Calvin scrunches his face and shakes his head.

Luis jumps into the ring, races to Calvin, lifts him up from his knee, and throws his arms around him. "You beat 'em all, Calvin!" he shouts. "Yo! You with me? You get a shot now! You get a shot!"

"What you talkin' about? No shot! No Cong. No leeches. No ear-beers. She's whispering in my ear. Beautiful."

"Stop talkin' shit!" Luis yells. "Listen to me. You're on your way to a title shot."

"When's this fight gonna start?"

# HAMMER AND NAIL

ABOUT FIVE MILES out of Vegas, Bobby took a left at a black cement-block building with purple neon running around the bottom of a flat roof.

TANYA'S—GIRLS, SLOTS, COMPS

Try that three times in a row.

*Peter Piper picked a peck of pickled peppers.* When Bobby was eight, Alice Cummings challenged him in front of her dollhouse to do Peter Piper as fast as he could and laughed at him seven words into his first attempt. Then they went inside the white dollhouse with sky-blue shutters her father had built for her eighth birthday, and Alice showed him her new pink panties.

TANYA'S—GIRLS, SLOTS, COMPS

Bobby passed the old salt factory on the right, which gave way to a five-mile stretch of desert on both sides of the road. He turned left at a sign for a trailer park called Cottonwoods.

On one corner of the turnoff, a car was parked in a sandy clearing. Three gray burros—white-splashed foreheads and chests—stood in wedge formation about ten feet from one of the cars. The burros were a local attraction, crossing the road from the large expanse of desert where they lived to panhandle people parked in cars. Two squealing kids in the backseat lowered the window, threw out pretzels and pieces of bread to the burros, and quickly rolled the window back up. The wide-eyed, grinning mom snapped pictures with a disposable camera from behind her shut window.

Bobby often drove to this part of the desert by himself to see the burros. He fantasized about catching one of the slime-buckets who shot them for kicks. His dream was to catch a perp and stake him naked in the desert in a scene from a John D. MacDonald novel, then smear him with Grandma's molasses—Nicky and Bobby's fave—an extra coating on more sensitive areas.

He turned left alongside the burros. A quarter mile later, he crossed a narrow wooden bridge, drumrolling the slats. The bridge jumped a shallow ravine he knew, but still found difficult to believe, could become a raging river in minutes and carry off a car. On the far side of the gully lay two mattresses spilling gray stuffing next to a whitewall tire and a smashed kid's red pedal car. There were only a few scraggly trees that didn't seem cottony at all to Bobby, not that he'd know cottonwoods from cotton candy. But the name seemed too warm and fuzzy for the desert. These trees, whatever they were called, were struggling to stay alive.

Bobby drove slowly through the trailer settlement's maze of streets until he found Amigo Street. Shades were down on the windows of the green-and-white double-wide. The front yard was scattered with patches of yellowed strands of vegetation, looking like wisps of stubborn hair on a cancer patient. To the side of the trailer was a fat propane tank on its side, stenciled in red letters "Desert Power, Inc."

Close to the curb in front was a rose-colored mirrored ball

that turned Bobby's compact car into a stretch limo. To the right of the walkway stood a lawn jockey in white face, a chain around its neck, dangling to a clamp around its ankle. In front of the trailer next door, a pink tricycle was upside down, resting on its seat. A sun-bleached red Honda with California plates was parked under a carport. Bobby knocked, rattling the aluminum frame of the closed screen door. He knocked again just as the door opened.

The strings on her pink V-neck peasant blouse were loosely drawn into a bow above full breasts. Her navy-blue shorts, cut in the style of 1930s tap-dancing pants, were sprinkled with white polka dots. She wore tan sandals, straps snaking around her ankles.

"Hi. I'm Bobby Trocadero. You must be Esme. I called a couple of days ago. Carlos Seguro said he called to vouch for me."

"Yes, he did. I'm still not sure this is a world-class idea, but you might as well come in."

Esme walked down the hall, her hips taking quick, efficient turns filling one side and then the other of her shorts—polka dots bouncing. From down the hall, Bobby heard a cartoon character's helium-gassed voice. She led him into the tiny kitchen, where a man, dressed in a white, sleeveless undershirt, sat in front of a small bay window. His black hair and thick goatee were speckled with gray. Raised scars in the shape of a tic-tac-toe box were to the side of his left eye. A box of mixed doughnuts was open in front of him.

"We have a guest, Luis. Time to pretend to be socialized," she said with a Colgate smile, dimples sinking into her brown face. "That's a difficult task for you, but it's good for you to get out of yourself once in a while."

"What does that even mean, girl? 'Get out of yourself.' It's not even English. You college girls." He shook his head and stuffed the end of a cruller into his mouth.

"It's women, old man. Stop trying to rile me. Clear off the table with those papers. C'mon, I'm not even asking you to put on a shirt, like civilized people. This man says his brother was with Calvin in Nam. He wants to see if Calvin remembers him."

Luis, his head down looking at the paper, raised his eyes over the top of reading glasses to look at Bobby. "Vietnam long time ago. You got new people don't know Nam from Spam, and old ones don't wanna remember."

"Would you like some coffee?" she asked Bobby.

"Thanks. That'd be nice."

She flicked her head toward the table for him to sit, then went to the cupboard above the sink and stretched to reach a plate and a mug, her muscles taut over full hips and long legs.

She put the plate and mug on the table. The mug was decorated with the Mirage Hotel's stylized logo of purple, pink, orange, and green splashes, suggesting palm trees.

"This grouchy old man," she said, waving her arm at the seated man, "is Luis 'The Viper' Castillo—at least in an earlier life," she said with a half smile. "Claims he was a fighting machine back in the day. Says he fought 'em all." She winked at Bobby.

"I did! I did! Woulda got the title they didn't take away my license because of a detached retina. My eyes. I shoulda made the call on that."

"And you'd be walking around with a white cane now, old man."

Luis chomped off more of his cruller, chewed, and washed it down with coffee.

"You were born in Vietnam, weren't you?" Bobby asked Esme. "I heard that or read it maybe in a story about Calvin."

"Yes. Of course, that would be the first topic of conversation about me." She pulled off a piece of a glazed chocolate doughnut. "Did they say 'Chink Chick' or 'Slope Grope'? Maybe it was 'Slant Slut'?" she said, popping the hole into her mouth and wiping her lips with a napkin.

Bobby took a sip. "That's pretty far out there. No?"

"The truth. That's what we were—are. Always will be to lots of people. These days they sometimes—sometimes—try to hide it."

"Not everybody thinks that way," Bobby said.

"Well, if they think differently, they're whispering it in the dark," Esme said, shrugging her shoulders, "so it really doesn't matter what they think."

He turned to Luis. "Does Calvin talk about Nam?"

"Not really. Alls I remember is Calvin saying he had a sweet setup, keeping White officers in booze and girls and watching out for brass not in on the deal," Luis said. "Said he got extra pay for helping get bodies ready to ship home. Said nobody checks what's in the caskets."

Luis gulped his coffee and held the cup in front of his mouth.

"Said no one wants to see those guys dead again. I 'spect was more than bodies in them boxes. You know, they say poppies grow real good over there."

"What are you expecting to find out from Calvin?" Esme said, locking onto Bobby's eyes.

"Your father and my brother were good friends in Vietnam, so mostly I'd like to know what my brother did over there and what he was like from someone who was with him and close to him."

"It's difficult to get close to anyone when you're just trying to avoid all the ways they're trying to kill you," she said, hard-staring at Bobby. "Maybe you don't want Calvin to remember."

"I think it's important to remember everything—the good and the bad," Bobby said.

"For some people," she said, nudging the doughnut box toward him. "Maybe it's better to remember only the bad, 'cause it's always there and you can always watch out for it."

"That's a tough way to look at things, at life," Bobby said.

"Good never stays around long," Esme said, pinching off a piece of doughnut. "Waiting and looking for the good keeps you from seeing the bad coming up on you. Good is nothing you can count on. Bad is."

Esme quickly stuffed the napkins into the mugs, put her fingers through the handles, stacked the plates, and carried them to the sink. Bobby watched the dancing polka dots. She opened the door beneath the sink and put the napkins into a garbage can. She squirted green dish detergent onto a pink sponge, turned on the water, and washed the plates and mugs. She slammed them into the drainer in the other sink.

She spun around to face Bobby, the water running behind her. "Calvin's been through a lot. I know I committed to you coming here, but I don't want him riled up by stuff that's best forgotten. By everyone. Probably you too, not that I know you or anything to say that. But still."

She turned back to the sink and shut off the water.

"I'd just like to talk to Calvin, to get his take on it all," Bobby said. "I want to know what the last days of my brother's life were like. Maybe that sounds weird or something, but that's my reason. I'd also like to talk to him about his boxing career. A great left hook and could take a punch. And why he never got a shot at a title."

"'Cause he was too good and not hooked up right," Luis said, staring at Bobby. "No promoter wanted to risk his guy against Calvin. So he had to take a lot of fights on short notice for short money—especially the last one. No money. Just a promise."

Esme snatched a dish towel from the fridge handle and kept her back to them, taking longer than needed to wipe her hands. She sighed her shoulders into a slump, threw the towel hard against the backsplash, and turned quickly to face Bobby.

"Let's go see Calvin now," she ordered. "Maybe we can find some hero stories about your brother."

They walked down the short hallway, past a photograph of Josephine Baker on the wall in her famous banana outfit, another of her in a garden surrounded by the children she'd adopted after exiling herself to France. On the opposite wall was a picture of Martin Luther King Jr., giving his "I Have a Dream" speech, thousands of people in front of him, craning their necks, trying to absorb his hopes.

Esme opened the door just beyond Josephine. Calvin sat in a tan recliner tilted back about forty-five degrees. He wore wraparound sunglasses, a blue-and-white exercise suit, and un-walked-in, cloud-white Adidas with red laces, perfectly tied with long bows drooping to the sides.

His fingers twitched in his lap, as Wile E. Coyote chased the Roadrunner on the big screen, set about two feet in front of him. Two speakers were on stands inches from his ears. Calvin was murmuring, his voice rising and falling, alternately shouting and whispering.

"The wall! Comin'! It comin'! You gonna hit it! Gonna slam you. Gotta get through it. Dance! C'mon, boy! It the tenth! You don't pick 'em up and put 'em down, he gonna put you down for good, boy. White boy gonna kick your sorry butt. Run! Run! Run! Run that hill. For sure that boy running!"

He was trying to lift his arms to throw punches but could only manage a few finger twitches and snorts.

"No pain no gain no pain no gain no pain no gain no pain

no gain no pain no gain no pain no gain no pain no gain no pain no gain no—"

"Daddy! Daddy! It's okay. It's okay to stop now," Esme said, gently taking his left hand into hers and stroking it with her other hand. "You did your five miles. Time to rest now. You rest now for Saturday. "

"Say again," Calvin said.

"Time to rest."

"Again."

"Time to rest."

"Again."

"Rest, Daddy. Rest. Rest," she said, patting his forehead with a towel.

"Gotta rest. Gotta rest," Calvin said. "He be resting and running, resting and running, resting and running . . ." His voice trailed off. Then it started up again.

"No punch, no lunch, no punch, no lunch, no punch, no lunch—"

"Daddy. Daddy, please, please rest. Rest. Please."

When he was calm for a while, Esme said, "Daddy, this is Bobby, uh . . ."

"Trocadero. Bobby Trocadero."

"Bobby Trocadero," she said slowly, stronger. Esme stroked her father's limp hand. "His brother was with you in Vietnam. You remember him? White guy? Says you two were tight."

"Nicky Troc," Bobby said, stepping closer to Calvin's chair. "Hi, Champ. My brother was Nicky Troc from Staten Island."

"You know me?"

"Saw you fight a couple of times."

"Saw me fight?"

"Yes."

"Say what?"

"Yes."

"Come close. Say again."

"Yes. I saw you fight."

"I'm the champ."

"Yes."

"Saw me fight."

"Yes. Saw you fight."

"Closer."

Bobby put his hand on top of Calvin's hand that rested on top of his stomach. Bobby watched the fingers of Calvin's other hand crawl on top of Bobby's and collapse.

"Know what that is?" Calvin said, twitching his fingers. "This my hammer." He twisted his other hand. "This my nail."

"Champ, do you remember Saigon and hanging with Nicky Troc?" Bobby said loudly. "You remember Colonel Mara?"

Calvin turned his head slowly toward Bobby. "Send back smack! Smack is back! Back is smack! *Ooooooooooo! Ooooweeee!* Could smack! Smack snack! Smack is back! Smack is us."

"You and Nicky Troc worked for him. He kept you in Saigon and sent Nicky to the bush. What'd he do to get that?"

Calvin seemed about to say something but was distracted, as if something flashier had rushed past his mind. He began slowly, almost imperceptibly, swaying his head to a beat only he could hear.

His wrists were along his thighs now. He managed small finger quivers that couldn't keep up with his swaying head.

Luis was standing in the doorway, leaning against its frame. "He done. No use trying no more."

Esme turned and followed, shaking her head.

Bobby took a long look at Calvin, who was riveted to the end of a cartoon—Porky Pig saying, "Th-Th-The, Th-Th-The . . . That's all, folks!"

Bobby left the room and went down the corridor to the

kitchen, where Esme and Luis sat at the table, hands clasped in front of them.

"I'm sorry if I upset Calvin," Bobby said. "That certainly was not my intention. I'd never do that to a friend of Nicky's—a really good friend."

Bobby let himself out into the desert and walked the path. He passed the dead bikes and the White lawn jockey. He passed the reflecting globe and turned back to look at himself in it—tentacles of long arms and legs and a twisted, lopsided face.

# ACKNOWLEDGMENTS

I'd like to thank some of the people who helped me on this audacious trip.

First, of course, is my wife, Robin Sidel, whose honest support, patience, and very smart writer's eye were beyond invaluable. As much as she could, she saved me from my more embarrassing attempts, which she made me understand I had to spike through their hearts. I am indebted to her in so many ways, beginning with "Yes, I will."

These stories wouldn't have gotten off oxygen support if it weren't for Jerry Izenberg's prodding, cajoling, and plain yelling at me to just do it. He believed when I didn't. I note, to the regret of some, that Jerry also has schooled me in the finer points of curmudgeonry.

Many thanks for Gary Alden's thoughtful guidance about his Marines and Vietnam, where he continued his family's proud legacy as a Leatherneck. Gary and legions of others are reminders that there were so many good guys who fought in a bad war with great courage.

Thank you to fellow Staten Islander Teddy Atlas. Teddy not only is a world-champion boxing trainer, he's a world-class person, always there to help. Teddy kept me from going "Hollywood," as he put it in describing the brutal, beautiful world of boxing.

Luck slapped me upside the head when Sam Douglas agreed to take me on to offer his editing genius—I think it must have been some kind of penance. His soft-spoken but demanding nudges, along with flat-out brilliance, made the difference. He never gave up on me even though I cost him gray hairs.

Thanks, too, for the unwavering support and encouragement of Elizabeth Luciano and Paul Lupinacci that mean more than I can say.

Thank you, Ivan Fuller, a new neighbor and new friend, who suffered my technical ignorance to help me with such patience and good humor.

Accolades to Tom Walsh, former longtime *Rolling Stone* editor, who entered in the bottom of the ninth inning for the book and hit a grand slam. His keen eye uncovered and resolved all manner of issues.

Of course, none of this would be possible without writer/publisher Lara Bernhardt giving these stories a home. Lara displayed tremendous skill, grace, patience, and support in ensuring the stories came together as best they could.

# ABOUT THE AUTHOR

John Phillips has led many lives: among them bartender, beauty-products salesman, union representative, and sportswriter. Running a bar was the best and worst of times. (Think sending a guy back to jail for burglary and having to pay off cops to ensure they'd be there when needed.) Of course, there were barroom dramas—good, bad, and just weird. All of it while trying to look the other way as Staten Island gave up guys to die in Vietnam and dancing as fast as he could to not be one of them.

As a sportswriter for Reuters, Phillips covered more than sixty world-title fights and their scenes, filled with a wonderland of characters—many tough, decent, and funny, others cold-eyed predators, always, always on the hustle.

Among other events he covered were the Olympics, World Series, Super Bowl, figure skating, tennis, and horse racing. He also reported from Cuba, where he spent three days in a hospital because he was dumb enough to drink unfiltered water at the airport.

Learn more about John at: johnphillipsstories.com

# MORE BY ADMISSION PRESS

Looking for your next great read?
Visit www.admissionpress.com